Día de los Muertos

A Day of the Dead Anthology

Día de los Muertos

A Day of the Dead Anthology

EDITED BY

Angela Charmaine Craig

Elektrik Milk Bath Press

Día de los Muertos: A Day of the Dead Anthology

© 2010 by Elektrik Milk Bath Press.

Cover art © by Dani

Cover design by Seraph B.

Interior layout and design by Seraph B.

Published by Elektrik Milk Bath Press. For Information please contact Elektrik Milk Bath Press, P.O. Box 833223, Richardson TX 75083.

ISBN 978-0-9828554-0-9

for Chrome and Frenchi

and Noodles and Hades,
and, of course, Mister Boo

Contents

Introduction

Sugar skulls... Marigolds...

These are the things that come to mind when I think of *Día de los Muertos*, and you will find them here among the altars and the offerings, the dancing and the music—all that has come to symbolize the celebration of the days of the dead.

When we set out to create this anthology, we kept the guidelines deliberately simple, asking only that the stories relate in some way to this theme. The result is the work of the 29 authors presented here, and they explore *día de los muertos* in a variety of ways.

Many of these stories offer a celebration of this holiday, sharing the mixture of jubilance and sorrow felt by those longing for a reunion with their loved ones. Others delve into the darker side of the days of the dead, and the horrors visited upon those to whom the dead may return. And there are a variety of characters present here: bikers, an assassin, an author, and the Queen of the Dead, just to name a few. Many of those you will meet are long familiar with this rich tradition, but there are those who are struggling, trying hard to understand.

These tales cross the boundaries of genre and culture. I think there is something here for everyone. I hope you enjoy.

Listen to the Wind
Día de los Muertos
The dead speak in tongues

—Stephen M. Wilson

Pan de los Muertos

Dru Pagliassotti

Take-Man strolled past Elysian Park, leather collar high, keychain rattling, mirrorshades reflecting the wildfires that chewed the Malibu hills, the San Fernando Valley, the San Gabriel Mountains.

He was Take-Man, dark beneath the orange glow of the October dusk, which was now starting to darken into ash and shadow. Take-Man, his hair ruffled by the whisper of tires humming over broken concrete. Take-Man, his heartbeat the engine tick; Take-Man, his laugh the sickening crumple of metal meeting metal at 65 miles per hour on a 15-mile-per-hour residential street; Take-Man, whose teeth had the shine of razorwire and whose voice was the rattle of discarded brass casings on pavement.

Take-Man had come to Los Angeles, and this was his month, this was his night, this was his hour. He'd rattled in over desert roads in his run-down Lincoln, over multiple lanes of barren freeway, and finally over chewed-up inner-city streets that glistened brightly with shattered windshields, broken brake lights and fractured turn signals. Red and yellow, the colors of October, fire season in Los Angeles, panic season, sizzle season, the right season for Take-Man to drop his chewed-up boot heels on the pavement of the city and look around and whisper to himself, "I claim this."

Dry laughter greeted his statement. Take-Man turned his mirror-maze shades on the old lady sitting on a bus-stop bench, orange and yellow marigolds spilling from her dark-skirted lap, miniature bursts of flame. The wall behind her was covered with concert posters that peeled off the weatherworn wood like curls of dry paper from a broken piñata, stirring gently in the warm breeze.

"What are you laughing at, old woman?" he asked, voice as cold and sour as the flavor of a blued-steel gun barrel. The white-haired old woman looked up and smiled at him with yellow *papier-mâché* teeth and bitter *pulque*-breath.

"Just because you have spread your shadow over our lands doesn't make us yours." Her laugh was old, her eyes ancient, her face creased with lines. "I know what you are, Take-Man. You cannot take this city."

Take-Man took a step closer, and somewhere a child shrieked, a door slammed, a needle plunged into bruised flesh.

"Every city can be taken," he said, face moving in shadow—first white, then brown, then yellow, then red, then black, then white again, an indeterminate color, the color of the many faces of the faceless crowd.

"The problem with mirrored eyes," she chuckled, "is that they reflect; they do not perceive. Lift your face, Take-Man. Lift your face and breathe my city."

Take-Man snarled at her. An empty beer can rattled down the narrow concrete sidewalk, fleeing before the gusts. She kept smiling. His nostrils flared as he smelled the burning-human scent of roast pork, the dry-adobe smell of sizzling masa, that surrounded her.

Take-Man straightened. Her scent was that of a foe. A foe, on this autumn night, the darkest of all nights, this night he intended to claim this city.

"Do you feel the heat?" she asked. "Do you feel the warmth? The states where you come from grow cold in October. In the cities that bred you, the people feel a chill. They sense the cold of the grave, and they fear your presence. But that is not the way here."

"All cities are the same," Take-Man growled. On the 101 a car spun out of control, tires screeching across four lanes before it slammed into the concrete center divider.

"But hearts do not freeze in *El Pueblo de la Reina de Los Angeles.*" She chuckled, a whispering sizzle of masa harina on a hot iron skillet. "They burn.

"October may be your month in the East, but here the rules are different. For the first weeks, maybe, there are days that drop into the 70s, and Los Angeleños begin to pull out their sweaters. But then, ah then"—the old woman gave her rictus grin—"then the Santa Anas, the winds of *la madre de María*, blow in. They are Heaven's breath, as hot as an arcangelo's sword, sweeping over the mountains to bring desiccation and wildfire. Every year they come, and October is as midsummer again."

"What is your name, old woman?" Take-Man asked suspiciously. He ran a large hand over the stiff leather of his jacket, suddenly feeling uncomfortably warm. Santa Anas shook the palm trees around them. Dry fronds rattled like old bones. He looked up, frowning. The fire-scent around him smelled of burning chaparral, charred pine—so different from what he knew: burning rubber, exploding jet fuel, smoldering insulation, molten glass, vaporized concrete. Gunpowder and asphalt, and the bitter fear of death's cold touch.

"Call me Calaca, Take-Man."

"Calaca." He sneered to mask a twinge of alarm. "Are you going to stand against me, Calaca? You—what are you, in this city of eternal youth? I am young, I am powerful. I am modern, I am urban. I am the nightmare on your screens and the despair in your music. I am the ignorance of childhood, the restlessness of adolescence, the violence of young adulthood. Your Los Angeles already venerates me, old woman. You—you are nothing to me. This city eats old women like you alive."

Calaca stood, and the Santa Anas swept around them, carrying smoke from the hills, exhaust from the freeways. Take-Man turned his face to one side as he caught the faint, sweet scent of melting dulces.

Marigolds fluttered from the old woman's black skirt and blew over the sidewalk, all except one. That one she held out to him. It was as orange as an ember, as orange as a pumpkin, as orange as October.

"Do not mistake the grimace of the *careta*, the mask, for the face that lies beneath it." She offered the marigold again. "Take this and leave. *Cempazuchiles* are all you can take from us, Take-Man."

Angered, uneasy, Take-Man slapped her hand aside. He stepped forward and wrapped a hand around her neck. Her skin felt dry and papery. She was warm, almost hot, against his cold flesh.

"If a wetback peasant like you is all that stands between me and this city, old woman, then I will own Los Angeles by midnight."

Dust and ash whipped up around them in an abrasive cloud. Chain-link and fence slats rattled. Faded posters flapped. Garbage shifted. Take-Man felt a furnace blast on his face and barked with cruel laughter.

"Heaven's breath," he mocked, fingers tightening around the old lady's sinewy neck. "A bunch of hot air."

The old woman pursed her lips and blew a quick puff at him. Her breath reeked of scalded sugar, copal, and agave. He recoiled, and the Santa Anas howled around them. Trees shook, palm fronds clattered, screen doors slammed, dirt flew. Sweat sluiced down the inside of Take-Man's leather jacket as the wind sucked all the moisture from his exposed flesh.

He released Calaca to turn his face away from the flying grit.

"I am not *all* that stands in your way," the old woman said quietly. "My *fieles difuntos*, my faithful dead, are with me." She held out a hand, and he saw the embers flicker across her fingertips. "Can mirror-eyes see my *angelitos*?"

Take-Man saw, and knew that the hot, dry October sparks, the autumn angels, thirsted for his blood, his lymph, his urine—everything inside of him that was still wet and vulnerable. Mirrorshades and leather, the cold shields of the impersonal city, were no protection against their insistent, all-too-intimate thirst.

Take-Man felt fear.

Calaca lifted her face to the wind and opened her mouth. The Santa Anas rushed between her jaws, drying the damp tissues of her nose, her mouth, slicing down her throat like knives and eagerly drinking the moisture from her lungs. Her flesh dried, mummified: hard gristle, charred tissue, burnt caramel.

"What the hell are you?" Take-Man asked, and for the first time he took a step back, back toward the cities of his origin, where the searing Santa Anas never stirred.

"I am an old woman," Calaca said, in a voice that rustled like shifting sand. "And where the Santa Anas blow in the city of eternal youth, the old are the *ofrenda*."

"The ofrenda?" He took another step backward.

"The altar that celebrates death and does not fear it."

Take-Man mopped sweat from his face. Blisters rose across Calaca's arms, then broke open and peeled back under the heat of the October winds. The October winds, the Santa Anas—the autumn fire-bringers of Los Angeles, which did not blow in the lands east of the San Gabriel and San Bernardino Mountains. In Take-Man's East, All Hallow's Eve was greeted by winds as cold as the grave. These unnatural gales, hot and vital, repulsed him.

Calaca's blistered skin peeled back like ashes. The tissue underneath sizzled and then surrendered to fire.

Take-Man stripped off his leather jacket, unable to bear the heat any longer, a heat like none he'd ever felt before, not even in explosions, in arson, in terrorism: not Take-Man, the October man, the autumn walker, the shadow-stalker, the harbinger of cold flesh and icy earth.

"And youth like you?" Calaca added in death's dry rattle. "Youth like you are the offerings on the altar. You are our *Pan de los Muertos*."

She lunged with blackened, skeletal hands. Take-Man flinched, but her sharp fingers pierced him, drove through his camouflage tank top, sank into his cold, dense flesh, and touched bones as hard and lifeless as chrome.

Take-Man screamed as she pulled him open and let the hot October wind inside. His blood poured onto the sidewalk, liquid darkness as thick and as rich as motor oil, as raw sewage, as dark mole.

"Now, isn't that better?" the old woman asked, and he screamed as she pulled off his face like a mask. His bones melted in the Santa Anas as though they were made of sugar. Fat sizzled and ran from his open body like candle wax. Heat burned within him like fire licking the inside of a hollow, lifeless gourd.

Flesh and bone twisted together into a mummified skeleton, as hollow as a piñata. Calaca effortlessly slid inside, drawing Take-Man's flayed flesh on like a dress.

He screamed, but there was nothing left to scream with, and as she smoothed his face over her own, his teeth and tongue became hers, and then he was empty of everything but Calaca.

"In the East," she said, opening his arms, her arms, to embrace the hot winds, "beyond the mountains, they are afraid of October. They are afraid of the cold, of death. But here, Señor Take-Man, here death is warm, as warm as our autumn brush fires, our winds, our blood, our altar candles. Here, Take-Man, we do not run from death, but embrace it."

Then she let the wind take her, and all that was left of Take-Man was a run-down old Lincoln parked along the street and a leather jacket lying in the shadows.

Marigolds slowly covered the jacket, blown by a wind that carried the smell of October ash and burning marzipan.

Susto

David J. Corwell y Chávez

Doña Ignacia straightened the marigolds on Enrique's altar and leaned against the iron railing of the porch to admire her work. Steaming bowls of *frijoles*, *chile verde*, and tortillas, along with a cup of hot *café*, were spread across the top, mingled with votive candles, Brach's cinnamon candies, and small tins of holy water. Her wooden crucifix was centered behind the offerings, propped up between the golden petals. *Santos* rested in the niches underneath. Ceramic hands molded together in permanent supplication, their bright, painted faces gazed at the arroyo to the left of the adobe. Her patron saints guarded against evil spirits creeping within the gully's shadowed recesses.

Día de los Muertos was a tradition best followed out of respect, but this year marked a personal celebration. Ignacia prayed that the Ancestors would honor her role as the community's *curandera* and bless a visit with her husband. She had healed all manner of physical and spiritual illnesses for three generations. Had she not earned some reward for her faithful ministrations?

Her face grew warm at the thought of Enrique's first homecoming, relieved that the opportunity had finally come. Eight months of silent rooms had drawn a shroud over her joy at starting each new day. More and more she paced the house, the quiet so overwhelming her thoughts seemed smothered. She longed for the deep sound of her *querido*'s voice to dispel her emptiness. His words always carried steady reassurances that brought her a deep calm. Soon now, they would be together again.

Smiling, Ignacia smoothed her flowered dress and brushed strands of white hair from her face, tying them into a braid, just as it had been the day they joined their lives together. She checked the altar once more, nodded her approval. Everything was perfect. Except for the finishing touch—the gift she had given him on their wedding day.

She pulled a handkerchief and Enrique's watch from her pocket, dabbed holy water onto the worn surface, and polished the gold with tender strokes. Admiring the chain's beautiful links, she wrapped it around her wrist. The watch radiated a comforting heat in the palm of her hand, a sign her *querido* was near, but she yearned for the full warmth of his loving presence. "Come home, *mi amor*," she whispered.

She snapped open the cover and gasped. The wedding photo inside shimmered away.

"Soon, *Señorita*, soon."

Ignacia recoiled from the hissed words, her wrinkled hands held up for protection, making the sign of the Cross as she choked back a frightened cry.

The porch was empty.

Startled, she dropped the watch, its descent stopped by the chain, a slow, twisting motion that made her head spin. She staggered into a kneeling position before the altar, arthritic knees creaking in protest; their rough skin scraped against cement.

"*La Llorona*."

The *bruja* was legend, a malevolent witch notorious for drowning unwary children. Ignacia had met her before, as a ten year old girl, and had lived through the experience. She had managed to bury that nightmare in the hushed recesses of her mind. But jogged free by *La Llorona*'s voice, the childhood memory swirled up into her consciousness, as vivid as the day she had lived it—and almost died.

CSEOCSEO

Ignacia had been making mud pies at the water's edge when she stumbled, head first, into the arroyo's murky current. Lying flat against the bank, feet dangling upward and arms flailing in the water, she had not been able to lift herself. Silt stung her eyes like salt rubbed into a fresh cut and seeped into her nose, her mouth, her ears. Her only true awareness was of sliding deeper, until the water covered her entire body.

She forced out a cry for help. Large bubbles brushed her cheeks as they rose past her face. The gritty sludge poured into her throat, gagging her. It oozed down, around her tongue, into her burning lungs, waves of pain spreading outward. The last of her air wasted.

She thrashed around, her arms and legs tiring, yet still grasping for something to hold onto. Branches, rocks, the bank itself. Something to push herself up. To stand up and gulp precious air. But she was surrounded by the current.

A throbbing agony roared through her ears; the tingling in her limbs grew more persistent. Her body soon stilled its struggling and drifted. Scattered pictures tumbled through her mind as her heartbeat slowed. She imagined her *abuelos* grieving over her lifeless form. Poor Grandfather and Gremma. Ignacia would have joined her tears to theirs if she had any strength left.

Gnarled hands appeared before her in the water. A larger shadow floated beyond, hidden. More images? Her thoughts dimming further, she couldn't be sure. Bony fingers, colder than the water, cupped her face and moved away, reaching for her wrists. "Come, *Señorita*, and rest." Sharp fingernails pricked the skin on her arms. "You must rest, my child." The voice was filled not with comfort, but menace. Ignacia opened her mouth to scream.

The water unexpectedly swept around her body, tugging at her clothes before releasing her. The hands fell away. And before her head left the water, Ignacia heard the voice growl, "I will come again. Soon, *Señorita*, soon."

An older boy had pulled her from the arroyo in time. In the daze that followed, she remembered coughing up clumps of mud and wheezing for air. Grandfather, bellowing the names of God's saints, had rushed her into the house before she knew no more.

A short time afterward, she had been introduced to her rescuer, a new neighbor boy named Enrique.

CRSORSO

The passage of many, many years had made Ignacia careless. She should have realized that *La Llorona* would never forget. The *bruja* had lurked just beyond the barrier between worlds, waiting for the right opportunity to return. Now Ignacia had unknowingly given it to her, by inviting Enrique home. She shuddered, rubbing her arms for warmth.

Black clouds bled into the sky's soft quilt of magenta and deep blue, blotting out the New Mexican sun's last golden rays. Ignacia knew she must hurry. There was much to prepare, for *La Llorona*'s full power would manifest under the cover of darkness.

But where was Enrique? If she could speak with him, perhaps together they could banish the *bruja* back to the spirit realm.

Lights flickered in the houses to the north. Still, the neighborhood was quiet. Subdued. The absence of Latino music vibrating her windows or of muffled arguments carried on the wind added to Ignacia's growing unease. The only sound came from the junipers and old piñon, sighing in the evening breeze.

The arroyo snaked along near the chain link fence that marked the south boundary of her yard, and she searched beyond it to the paved road on the other side and then east, to the highway and to the tunnel underneath where the sharp curve of the gully disappeared.

Had the *bruja* snatched him away?

Ignacia jumped at sudden movement within the arroyo, clutching the watch like a talisman. She slumped with relief when Enrique, dressed in his gray burial suit, emerged on the near bank. He waved his hand at her, and she returned the gesture, holding out her arms. She hobbled to the edge of the porch, the urge to draw him close soothing her.

"No. Stay back."

She stopped, puzzled and hurt by the command. "*Mi amor?*"

Enrique gave no smile of greeting, and his eyes were shaded from her. "Beware, *querida*. Do not drop your guard, even for me. *She* is near." His legs blurred with movement, but he never strayed from the arroyo's rim.

Ignacia followed his questioning glance. A wet stain spread out beneath his feet into a widening puddle.

"'Rique, watch out!"

Dark water swirled around his pinstripe pants, preventing him from drawing closer. It continued higher and higher, until its dizzying spin covered Enrique's chest. "*Querida*, our love—"

The whirlpool swallowed him up.

Ignacia collapsed against the railing, gripping the metal to prevent herself from pitching into the yard.

Menacing eyes, glowing embers of coal, watched her from within the twisting funnel. "Shall you join your husband?" The water suddenly crashed to the earth, splashing everywhere.

Grabbing her crucifix, Ignacia backed away toward the front door. "Begone, cursed spirit. You are not welcome."

A sudden gust of wind toppled Enrique's altar onto her hip, knocking her to the floor with a thunderous shattering of glass. Burning, stabbing pain exploded in her knees, legs, and hands. The altar's wooden frame pressed into her back. She pulled the crucifix, snapped into two pieces, out from under her, wincing as the jagged edges scraped against her ribcage.

Cruel laughter floated through the yard. "Soon, *Señorita*. Very, very soon."

Broken plates, scattered food, and cooling wax covered her from the waist down. The sweet fragrance of crushed marigolds mixed with the smell of snuffed candles and sweat. Tiny shards of glass, the remains of her *santos*, stuck out from numerous cuts in her tanned skin and littered the floor. Her right knee fared the worst; the skin was stretched tight over a swelling bruise.

Ignacia dragged herself toward the front door, slowly pushing herself out from under the altar with her good leg. With each motion, glass rubbed against her, creating new spasms of agony. Her legs clear of the rickety wood, she sat up and took several calming breaths.

She yanked the protruding slivers from her hands, pressing them against her thighs until the bleeding stopped. Then she pulled herself into a standing position, hugging the wall for support. The injured leg wobbled, spurts of pain shooting down to her toes.

Ignacia clasped Enrique's watch close to her breast, hoping that Enrique somehow remained nearby, safe from *La Llorona*'s snare.

The watch was cold.

Her eyes blurred with tears. Fear for his soul—and hers—stirred in her heart, followed by a gnawing doubt. Could she fight the *bruja* in her condition? She had been weakened in the attack. This had been *La Llorona*'s intent all along.

Holding back her sobs, she opened the door. She had to remain strong for Enrique; if not, he would be lost to her forever.

Ten minutes later, Ignacia had lifted the altar and pushed it against the house. No need for further surprises. A pile of *remedios* littered the surface; these healing substances would repel hexes and *mal de ojo*, the evil eye.

She worked as fast as the aches would allow. Her knee was now wrapped in a tight bandage. The menthol ointment numbed the pain, and she could limp around if she kept her full weight off the joint.

She began by tucking a vase filled with juniper berries at the bottom of the altar to guard her home. Then she placed burning piñon incense at the edge of the porch for good luck. Dabbing the tip of her cedar broom in a *yerba anise* ointment, she leaned it between the wrought iron bars of the kitchen window. The scents of sweet wood and tangy herb lessened the shaking in her arms and legs.

Along the window sill, she lit black, blue, and red candles, representing freedom from evil, harmony, and love. They sputtered in the fitful breeze. Reciting the Lord's Prayer, she sprinkled holy water on each wick. The flames sizzled and dimmed, then sprang back with a steady flicker. She repeated the process with smaller votive candles on the altar.

Next, she hung strands of *yerba buena* from the clothesline under the porch's tin roof. The peppermint aroma was strong and soothing; a burst of energy rushed through her body like desert flowers soaking up newly fallen rain. Renewed confidence blossomed in her mind.

Ignacia knelt before the altar, careful to shift her weight to the left leg. Holding Enrique's watch, she prayed to *Santa Agrippina* and Raphael, the Archangel:

> *Guardian Angels from heaven so bright,*
> *Fold your wings 'round me,*
> *Guard me with love,*
> *Keep me from evil,*
> *And guide from above.*

She dabbed more holy water onto the cover and rewrapped the chain about her wrist. The combination of incense, herbs, and prayer would be enough to protect her, as long as she maintained her strength.

Done with the ritual, Ignacia faced the yard, surprised she had not been attacked. Was *La Llorona* mocking her efforts? A dull anger smoldered in her chest.

Thunderclouds drifted overhead, hanging like thick drapes, ready to smother her. She sensed the *bruja*'s presence within the shifting cauldron in the sky. Ignacia had no doubt that *La Llorona* had brought the storm; the *bruja* probably controlled it. Spider legs of light streaked across the sky, and thunder hammered the air. The smell of approaching rain permeated her nostrils.

The sun dipped below the horizon. Its light faded from magenta to periwinkle and then died out altogether.

A few icy drops of rain touched Ignacia's shoulder, and she shrank away, closer to the house. Grabbing a tube of camphor, she squeezed the ointment into her hand and massaged her chest, willing her heart to slow its rapid beating. The comforting smoothness of Enrique's watch pressed into her other palm.

Another flash of lightning blinded the sky. With a deafening crack of thunder that rattled the window panes, the clouds released their burden. Large drops pounded on the tin roof with such fury that Ignacia wondered if the *bruja* was beating the metal with her own hands. Sheets of wind-driven rain drenched the open end of the porch. Water dripped from the roof onto the altar, then formed small pools on the floor.

The darkness hid the arroyo from sight, but Ignacia heard the water gathering in its parched bowels. A flash flood soon roared from the highway tunnel; the rushing current rose higher. She huddled against the house, the haunting images creeping forward once more.

Sliding into the water head first.

Floating in the current.

Blinded, choking on thick muddy water.

Can't breath. *Dios mío, I can't breathe!*

Ignacia shivered uncontrollably, gasping for air. She was seized by an overwhelming urge to run into the house, but her body didn't respond to her mind's frantic pleas.

The red eyes reappeared, two points of light emanating from a shadow that hovered above the chain link fence. "Almost like the first time."

Ignacia cringed, struggling to gain control of her thoughts. She focused on her anger, repressing the memories until she could speak. "No, not the same. I'm no longer a scared little girl."

"I see a frightened old woman. Alone and weak." *La Llorona* laughed.

"And there is no one to save you now." The *bruja* held out her hand.

A deadening grip stiffened Ignacia's body, and she slid down the wall into a sitting position on the floor, legs splayed outward. Her head lolled forward, and her eyelids drooped.

Susto!

The loss of one's soul.

Ignacia forced herself to blink, realizing the terrible danger. In her long years as a *curandera*, she had only seen the condition twice. Those patients had nearly died, and it had taken all of her concentration to ease the numbing shock to their bodies before calling their souls home.

Ignacia's spirit was already detaching itself from her flesh. A deep cold settled in her limbs, and her rasping breath stopped. She concentrated her ebbing energy on willing her essence back into her body. A small portion trickled back, but the *bruja* grasped Ignacia's spirit and pulled again. They waged a continuous battle of mental strength, but Ignacia's will was slowly crumbling. "I must reach the broom," she wailed inside her head.

She visualized air flowing into her lungs, the tissue expanding and contracting with each breath. Exerting her thoughts on that specific action, she was rewarded with a loud wheeze.

Her arms and legs, robbed of their heat, ached to the center of her marrow. Again she imagined the coordinated action of bone and tendon working together. Quivering to life, her muscles felt like they were tearing with each tiny movement.

Ignacia crawled toward the broom.

Inched forward.

One flicker of progress, followed by moments where her body would not respond.

Her numbed hand, weighed down by a lethargic arm, reached for the handle and missed. She sprawled flat on the floor, splashing in a pool of water.

She pushed herself up, not only fighting the weakness in her arms, but now the added weight of her drenched clothing. The strain was too much; she fell again.

Ignacia would not give up. Taking a deep breath, she pressed her palms against the cement, raised her body again on quaking arms. She reached for the broom.

Her fingers closed on air, but she managed to steady herself. She stayed up.

Another try.

More air. No handle.

Her hand, tingling back to life, finally wrapped around the rough wood of the broom. Dropping back into a sitting position, she jabbed the straw tips into her legs, driving out the unnatural weariness.

Still not enough.

She brushed herself from head to toe. The fiery odor of *yerba anise* seared into her nose. Her skin flushed, more of her essence seeping back into its earthly shell.

"I believe in the Holy Spirit, the Holy Catholic Church, the communion of saints, the forgiveness of sins, the resurrection of the body, and life everlasting. Amen." She struck the porch floor with the broom. "*Venga*," she cried and then answered herself. "I come."

Sweeping, reciting the Apostle's Creed, and striking the broom on the floor, Ignacia commanded her soul to return twice more. Each time she became more wary, stronger. Pain cascaded from numerous cuts and bruises as her nerves came alive, and her bandaged knee pulsed with an aggravated soreness. Sucking in another gulp of air, she relished the water soaking through her dress and dripping on her head through small cracks in the roof. The cold was outside of her now.

"You will not escape," *La Llorona* howled. The *bruja* was nowhere to be seen.

A steady rain fed the swift current within the gulley. The sound reminded Ignacia of a waterfall. It flowed on and on, never ending. Murky water flooded over the bank, into her yard. Her magnolias and geraniums disappeared under the choking waves, as did the base of the junipers and old piñon. The water sucked at the first porch step and continued to rise past the second. Soon the floor would be submerged.

The paralyzing fear of drowning swept through Ignacia again. She squeezed her eyes shut to block out the images, but now a new scene unfolded in her mind. Her dead body floated in the current, her rotting face a mixture of sorrow and horror. Enrique held out his arms, but the treacherous water pulled her out of his reach. Tears clouded his eyes, and she would never wipe them away—their love forever ripped apart.

"No," she shouted. Enrique's love had sustained her for most of her life. Would she surrender it all to a terrifying vision? She wasn't drowning yet. Rising anger pushed away her fear and doubt. She dragged herself to the railing and stood up. "What would you know about love, wretched *bruja*? *Vete*! Go! Give me back Enrique. He doesn't belong to you."

"*Señora*, love brought me to this fate." A column of water rose from the top porch step, forming into the shape of an old, deformed woman. *La Llorona* grinned. "Your pitiful love will also be your undoing."

The *bruja* had addressed her as *Señora*. Why now? Ignacia was emboldened. "Perhaps," she said, "but you have always brought death and sorrow upon yourself. You were forgotten and scorned, never freely loved in return as I have been."

La Llorona's eyes lost their bright spark, the light muted from before. The *bruja* seemed to hesitate.

Hope surged through Ignacia's heart, and she thought frantically for the answer to this new riddle. Enrique had tried to say something about their love before being swallowed up in *La Llorona*'s trap. Of course! The love she shared with her *querido* would not be their undoing; it was the means to force the *bruja* back into the spirit realm.

"Love? What does it matter? Prepare to meet your end, the way you should have as a child." *La Llorona* spun into a churning whirlpool and lunged toward Ignacia.

A liquid mouth filled with sharp teeth descended upon her. Ignacia held up Enrique's watch, high above her head. She poured her memories into it, tempered it with her love, and filled it with every image of Enrique that she remembered: their courtship, wedding, anniversaries, birthdays, years of joy, of sickness, of sadness. Everything that combined their undying devotion. The watch flared in her hand like a miniature sun.

"I do this for you, *querido*." Ignacia plunged her arm into the opening. Her heart fluttered at the icy grip sucking at her skin. Slipping in the deepening pool of water, her arm wrenched free, and she landed on her backside. A new ache to add to the others.

The watch danced within the whirlpool, stopping its forward momentum. The gold hissed its defiance and glowed brighter. The darkness of the water lightened, becoming pale and then transparent.

An enraged shriek shattered Ignacia's kitchen window, covering her with a fresh layer of glass. As the spirit of *La Llorona* was banished, the water under the *bruja*'s control plunged over the porch, sweeping candles, herbs, and the other *remedios* into the yard.

C3ᔓC3ᔓ

Ignacia leaned against the iron railing. The storm had lost its power the moment *La Llorona* was transported to the spirit realm, and the moist night air was peaceful.

Sensing new movement, Ignacia tensed for a new confrontation. Had the vengeful shade found another way to return so soon?

A figure stood under the old piñon. A gentleman in a gray, pinstriped suit. "Enrique!"

"Yes, I am here." He floated toward the porch, his blue eyes twinkling with merriment. A playful, comforting smile shone on his face. "*Mi* 'Nacia. In life, you were my miracle. Now you have become my salvation."

Enrique stopped in front of her. "But you must rest. Sleep, *mi* 'Nacia. I will be waiting for you when your time here has passed."

Ignacia closed her eyes, content at the warmth tingling along her cheek.

"*Gracias, querida,*" he whispered and was gone.

Ignacia stared into the yard long after her *querido* disappeared, dabbing tears from her eyes with the sleeve of her dress. She reached for the handkerchief, but instead found something solid in her pocket. The gold watch glittered on its chain. She opened the cover with trembling hands. A young married couple smiled up at her from within. The heat from the watch warmed her palm.

"*De nada, mi amor,*" she said and blew a kiss into the yard.

Julia

Maxine Anderson

*T*wo *candles melting slowly into hot puddles, staining a pattern on the fabric.*

One Tuesday, I woke up and there was cold rain blowing in my window and a brown bird on the red sill, and I did not believe that I was real and I did not comprehend that I was alone in the room. I threw a mediocre novel about a woman who fell in with the wrong crowd at the quietly huddling bird to keep it out of my room and it flew away into the storm. I felt much too guilty, but my novel grew wings and soared out the window, never to return. There was a note on my pillow but I could not read it because I did not have my glasses on and I could not find them. I could only think of one explanation as I held the note up to my eyes and squinted blindly. I tried to read but could not see and could only think of the fact that, later, there would probably be mushrooms growing in my carpet. "Julia," I said, because only Julia would—

Oval loaves of bread, becoming cold and stale as the moon set.

"Off to seek the American Dream," it read, and a door slammed somewhere, maybe downstairs, maybe next door, maybe at my friend's family's house in Colombia, it didn't matter, because Julia was nowhere and everywhere. I did not know what Julia was seeking or where to find her, but I could not let her go off in search of an ideal that I did not believe in, even if the self-imposed loneliness was the reason for the note, and for Julia's escape. I did not throw the note like I threw the novel; instead I trapped it under a telephone that had never worked and I sat. I sat down on the red windowsill and my feet dangled out into the rain, and my pants became soaking wet. Eventually, I stuck my head out under the grimy water falling from the sky and from the roof, and even though my hair dripped into my face and I saw fantastical patterns in my stinging eyes I could not see Julia there, because she had left this place, and, shivering, I went elsewhere with no plans in mind.

Carefully draped lace, now damp with salt spray from the edge of the earth.

"I saw her in a dream," a bearded man under a bridge told me when I asked of Julia. He was wearing shoes with holes in them, and a pink and black coat with one torn pocket and sleeves that were much too long, and he made sense and did not make sense at the same time. "She is the Archduke of Irrationality with a pinstriped mustache, and the camera loves her like the fast cars do." I couldn't ask whether he meant to say that she was the Archduchess, or whether there was such a title, because the river carried me away, rippling endlessly, and not for the last time I wished I actually had a boat. The man kept fishing for something as I looked back, scooping and scooping the river with his silver net, exhaustion in his face and in his shoulders. He showed just as little expression as I left as when I had first floated by him, holding my umbrella and lazily kicking my legs.

Simmering peppers and spices still smelling strong as the hours progressed.

I was stuck in some city I could not name, lost in the financial district among men in suits with the world on their shoulders, but they did not know that the world was on my shoulders too, because I was looking for Julia, looking for her in every window of every skyscraper and every face in every car. I bought ice cream from Julia on a busy street, a street where I could understand no one and faces appeared on the brick walls, and everyone was sweating in puddles around their feet, or flocking to the giant walls overlooking the river to sit in the shade. I could not see the river, because I could not stay in the city, because it was not where I could be with Julia and bring her back to me. I tried to leave because I thought I heard her voice far away but close, but I could not get through the turnstile to get on the train because I saw Julia in the child with braided hair in the distance, and the angry commuters yelled since I did not have a train ticket and I was staring at the quick-witted girl with flowers in her hair, a girl who would never grow up and would never be unhappy, a dangerous girl with the world contained in her delicate dancing steps, turning under her feet.

Children's toys abandoned on the wooden pier, rotting eventually like the pier itself.

There were birds when I left the city, left the oppressive heat for the terrifying thunderstorms, and there were birds when I finally slept. I thought

I had found the place I should be, the end of the earth among the silent birds and silent stone walls, but the storm changed it all. A police officer came up to me and asked what I was doing, as I sat in the lightning and noise looking up at the sky, and I was angry at him for interrupting something I really did not know how to explain; certainly not at the point he walked up to me, if ever. He was a man who really enjoyed telling others what to do, and though I was afraid of the questions he asked, I told him I was looking for my novel in the patterns of storm-birds, and he did not understand, and thought I was joking with him. "Julia," I told him, and he did not look at me again, but only frowned at the storm. "I once knew a woman named Julia," he said, and he left me alone in the rain. He was not evil, because Julia was there.

Marigolds wilting, their petals imperceptibly turning brown and limp and falling.

Julia was the woman on the bus in Kansas, rattling across endless roads that were not as flat as any breakfast food, singing a song under her breath as the passengers looked away from her embarrassing actions, her embarrassing appearance. She was old, yes, old and tired with two miserable, dirty babies that may not have been hers, and she was alone and had no name, but she was Julia too, and not only that. She had a story to tell, which was why she was Julia so far from the ocean, but although she was more, Julia was more too. Julia was the babies and the water under the bridge and the fire in everyone's eyes that I had seen and had yet to see, and Julia was the dust blowing across the drought-parched grass, and Julia was in the rain that did not come and the rain that eventually would flood the country, and Julia was in every piece of paper thrown out of the bus window, and the woman's gold tooth, and Julia was in that photograph of your parents at their high school prom, and Julia was here and there and nowhere.

The wind blew the altar away, piece by piece, and the waves came up the beach relentlessly.

Millions and millions of stars and grains of sand and androgynous people with sparkling eyes like fire—of course there was fire, there was a car accident, and people I did not know on the beach, people who said they understood, said they knew. That's how it was, that night I found Julia. Beautiful people I had never seen all came together with glowing faces and glowing candles, and prayers came from those who did not know, and only tears from those that did, and no one spoke to me even though I had been searching for weeks. I was invisible among these people, but really, we were all invisible, because it was not about us, not about connections lost or never made or lives that would never touch again. It was Julia. It was Julia on the beach, Julia in photographs and Julia in candy skulls and rosary beads, and Julia came like the winter came, and the city slid into the sea. As I came up for air I saw different marigolds and different photographs, because I knew, if no one else did, that Julia was here and there but never really *here*.

Day de los Muertos

Chris Blocker

For the past eight years, Señor Ambrose has descended from the Sierra Planchadas, reprising his role in our Day of the Dead festivities. This year is no exception. Just as in those years past, he sits on the edge of our tiny civilization and, lacking any countenance, stares at the spot where he had danced with his son. Our celebrations continue late into the night and his focus never wavers; his septuagenarian body does not tire. The children, consumed by sugar, know to let him be. He was sardonic in life, but his passing has only found him apathetic—incapable of recognizing us as any more than wild coyotes, scavenging from the remains of death.

Every year, once the celebrations of our village have turned from somber soliloquies to drunken revelries and beyond, we retire to our abodes. Without looking back, we know that he has taken our place in the dark, attempting to communicate with the spirits of yesterday. He performs the same rituals yearly. Not once has he departed until the last of us have fallen asleep; he remains unseen until the following year, when the scent of the *cempazuchitl* and of copal incense again fills the air.

This year, I am determined to witness his departure. Without fail, Sr. Ambrose has eluded even my great vigilance year after year. The last two, I have remained sober, getting well rested ahead of time and keeping distracted by reading the translated works of Coleridge. The verse had made me sleepy, however, and in my dozing, his silent wake ended abruptly and he disappeared into the night. My attention will not move from his broken form in the blackness of the night. Even now, knowing that he is just beginning his nocturnal ritual, my eyes remain on his barely recognizable silhouette.

Sr. Ambrose has not changed since the day he arrived in our village in the spring of 1914. His wavy white hair reaches down and almost seems to connect with the tufts of hair creeping out of his hanging ears. The same tattered brown coat clings to his back. Perhaps the only thing that has changed is his mocking smile and the inquisitive rise of the eyebrows he once carried proudly.

☙❧☙❧

The first time he came into the valley was the day I buried my only son, Alberto, a victim of Madero's Revolution. Being a new town, the soil at the cemetery had hardly been disrupted; in the previous three years, however, its size had doubled. In the three years following, it would double again—twice. Sr. Ambrose seemed indifferent to the fact he had journeyed into town during such a solemn occasion; yet, the gringo never took his eyes off me from that day forward.

The same day, he told some of the villagers that he had come to the valley to defy old age, to join the revolution and to die "a martyr or a traitor, depending on your outlook." Yet there was hesitance in his statement. He said that he had just come from Ojinaga, where, if he had wanted to die a hero of the Revolution, he could have done so. The truth was evident in his eyes—at the end of his life, a life where he had always had the answers, he finally had questions. He wasn't aware of this, however. They were questions deep within his soul; questions that even his brilliant mind could not completely envelop.

While I was still in mourning, Sr. Ambrose asked to see me. He insisted. So Tuesday morning I invited him into my home. He asked for nothing but water, and proceeded to tell me that he had been a writer in a former life. He spoke in a tone much different than he had with my compatriots, as if he were challenging me and revering me at once.

"Dear sir, you have lost a son," he began after a rudimentary level of comfort had been established between the two of us. "Alberto, I have been told."

"Yes. He was seventeen."

"Died as a result of the war, correct?"

"Yes. He was a member of Villa's army."

"It's been several days, and still you mourn him. Without sounding insensitive, may I ask why?"

His question seemed distant, as if it had been spoken from a faraway land, yet it was close enough that I felt its hardness. Its unyielding grasp of my lungs must have been apparent, because he changed his tone and added, "It is the aspect of the devotion that intrigues me. I am having difficulty understanding a devotion such as yours."

"So you have never had a child, Señor Ambrose?"

"On the contrary. I have been father to three."

"And you wish to understand what it will be like if one of them precedes you in death?"

"Two have already passed on. Only Helen, my daughter, remains."

I did not understand the logic of Americans, but I had thought they shared the same basic emotions. His response made me wonder if perhaps I had misunderstood their culture.

"Day, my eldest son, died when he was seventeen," he continued. "The same age as Alberto." It was our common link. We had both lost our sons suddenly at the age of seventeen, but my companion, who had buried his son twenty-five years prior, still questioned his role as a father.

It would become a season of exploration during a time when, periodically, Sr. Ambrose would talk about joining the revolution and having his body riddled with bullets from a firing squad. And I believed he would, but not until he found his son.

He seemed greatly intrigued by how involved I was in my son's life. He asked if I had been there every day of his life, which I had, until the day he left for the army. He asked about the things we did together and I found joy in telling him of our many adventures.

"When Alberto was very small, he and I would climb up into the hills at the time of the year when the small fairies came out. We would run over the hills and catch them in our hands. And every time we caught one, we'd come together to look at it; but every time that we would open our cupped hands to observe our catch, we would discover that it had disappeared into nothingness.

"Over time, Alberto got too old for such games; perhaps I did as well. And then the fairies disappeared from the hills altogether. No one really noticed when the fairies stopped visiting—it was such a gradual process and we were so busy in those years.

"About a year before he left to join Villa's army, I remembered those times and how much enjoyment they had brought. One night I roused him out of bed. 'Let's go chase fairies,' I said. Knowing that the fairies had left many years prior, he thought I was crazy; being a teenager, he was reluctant; but deep down he really wanted to go. And so we did. We ran around grabbing at the air and every once in a while we would pretend we had caught one. And when we would open our hands, we could almost see the faint image of a fairy, unaffected by its capture."

Sr. Ambrose was clearly pondering the realities of what others called our Mexican mysticism when I added, "You *must* capture every moment. We looked crazy in those hills, but we didn't care. Both of us were forever shaped by that event.

"A soldier who was on the battlefield with Alberto said that right before my son died, while he was lying on the dirt mortally wounded, he reached up and said '*Para mi padre.*' The soldier said that when he opened his clutched hand, stained with blood, that there was nothing in it. But I knew that he had finally caught a real fairy."

On many different occasions Ambrose's questions returned to whether I thought I'd see Alberto again. "Of course," I would respond.

"In Heaven?"

"In Heaven and here on Earth."

"So you believe that the dead can make themselves palpable to us?"

"Certainly."

Ambrose stroked the hair on his face and asked, "Then how can we distinguish the living from the dead?"

I had seen the dead many times, but the only reason I knew they were dead is because I had seen their lifeless bodies, or I had heard of their death. Besides, their actions did not speak of the living. My reply was unsatisfactory, "I do not know, but I have seen it."

"When?"

"Many times. Last year I saw my father, Aunt Carmen, and my niece who died from Diphtheria when she was seven. It was *el Día de los Muertos* and my—"

"Ah yes! *Día de los Muertos.* A day where the dead are consecrated with the virtues we hold so dear in life—gluttony, drunken misbehavior, and the unrelenting ego." After he said this, however, his mocking expression melted into something altogether different. "I feel that my energy has left me," he lamented, retiring for the night.

The following day, Señor Ambrose disappeared from our village. He had been riding on his horse when the muddy boots of a small group of soldiers dirtied our clean streets. Talk of spies and traitors was abundant and suddenly the market was filled with elderly women and soldiers, former silver prospectors and politicians. A thief took off with a chicken. Gunshots were fired. In the midst of all this, Ambrose's horse threw him off and he fell to the ground.

Minutes later, as I sifted through the chaotic but dispersing crowd, I made my way to the spot where he had fallen. A small dab of blood stained the rock, but no other remnant remained of the gringo. Naturally, I asked others, but the event had been so riotous that no one was sure. An old man said that the visitors had carried him away; two others said that he was eager to leave with the soldiers; an attractive young woman insisted that he had walked up into the mountains. Señor Ambrose was gone. I would not have the privilege of seeing him again for nearly four months.

CREECREE

It is now late, and the silly old gringo has continued his typical spectacle. He stands awkwardly at the stone where he saw his son nine years ago, his feet tapping to an imaginary beat. His hands reach out clumsily to be taken by another, but they shake nervously in the cool night. Yet he continues to stand there, a statue in the desert. When Day does not come, he begins to dance, hoping this year he will find the right step, that he will lose his balance at just the right time and fall to the ground, that a hand will reach down for him, and that he'll look up into the eyes of his son, seventeen, but with a hole through his head.

After performing this ritual for near twenty minutes, he'll fall to the ground and begin sobbing. He'll look around and make sure that he has the right location. Perhaps his son has been standing behind him all this time. Perhaps Day is just late. Maybe he has the wrong day and will realize his mistake and show up any minute now.

It breaks my heart to watch him, knowing that his son is not coming. Nine years ago he passed through this world. But I don't believe that he will ever again.

CB∞CB∞

The tombs were decorated, the bells had been rung, and the light of a thousand candles filled the sky. Just as he had come earlier in the year, Sr. Ambrose came down from the Planchadas and entered into the village as if he had never left.

"Señor Ambrose! From where have you come? Where have you been?"

"I have come to see your dead. To join in your festivities." An exuberance overflowed from his speech, and his appearance had changed dramatically from one that months prior was glossing over with doubt and hopelessness.

"But where have you been, my friend? I looked all over for you."

"That conversation will have to wait." He poured himself some *atole*, drank it swiftly, and began to mingle with the crowd.

The nightly festivities went as they always did, but I could not take my eyes off of my gringo friend. He was different, yet he had not changed since the day he left. He talked openly with everyone, and participated in every aspect of the celebration that he would have censured before.

As the night was beginning to wane, Sr. Ambrose ran to the edge of the darkness and as he returned, he exclaimed that he had found him. From the dark, a mysterious figure appeared, and I knew before seeing the hole through his head lent by a revolver that Day had come.

Father and son embraced and, without warning, the elder took his son and danced with him. Uncontrollably. Laughter encompassed the darkness as their antics appeared quite humorous; at the same time, however, tears clung to the faces of even those who had barely known the old man.

Ambrose and Day continued dancing, singing, and running around the village together. There was no meaningful dialogue between the two. Nothing expressed to make up for lost time. No questions asked. They were merely two souls playing in the realm of the dead.

They continued while the rest of us, quite tired and feeling intrusive, decided to retire. When the village awoke, both were gone. Señor Ambrose returned the following year to recapture that moment; Señor Day did not.

⊰⊱⊰⊱

It is now morning. I have just dozed for a few minutes, and in that short span of time, the valley has once again become vacant. Next year, perhaps, I will try to wake early. Or perhaps I will just leave it be.

Regardless, another year has passed—and Señor Ambrose has danced around in the desert and found only disappointment. He is plagued by recapturing that one moment. And it concerns me greatly, not only for his eternal soul, but mine as well. For he has taught me that sometimes, even in death, we can be separated from those who are departed.

Since the day Alberto died, I have hunted for fairies many times. It is such a strong passion that I cannot help but wonder if I will spend eternity chasing these creatures. What scares me most, however, is to know my intentions are not simply to catch one and observe it; rather, if I do catch one, and I am sure that someday I will, I will shit on its face and crush its delicate wings inside of a fist that will never again relinquish its wrath. God help me.

Mexican Moon

Edward DeGeorge

Vic's head was pounding. The crew was treating this like a leisurely Mexican retreat rather than a tight shoot. Was he the only one who saw disaster in the wings? Worse, he could hear the plaintive whining in his voice, and he hated it.

"This dress is wrong. The costume needs to fit on her backwards. We're trying to make it look like her head has been turned around backwards."

The flimsy garment rack swayed to and fro as Miriam pawed through the outfits. The rack looked like it would collapse at any moment. "Relax, chief. We've got two of them. There's another one fitted for the special shot." She was a tough old bird half Vic's size and she looked like she wanted to stuff him in a trunk. The cigarette she waved about issued stale smoke that both repelled him and fueled his own craving to light one.

"Jesus Christ, how hard can it be to find? It's green." Vic stamped away. He felt like the garment rack, ready to collapse at any moment. Sid still hadn't secured additional financing for the film. They had a ten-day shooting schedule with enough money for no more than eight days of film. And that was stretching it. Plus, they were already a half-day behind schedule, which would mean dropping scenes or additional rental on the villa and salaries for the cast and crew. Vic was well into his why-did-I-ever-get-into-this-business mode that usually didn't kick in until the second week of shooting.

He pushed through the double doors of the study. The Mexican sun blinded him as he stepped onto the patio. He strode to the edge of the patio, placed one foot upon the low, decorative wall that surrounded it, and looked out at the gulf. Beyond the wall the earth fell away steeply. Fifty yards below the villa was a narrow strip of beach that was more rock than sand. The waters of the gulf crashed against the shore with a mighty *shush*, celebrating its own violence with a gusto that was infectious. At the same time, the steady tempo of its assaults on the beach was relaxing. Vic heard the lonesome cry of a seagull, but he did not see the bird. He wrestled with his craving for nicotine.

They were lucky to have found this villa that provided them with a shooting location and housing together. An isolated estate south of Guaymas with an old colonial main house and four outlying buildings, it lay nestled between the shoreline and jagged hills speckled with saguaro.

The furnishings and décor were authentic old world Mexican. The house stood empty most of the year and the owner had been overjoyed to rent his family home for a movie production.

The *flip-flop* of rubber thongs on the patio flagstones heralded his assistant's approach. Cathy moved to his side and they murmured "Hi" to each other. "Mike wants you to check the set up in front of the villa." Cathy brushed an errant strand of long blond hair from her face. The ocean breeze played with it, swept it back across her cheek.

Vic glanced at her. She was slender and shapely, almost a perfect product of California. She wore smart emerald shorts that barely covered the sweep of her buttocks and a short-sleeved cotton top that rippled in the breeze. Huge round sunglasses perched on her head, much too big for her small face, yet marvelously kitschy when she wore them. She clutched a clipboard— heavy with the detritus of filmmaking—to her chest, concealing the svelte curves of her meager breasts. If she'd had a boob job five years ago she'd probably be an actress instead of a director's assistant.

"I'm sure it's fine. Round up the actors and I'll meet you out front. We need to nail those two scenes before dinner."

"Ten-four."

She scurried away, barely lifting her feet so her thongs wouldn't slide off.

The lead female character was being played by Francesca Dellabueno, an Italian model, barely eighteen, as she endeavored to parlay her four years of European magazine covers and commercials into an American film career. That her first acting assignment landed her in a cheap horror movie did not seem to trouble her.

Vic fought with the frustration that her poor command of English engendered. At the end of every take she dashed for the haven of an umbrella like the word "cut" was a starter's pistol. "*Il sole e il peggio nemico della donna,*" she said. *The sun is a woman's worst enemy.*

Dinner was a salty plate of shrimp with rice and beans. They shared a platter of steamed clams. Vic contributed little while Pat, his director of photography, laid out plans for tomorrow's shoot. Cathy had kicked off one thong and stroked Vic's ankle with the top of her foot.

Vic's mind drifted. He had fought with Marjory again before he'd left for Mexico. Money, time spent together, the kids: she had all the arguments down pat for a beat-up, twenty-year marriage.

And here he was, Victor Reynolds, not even a footnote in cinema history. He'd wanted to be a John Sayles, a Robert Altman. Instead he had become a third-rate Roger Corman.

That evening Vic held Cathy close to him as they swayed slowly, a private dance in his room, the master bedroom of the villa. The portable CD player ground out the pensive strains of a female singer too young for her melancholy.

The old fashioned phone on the nightstand jangled. Vic switched off the CD player in passing and picked up the phone.

"Marj, hi. I was just getting ready to call you." Cathy sat in a chair in the corner of the room, watching him.

"What did he do? What's wrong?" Vic shrugged his shoulders and flashed a regretful smile at Cathy.

"Did he smash the car? Then what's the big deal? It's just a ticket. Marj, he's seventeen; he's going to have a few beers. No, I don't think it's all right. It's just how it is. What do you want me to do about it? I'm 500 miles away."

Cathy stood. Vic waved her to sit down, his hand flapping like a wounded bird. "If he loses his license maybe he'll learn to be more responsible."

Vic watched helplessly as Cathy walked to the door. He wanted to go to her, but the phone cord tethered him to the wall. He winced as the door closed forcefully behind her.

"Was that the door?" Marj asked, her voice tinny and sharp in his ear.

"Yeah. The wind blew it shut."

They argued for another twenty minutes. When they said good night, her voice was distant, unreadable. He could feel the gulf of miles that separated them.

He threw on a shirt, but didn't button it. The hall outside his room was dark. The end of the hall held a pool of preternatural light, like some desert mirage. He traversed the length of the hall, stepping into the light as he reached the top of the staircase. From tall windows at the front of the house, moonlight poured over him. The moon itself stared down at him from the heavens like the eye of some fierce goddess.

Vic padded down the stairs silently, unmoved by the magnificence of the heavens. He crept to the back hall and slowly negotiated the dark passage. Though it wasn't terribly late, everyone had retired for an early start in the morning.

Vic found Cathy's room and knocked gently. A sudden fear gripped him that he had the wrong room. This was only their second day at the villa. If he had counted wrong . . .

The door swung open and Cathy smiled at him wanly. She stretched up to kiss his cheek, but Vic turned his head and their lips brushed briefly. Vic studied her face. Had she been crying?

Cathy squeezed his arm. "I'm really tired. Why don't I see you tomorrow for breakfast?"

"Sure, that's fine," he said, his voice husky. "Get some sleep." He kissed her again, longer, deeper. She returned the kiss, let him be the one to break it, giving him at least that much reassurance.

Vic plodded back to the stairway. The great windows showed the moon banished behind dark clouds, perhaps sulking. As Vic's hand touched the banister, he glimpsed a pale illumination that his mind could not identify. It was like moonlight sprung from itself, pure and white, confined to the span at the top of the steps.

He stared at it in wonder. It filled him with a primitive awe that only nature, with all its myriad splendors, could produce. The moonlight swirled, danced, pirouetted slowly.

As Vic stood rapt, the moonlight changed. He couldn't identify the point at which it stopped being mere light and transformed into a little girl.

He saw her distinctly: a little Mexican girl of seven or eight, standing at the top of the stairs in her nightgown, clutching something in her arms.

She was made of moonbeams.

Vic's mind told him this could not be. This was some practical joke the crew was playing on him. He tried to seize on that solution, but he knew it wasn't true.

The girl began to descend the stairs. Right foot, then left foot, one stair at a time. She held the railing with one hand and cradled her treasure in her other arm.

Vic staggered back against the wall. It braced his weight as his knees threatened to give.

The little girl did not look at him as she came toward him. Her face was beautiful, angelic. Vic could see through her like she was only half there.

He now saw what she carried so tenderly: a rag doll, yarn for hair, buttons for eyes, one arm missing.

She passed by him slowly, never looking at him. A strong scent of roses filled the air, then vanished. Her measured steps took her around the corner and out of sight. Her aura of light blinked off.

Vic swallowed dryly and sought to calm his heart as it pounded in his chest. Why had he been so frightened? Nothing about her had suggested a threat.

He followed her path to the back hall, but found no sign of her. Watching for any manifestation that might greet him, he returned to his room. Once inside, he felt safe. The room was mundane and, even after only two nights, familiar. He slept like the dead.

CR&OCR&O

The company rose before dawn and ate a breakfast of eggs, ham, and tortilla shells. The actors and the crew divided unspoken into gangs. Most of the crew wore some form of simple costume, mask, or make-up in honor of Halloween. They had lobbied for a full-blown party, but—morale be damned—there was no room in the shooting schedule for late night celebrations and hangovers. Vic felt a little unnerved by his encounter of the previous night. But what a story it would make. *After* they had safely left the villa . . .

In the glum, pre-dawn sky, sporadic clouds threatened to block their sunlight, but they set up on the patio with unwarranted optimism. They were rewarded with a clear sky and worked at capturing the four scenes they needed.

During lunch, Vic and Cathy ate strawberries in her room and made out like high school kids. She resisted his every effort to peel off her clothes with the promise of, "Tonight."

The afternoon was too hot for working outdoors. They set up for a shot in the study of the villa. Fans cooled the room and would be used while filming to simulate the telekinetic energies of evil as a sorcerer's damned soul tried to possess the lovely maiden played by Francesca.

Vic's thoughts went to his experience of the previous night. The irony of filming a horror movie in a remote Mexican villa where the ghost of a young girl wandered the halls did not amuse him.

He walked through the scene with Francesca. She wore the billowing green party gown of another century and an ostentatious faux diamond necklace that, despite being costume jewelry, was in itself quite expensive.

Francesca stood centered between the open double doors that led onto the patio. Though this room was on the ground floor, this scene would be matched to a balcony exterior that would make it appear to be on an upper story.

Francesca held her arms at shoulder height and her hands gripped the doorjamb at either side.

"Lean back more." Vic slipped behind her. "It's as though the winds will blow you away."

He put his hands above hers on the jamb and demonstrated for her. She covered his hands with hers and leaned back into him. She let her body rest against his. Her head lolled back so that his face was buried in her hair. "Like this?"

He pulled himself forward, carrying her as well. His hands went to her waist as he spoke softly in her ear. He came around to face her, letting his fingertips slide across the small of her back. As he gave her direction, he searched her flawless face: her large brown eyes, razor-thin eyebrows, pouting lips, and her olive skin that had him mystified as to why she hid from the sun.

She did not shrink from his scrutiny, but instead met his gaze boldly. Her silent demeanor stirred his blood as he continued to babble instructions that grew less and less meaningful. She took a short step that brought her against him with the barest contact. Or was it simply her full skirts that brushed against him? Pat called out from the camera set up. "We're ready to roll, chief."

Vic backed up a step, back to reality.

They broke for a quick dinner and then shot for a few hours more. When everyone was tired and short-tempered, they called it a night. Cathy begged off with a headache. Vic thought she looked drawn. He felt exhausted as well and fell into bed without undressing.

He woke with a start from a nightmare of darkness surrounding him like a fist. He felt disoriented, lost. His bedside clock told him that he had dozed for only forty-five minutes.

He got up and brushed his teeth and splashed tepid water on his face. His bedroom was empty. When he gazed out the window, the world looked empty as well. He slipped from his room with the notion of slipping into Cathy's bed.

As he walked down the steps, his fingers caressed the banister that the ghost child had clung to the night before. As the bottom of the stairs he paused to see if she would appear.

Standing there, he recalled the way Francesca had leaned against him. Impulsively, he made his way to the side door.

Francesca's quarters were in one of the four outlying buildings that had once housed servants. Vic strode across the grounds beneath a brazen moon. The ocean surf whispered to him, urging him on. When he reached her quarters, his courage flagged. After an uneasy deliberation, he tapped at her door.

He feared his faint knock had gone unheard. Just as he decided to leave, the door opened abruptly and Francesca stood in the narrow gap.

"It's late. What do you want?" She looked sleepy and cross as she stared at him, clutching her robe shut around her.

"I was wondering . . . ." He had to clear his throat. "If you wanted to have a drink."

Her lips curved into a brief and mocking smile. "But you didn't bring anything with you."

Vic shrugged. Francesca tilted her head to the side, smiling wryly. "I wish I had something to offer you," she said. "But I don't."

He marveled at the facility with which she spoke English this night. He wanted to reach past the door and cup her chin, but the narrow gap was a course he didn't know how to negotiate. "Some other time, then."

She flashed her small smile again. Vic wondered if she had someone in her room. "Good night, *Signore* Reynolds." Her eyes held his gaze as the door slowly closed. He heard the deadbolt slide home with undisguised finality. He plodded back to the villa, hands deep in his pockets, the landscape as desolate as his heart. At the foot of the stairs, he waited twenty long minutes before going up to bed.

CB&)CB&)

In the morning they shot exteriors. Francesca made no mention of his visit last night. Her English, however, lapsed to its previous unwieldy level.

During lunch he called Marjorie. They argued over the lawyer she had retained to handle Eric's DUI and naturally moved on to what a son of a bitch Vic was. All their arguments led logically to that conclusion.

The afternoon saw Cathy retire to her room with cramps.

When they broke for dinner, Vic sought out the villa's caretaker, Miguel. Well into his fifties, he was a spry man with sparkling eyes. The top of his head barely reached Vic's chin. His black curly hair was overrun with gray.

"This is a very old villa, isn't it?"

Miguel grinned vapidly. "*Oh sí, Viejo.* Two hundred years and older. My *abuelito*, he was big boss here for owner."

"You grew up here?"

"Oh, *sí*. I play, I school, I work all my life."

"Have you ever seen a ghost here?"

"*Que?*"

"A ghost. Um—el spectro."

Miguel tittered as though Vic had told a hilarious joke. "*Un espírito.* No, *señor.*"

Vic's face darkened. "You're sure? A little girl?"

Miguel waved his hands. "*No tenemos espíritos aquí. Todos esta mos feliz.*" *Everybody is happy.* What did he mean by that?

Miguel poked Vic's chest with a rigid finger. "*Señor* Vic. We have no ghosts, but I show you something."

Miguel led him out to the patio. He walked to the northern corner where the low stone wall that bordered the patio butted into the villa. When Vic hesitated, Miguel waved and said, "You come!"

Vic joined him at the edge and found himself looking down at narrow stone steps. Miguel smiled and motioned to him. He stepped over the low wall, then trotted down the steps with nimble feet. Vic followed slowly, brushing against the villa on his left and away from the open right side. The tall steps were made for shorter feet than his. The overall effect was a steep descent. Vic counted thirteen steps. But did the last one count since they were on level ground?

They doubled back now, following a gently sloping path toward the gentle susurrus of the surf. Grotesque saguaro lined the path, planted in a dense wall that made an effective fence. How had they missed this area of the villa? It had been hidden here all this time. Vic's mind started working on ways to incorporate it into the film: perhaps the scene where Bert lost his soul. The caretaker trotted ahead of Vic with gay steps.

The wall of cactus took a sharp left and the path followed. Vic stepped around the corner and his feet ground to a halt. In the clearing before him lay a cluster of gravestones. He stared numbly at this hidden area of tranquility. His eyes took in the carefully tended graves, and the various shapes of the headstones. They were mostly rectangles with two—no three—crosses and a lone angel. A low, wrought iron fence contained the three sides of the private cemetery, but the path was wide open to it.

Vic entered carefully. He had to walk around the stones to read them. They all faced the ocean, away from the villa. The sound of the surf was a gentle serenade. He counted seventeen graves. The most recent burial had been in 1906.

He scanned each set of dates carefully, doing the math. He found that most of the graves were marked with more than one name. Judging by the standard width of those graves it would seem the occupants were stacked on top of each other. Several graves were decorated with little statuettes of the Virgin Mary.

Except for one grave, they were all adults, the youngest, a man of twenty-three. The sole child's grave was for Constance Paloma, 1899-1901. Two years old, and the diminutive size of the grave reflected it.

Little Dove, Vic thought. He said a prayer for her, then turned away. Miguel waited patiently at the path.

Vic made a second tour of the stones, looking for something he had missed. He was certain there should be a grave for a seven or eight year old girl. But he found nothing.

After dinner they started shooting the scene between Bryan and Francesca. Bryan played the evil sorcerer attempting to seduce the ingenue's chaste character. Vic felt distant from the action.

They replayed the scene from different camera positions. Vic felt a dull pang of jealousy each time Bryan pulled the struggling Francesca against him.

When they had wrapped for the day, he took tea up to Cathy. He shook out two Ibuprofen tablets for her and told her how the day had gone. He stroked her hair softly while she lay back with closed eyes.

Vic closed the door quietly when he left. Restless, aimless, he wandered out to the patio. He sat on the low stone wall that ran the perimeter and let his legs dangle over the edge. He sat for over an hour, undisturbed except by his thoughts.

He thought of Marjory, a good wife saddled with a poor husband. He thought of how jubilant they had been when they had taken their newborn son home seventeen years past.

At nine, Eric was plunged into a battle with encephalitis. Vic remembered too well the fevers and the pain-wracked little form. It seemed a miracle when he had begun a slow recovery. What if they had lost him? What if he were walking through halls, night after night, never finding peace?

Vic's face crumbled and tears spilled from his eyes. His body shook with sobs that he managed to keep silent. The crying jag passed quickly. It left him feeling tired, drained of energy, yet thankfully, drained of emotion as well.

He searched the sky for a long time, examining each star for the individual beauty it possessed. So many, yet all so different. It seemed that there must be more stars out there than grains of sand here on Earth.

He hauled his legs in, surprised at how stiff his muscles felt. He crept into the silent villa, careful of the cables and lights that littered the study. At the foot of the stairway, he stopped.

He stared up its wide expanse. He wanted to see her again, the little ghost girl. Would she come because he wanted her to come? Did she appear at a certain hour of the night? Or only once a year on some forgotten anniversary?

Had he imagined her that night?

He tried to calculate what time he'd seen her, but found it impossible. At each creak of the villa's timbers, he imagined the shuffling footsteps of unquiet spirits.

When it happened, that gathering of unearthly light, it was so subtle it didn't register at first.

A nimbus grew at the top of the stairs, moonbeams woven into some ethereal fabric. Again, the drifting light shaped itself into the form of a little girl.

The same heart-pounding fear gripped Vic. Maybe this wasn't such a good idea. He watched her step down the first stair, right foot, then left foot. Her hand gripped the banister as those delicate bare feet carried her closer. She hugged her precious rag doll, her only companion in a lonely afterlife.

When she came eye level with Vic, he said, "Wait." His voice was a croaking whisper. He repeated that single word, louder, steadier.

She did not pause in her descent, did not acknowledge his presence. Her face bore an expression of single-minded intent. Her fine hair cascaded over her shoulders.

She climbed down the final stair and turned her back to Vic. She was close enough that he could reach out and touch her, but his arms hung at his sides uselessly. "*Muchachita*," he said. She paced away from him with measured steps. The sweet scent of roses followed in her wake.

"Are you lost?"

The little girl halted. Vic's chest felt tight; his lungs were in a vise. The little girl turned slowly. She faced him directly, her eyes pinning him with unremitting ferocity.

On trembling legs, Vic took the few steps that separated them. She raised her head as he approached, her gaze fixed on his.

He extended his hand to her slowly, the way you would so as not to scare off a small bird. She reached up and placed her tiny hand in his. It was neither icy cold nor fiery hot, but it had weight and he felt the slight pressure of her grip.

He led her in a new direction. They retraced his steps to the study and then to the patio. She walked beside him in unquestioning trust as he took her to the low stone wall around the patio and he stepped over it. He looked back at her, still holding her hand.

When she did not move, he reached down and put his hands in her armpits, lifting her over the wall. She came up easily, weightier than a moonbeam, lighter than a little girl. Instead of putting her down, he sat her in his arms. Her arms encircled his neck and she laid her head on his shoulder.

He carried her down the treacherous stone steps and along the hidden path. The wash of the surf served as her lullaby. He carried her into the cemetery where the Mexican moon bathed the headstones with a glorious light.

He set her down and watched while she drifted between the markers, studying each one the way he had earlier. Her pale form blended in and out of the moonlight. He sat and watched her as she paced up and down the short rows. The sound of the ocean soothed his mind.

He awoke to bright sunlight and the stiff muscles of sleeping on cold earth. As he stepped over the low wall onto the patio, Miguel saw him. The caretaker hurried to him, concern large on his face.

"*Señor* Vic, were you lost?"

Vic squeezed the little man's shoulder. "Yes, I think I was."

The patio was festooned with strings of orange marigolds to celebrate *Día de los Muertos*. Charlotte in craft services had fashioned dozens of bite-size skulls—some from sugar, some from chocolate—and set them out at each table. Breakfast was set up and the crew wandered out one by one to fill their plates.

Vic felt glad to be among them, the living.

Ya-acawa

Sheri Sebastian-Gabriel

M ago shoved a sugar skull, bedraggled marigolds, and a sack of dollar-store votives into his saddlebag and slapped it shut before looking up at us.

"What are you assholes just standing there for?" he asked, eyebrows pushed together.

"Remind me why we're doing this again," Spike provoked, arms crossed over his leather-clad chest.

Mago opened his gap-toothed mouth and pointed a dirty brown finger, accusatory.

"Same reason we did it last year. And the year before. *Día de los Muertos.* You can talk to the dead. Show some fuckin' respect for Fox, man."

His eyebrows relaxed, but he gave me a bone-chilling stare before getting on his Harley.

Fox didn't speak to us last year and I was skeptical he'd say anything this time either. He hadn't been doing much communicating since he crashed head-on into that tractor trailer out on Route 46.

Still, I buckled my saddlebag and hopped on my bike, pure curiosity and boredom driving me over any real hope of hearing from our dead friend. Spike followed suit and we roared off down the dirt-paved road toward Morningside Cemetery and Fox.

The sun traced an orange-pink glow over the hillside, the dusty plateau looking down on the stiffs like a monolith. The lines of shadow-darkened headstones made me shiver in spite of myself. The thought of all those dead bodies just feet under the ground gave me the heebie-jeebies. I ain't scared of nobody, but messing with the dead is another story.

The girl appeared along the path, near the cemetery gates. Her dark hair spilled down her back and her jeans-clad bottom swayed with each step.

Mago's bike slid to a halt just ahead of her, and the acrid smell of exhaust and dirt assaulted my nose.

Spike and I stopped our bikes as well and I said, "Shit, man. Now we're stopping so he can get some ass?"

She approached the bike tentatively, and Mago looked her up and down. Pale-faced with small breasts, he must have approved because the two exchanged words we couldn't hear and she climbed on the back of his hog.

Mago and the girl led the way down the cemetery path, buzzing echoes bouncing from tombstone to tombstone. If the Day of the Dead won't wake up Fox, I thought, maybe Mago's bike will.

We pulled up to the stone and Mago lifted the skull, marigolds, and votives from the saddlebag, and methodically, ritualistically spread the candles out at the foot of Fox's tombstone. One by one, he lit the candles with his silver lighter. Then he rested the sugar skull atop the stone and placed the flowers at Fox's head. The girl stood, hands crossed behind her back, studying the ritual curiously. A slight smile spread across her small, delicate features as she stared—a little too attentively—at this strange display.

Spike and I exchanged uncomfortable glances as Mago eased himself onto the chilled, browned grass and muttered something incomprehensible near where Fox's ear might have been, under tons of dirt and rocks and maggots and worms.

The girl—her name was Jane, Mago told us—seemed unfazed by this peculiar display. In fact, she knelt down next to Mago and placed a bone-thin hand on his shoulder as he babbled in some strange language to the corpse underground. Spike and I both grew up in Laredo, and we knew enough Spanish to hold conversations with Mago. The language he spoke to Fox's remains was not Spanish.

I eyed Jane with trepidation and was amazed when she, dead-eyed and pasty, began chanting in the same odd language. The two sang some weird monotone song, using some of the words I'd heard in their chant. *Ya-acawa.* They repeated that over and over again in this song. *Ya-acawa, ya-acawa.* I'll never forget that word. To this day, I don't know what it means, but the thought sends a chill down my spine.

The glow from the votives seemed to rise, and Spike and I both took a few steps back, genuinely hoping nothing would happen. Darkness crept upon the cemetery slowly, and the candles flickered and danced in the November wind. Besides the hum of the song, the cemetery was quiet. Unless he was whispering something only Mago and Jane could hear, Fox had yet to speak up.

Mago pushed himself onto his knees and brushed his hands together. His eyes were wide and his dark hair was wild, in all directions. Jane remained kneeling at the gravesite and slowly moved her eyes toward us. Those large, chocolate brown eyes seemed to hold the answer to everything, but she sat cast in a white glow by the candles, lips closed tightly.

"So?" Spike said, braver than I, inching closer to the gravesite.

"It's going to take more than chanting," Mago told him. "I need something else. Fox didn't give a shit about some flowers or candles."

He stood and grabbed a flask out of his pocket, and he took a long, hard swig. Vodka, I suspected. Mago was a vodka man. He upended the remainder of the vodka over Fox's grave, perhaps an offering.

Mago clutched Jane close to his side and whispered something in her ear. She nodded slowly and then he shoved his tongue in her mouth. Jane stared icily at us, Mago still stuck to her mouth, with narrowed eyes. There was something about her that made me very uncomfortable, and so I was relieved when she and Mago began walking toward the plateau.

The two shadows edged through the brush and past the headstones. Spike and I watched them ease up the side of the blackened mesa.

"You think we should get the hell out of here?" Spike asked once they were out of earshot.

"I don't know, man. There's something weird about that girl. Maybe we ought to wait."

Spike didn't respond and we both sat on the chilly ground next to Fox's grave. The silence between us lingered until Spike said, "You think he can really talk to us?"

I sniffed and replied, "You really believe in this crap? C'mon, man. Be for real."

"What about all that stuff they were saying? You know, to Fox. What was that?"

I shrugged, still halfway watching the two figures move up the side of the hill. The outlines neared the top of the plateau. Mago's stocky shadow arrived first and a darkened arm extended to pull up Jane's wispy frame.

"I have no idea," I replied, taking my eyes from the plateau and focusing again on Spike. "I was wondering the same thing. Could you figure out what language they were speaking?"

"Beats the hell out of me," Spike said and reclined on his hands.

The remainder of the sunlight had been swallowed by night and I could no longer see the shadows on top of the plateau. I was secretly grateful for the candlelight, though I never would have admitted that to Spike. I suspected he was happy to have the light there too.

I ran a palm over Fox's headstone. The candles still burned bright enough to reveal its inscription. Jose "Fox" Martinez. Born May 21, 1962. Died Sept. 12, 2006. Melancholy grabbed at me for a moment and I could see his face in my mind. He had been a good friend to all of us and it would have been nice to talk to him again. I secretly hoped this voodoo junk worked and that he'd say, "Hey, you assholes. Stop moping around." That's just the kind of thing Fox would say. Spike must have sensed my sadness, because he stood and put a hand on my shoulder. It made me jump; I was afraid that strange girl had come back from the mesa. I didn't want her touching me or coming anywhere near me for that matter.

Voices broke the silence, echoing in the distance, and Spike and I wrenched our necks toward the plateau. The black hill was surrounded in navy, and if any people were still atop it, they were obscured by the dark.

"*Ancewa*," a voice that sounded like Mago's said. "*Ya-acawa*."

My guts twisted and I wished Mago would finish up whatever he and that girl were doing so we could beat a retreat already. Spike's eyes widened and glimmered in the fast-dimming candlelight.

Soft and sweet, at first, a female voice began singing another song in that same weird language. The voice became more and more agitated until the words came out in grunts that sent choppy echoes bounding off the headstones. A scream shattered the air. It was Mago.

"*Dios mío!*" he yelled. "No, no, no!"

This plea was followed by a lengthy scream and the two of us ran down the cemetery path. Spike took off down the center of the cemetery, hurtling over the tombstones, vainly feeling them out in the dark.

"Wait," I shouted out. "You're going to kill yourself."

Spike flipped over a stone and landed headfirst against the ground. I saw him pull himself back up, but I could tell he was hurt.

"Go on," he gasped. "Get Mago."

I dashed on into the night, following the pitch-black path by dead reckoning, hoping to find Mago by his cries. Silence pervaded. It was as if he had been swallowed up by the earth.

The path wound around the far end of the cemetery at the edge of the plateau and I saw the heap lying there. Against the shadows, I found his limbs outstretched in all directions, pointing unnaturally at angles. His chest moved slightly, irregularly, and I nearly tripped over a headstone myself to get at him.

"Mago," I shouted. "What happened? Talk to me, brother."

I tried to find his eyes, but he was a dim shadow of a person, broken against the graves. He sputtered slightly and I tried to make out what he was saying. His breath was labored and he murmured a few words I could barely understand.

"Girl. Get girl. Knife. Sacrifice me."

Each word was punctuated by a horrible wheeze, a begging breath for life. I saw his Bowie knife sheathed in his belt and I grabbed it. I put a hand on his bloodied chest, desperate for him to move, to breathe, to get up out of this place and ride home with us. The movement of his chest stopped. I turned, determined, and tucked the knife into my belt.

I heard some scuttling noise as I made my ascent up to the mesa and my heart pounded as every muscle strained to find the sound. My eyes ached against the black night and my arm was slightly pelted by tiny rocks. Eyes straining, I looked above me to find the girl calmly making her way down the side of the hill.

"You wicked bitch," I shouted, surprised by the loudness of my own voice. "You killed him."

My body slid back to the edge of the cemetery and she coasted the remainder of the way down the hill. I dashed toward her with the knife and held it inches from her form. She held out a hand and clutched my wrist with a strength that belied her bony physique.

Her face was luminous, emitting its own light against the depths of blackness, and her smile gleamed.

"I'm afraid you have it wrong," she said, her voice clear and even. "He was trying to kill me. I was going to be a sacrifice for Fox. Too bad he failed. I needed a sacrifice too."

Her giggle made my skin crawl and I swallowed hard, my throat dry. I watched her walk off, engulfed by the night.

When I found Spike, he was a bloodied mess, nose busted and face oozing from the scrapes he'd gotten from the tombstones.

"Well, what happened? Where's Mago?" he muttered frantically.

"I'm afraid he didn't make it," I said diplomatically, certain he'd think I lost my marbles if I told him about the girl. "Looks like he fell. Come on. We need to get the police out here."

Spike limped to my bike and hopped on the back. The two of us buzzed down the path in silence, knowing our friends would never speak again.

The Courtyard

Maureen Wilkinson

I'd walked the length of the street a hundred times and never once noticed the opening, or the name plaque in the old stone archway that read Flower in the Hand Yard.

A shaft of sunlight polished a path through the blackened arch. Many times since, I've wished I had walked on, but curiosity overcame me and I stepped through.

I found myself in a small square. On each side, the buildings stood four floors high. Two white-framed windows and a pair of French doors leading onto a small wrought iron balcony marked each separate apartment. Window boxes adorned the frontage, flowers spilled over the edges in a tangled riot of colour and perfume.

The cobbled courtyard was empty, except for a curved bench that wound a dark circle around a miniature fountain. In its centre, a statue of a woodland nymph held a cupped flower above her head. Water flowed in a soft trickle down her body and gave her grey-green metal contours a life-like sheen.

A slick of slimy, yellow-green fungi coloured the courtyard cobbles and also covered most of the bench. I ran my fingers along a small patch of wood that received some sunlight and felt the dust of dry unvarnished slats.

The smell of damp vegetation and flowers hung heavy in the air. There was something about the cool tranquility of the courtyard that made me want to linger. I settled on the dry patch of bench, lit a cigarette, and scanned the blank-eyed windows. On the upper floors a few shutters were drawn against a slither of sun that edged over the rooftop. Silence, broken only by the soft gurgle of the fountain, pressed down like a comforter. My eyelids felt heavy and, reluctantly, I let them droop.

I must have slept for quite a while, for when I opened them again, the patch of sky above my head was deep blue and a few stars shone faintly in the half-light. I jerked upright, feeling a fool, and scanned the windows to see if anyone had witnessed my behavior. Although there were no lights to indicate the flats were occupied, I had the feeling there were eyes watching me. Watching from shadowed recesses in the rooms behind the blank glass. I straightened my long frame from its unaccustomed position of sleeping upright and moved stiffly out through the archway.

❦❦

In the kitchen of our modest West London house, my wife Jane put the finishing touches to the evening meal. She raised a cheek for my customary kiss. Her pale hair, a contrast to my own dark locks, smelled of orange and coconut shampoo.

"You're late tonight. Had a good day?" she said, her fingers busy arranging a bed of lettuce in the base of a salad bowl.

My intention of telling her about the eerie Square froze in my throat. I found I didn't want to share the experience. I wasn't sure why, but it felt as if I would be giving the keys to my house to a stranger. "The usual—the kids ok?" I replied, mentally shaking my head at being a fool. Why should I wish to hide such a casual occurance?

"Yes, they've eaten and they're both upstairs doing their homework."

"Just us, then?" I said and moved to the cutlery drawer.

The clock on the wall ticked loudly as we ate, and the sound enhanced the unaccustomed silence. Jane tipped her head to one side.

"You're quiet, you okay?"

"Yep, just tired I guess."

She grinned and filled my wine glass. "Get that down your throat, it'll soon liven you up." She gave a saucy wink. "The kids are going out tonight and I have plans for you."

We made love that night with passion that I hadn't felt since the first days of our marriage. I turned my mind to other things as I endeavoured to make the moments last. Balconies filled with flowers, shadows across empty windows, a fountain spouting water towards a ray of sunlight. And underlying these visions was the inexplicable feel of an unopened birthday treat, something waiting to be discovered.

❦❦

It was several months before business took me once again into the vicinity of Flower in the Hand Yard. The late autumn air had a slight chill, and I pulled my jacket collar close about my neck. I'd concluded my business selling first edition books to the bookstore and, as all sales had gone well, I started for home with a light step. I had almost forgotten the archway and the courtyard.

It was the smell of flowers that made me turn my head. Although I knew what was on the other side of the passage, I felt an overwhelming compunction to take another look. I wandered toward the fountain; my eyes took in the surroundings and noted nothing had changed. I was about to turn and leave when a movement in one of the upper windows caught my attention. I paused and stared upwards.

A young woman was framed in the window, dressed in some sort of filmy white gown. She seemed oblivious to my presence as she brushed her long dark hair with smooth rhythmic strokes. The elegance of her movements held me to the spot and something unfathomable stirred deep in my consciousness. I watched, spellbound, as she tied her hair back from her face with a scarlet ribbon, winding it around neatly until it resembled the decorated tail of a show horse. I was so lost in the sight I wasn't ready for the swift turn she made towards the window and the dark eyes that held my own. She smiled and I saw a flash of small, snowy teeth against the perfect bow of her lips.

CRLGCRLG

Throughout the spring and summer I organized my life so that I could spend at least some part of the week in Flower in the Hand Yard. I sat on the round bench gazing up at her window in hope of seeing her. Sometimes I fancied I saw her shadow behind the glass. I'd lie silent beside my sleeping wife and fantasize that the strange dark beauty I'd seen so briefly came to the window and rewarded me with a smile. On these occasions my heart beat in my throat and my pulse raced.

I couldn't get her out of my head and I researched the building. The flats were mostly occupied by the poor of the city, mostly immigrants and the unemployed. At the end of the eighteenth century, the land belonged to an aristocratic family. A series of tragic events, death in child birth and suicide, left it without an heir and it reverted to the state. The buildings, including the mausoleums, were razed to the ground and replaced with houses to accommodate the influx of French and Spanish citizens fleeing unrest in Europe.

CRLGCRLG

Iced stars laced the midnight blue sky, frost sprinkled the streets in icing sugar whiteness, bringing with it a reminder of impending winter and that it had been almost a year since I first came to the courtyard. A family holiday and then a business trip had kept me busy, and it had been two months since I last visited. I walked through the arch and, to my surprise, once again the courtyard had not changed, no sign of November. The frost had killed off most of the flowers in my garden and yet here the flowers were still lush and in full blossom on the balconies. The continental flavor of the architecture was clear to me, now I had explored its history. I settled onto the bench, prepared to view the buildings with my new knowledge.

I raised my eyes. This time she was at the window as if she had been waiting for me. She smiled, beckoned and pointed to a small door in the side of the building. With my head spinning in disbelief, I followed her pointing finger, passed through the door and found myself at the bottom of a flight of stone steps. Shadow in the unlit hallway enveloped the upper floor and yet somehow I knew she was standing there, waiting. I felt a wave of anxiety and a sick sinking in my stomach. What was I going to say to her? Hello, my name's Chandler James, I'm a married man with two children and I want your body. Is that what I really wanted, her body? Yes, I wanted her, but there was something more and I couldn't put a name to it. Yet I felt it, violence, a wolf about to spring on its prey, savouring the moment of tearing flesh and the metallic taste of blood.

She moved forward. "Come in Chandler," she said and took my hand. I didn't question that she knew my name.

On a table close to the window stood a large metal cross, and placed before it like small gifts were flowers and fruit. One candle threw flickering shadows in a far corner of the room. The furniture was sparse. A dressing table and stool were situated close to the window and a huge bed dominated the central area.

"I'm . . ." I began.

She put her fingers to her lips in a command for silence and pulled me towards the bed. I felt her cool, smooth fingers against my skin as she helped remove my clothes. No smell of shampoo or shop-bought perfume emanated from her closeness; and yet a sweet pungent odour, a scent like no other I had encountered, bathed her body.

She held out slender arms and desire took over, my blood ran hot. I ripped the delicate linen shift from her body. There was no thought of foreplay as I flipped her to her stomach and entered her from behind. I took her in frenzy, bit into her neck and felt skin split beneath my teeth, liquid—salty and foul—trickled into my mouth and down my chin, the taste only served to heighten my passion. My body was slick with sweat as I lunged into her with no words but the grunts of a rutting animal.

Then it was over and I collapsed at her side, my desire spent. I looked up at the flickering shadows on the ceiling and shame swamped me. I must have hurt her, but she had given no sign. I needed to apologize. My throat was tight with tears of remorse and I wasn't sure if I could speak. I turned to her and shock kicked me in the stomach and rendered me speechless. She smiled; grey teeth rested against her bottom lip. Coarse spiked hair sprouted from decayed skin, gathering in the wrinkles around the empty sockets of her eyes and shriveled mouth.

"Oh Jesus!" I screamed and rolled out of bed, landing on all fours. "Who are you?"

Her breasts hung, leathery and thin against her thighs as she crouched on the bed. "I'm your lover." Her eyes glowed yellow and her breath spoke of inner decay.

I dry retched and reached blindly for my discarded clothes. "Oh God help me," I moaned. I pulled on my clothes and scrambled towards the door.

"I'll see you again, Chandler. Very soon," she whispered. Her voice gritty, as if from long disuse and rusted in her throat.

"No, no never again," I babbled as I fumbled in the dark for the handle.

She gave a low laugh. "Oh, yes, I'll see you again. Next year, on the day of the dead, you'll come to me."

I ripped open the door and plunged into the dark corridor. At that moment I had no idea what she meant—but now, as I make my way to Flower in the Hand Yard and some dark instinct pulls me inextricably into ungoverned depths of depravity—I understand.

Gabriela

Mary Fernandez

Her eyes are wide open when they unlock the trunk. Two glass marbles with strands of dark and opaque brown swirl around a translucent base, similar to the glassy eyes owned by Gabriela, the muñeca tía Raquel sent us from the convent in Culiacán. These eyes look straight up to the ominous sky. Gabriela was to stay up on the shelf, standing straight up on her doll stand, not to be touched. The nuns twisted up her long brown braids into two loops, the ends, thick finger-rolled curls hung at each side of her head, long red ribbons tied up in bows. The long sleeved, high neck dress was hand stitched together, full of ruffles and laces, a Cinco de Mayo dress. Bright rainbow colored stripes on the ruffles fanned out by her tiny hands exposed a red corset with tatted trim, black silk stockings and black velvet high top shoes. Gabriela had a sweet closed mouth with an accent line drawn between her lips, rosy cheeks painted on her caramel complexion. It had fallen off the shelf and a large portion of her shoulder broke off, but it was below the base of the neck and did not show when she was dressed. There were a few small holes and some slight stains on the dress and a small tear in the bodice that mama readily mended—mama was always mending that dress. The black stockings, worn through in a few spots, revealed red legs. A little of the paint had rubbed off of her face, the porcelain cheek shattered. Her lifeless body lay broken and torn inside the trunk on top of a pile of tattered and soiled rags. Her brown, glass marble eyes look through me, straight up to the heavens, the authenticity certificate long ago lost; she is no longer my sister.

CʒEᴏᴄʒEᴏ

    I see the barrel of shotguns through the window with the almost drawn curtains more clearly as I walk up the boiling hot pavement to my sister's house. It is Tucson hot. I put my hands up and cup them around my eyes to remove the sun's reflection from the window. My face to the window, I see the black finished, aluminum alloy butts of the guns sticking up. A shotgun lay across my sister's boyfriend's lap and, sandpaper in his hand, he is scraping off something above the trigger. I had not noticed a man sitting in a car parked by the mailbox. He drives off as I approach the door. Before I knock, she opens it and comes outside.

"Hey, what are you doing here?"

"Can't I come and visit my sister?" I take a step closer to the door.

"It's too messy inside to come in right now."

"I came to see if the kids wanted to come over and spend the night." There is stirring inside, something being dragged. My sister looks inside the door and opens it. "Fine, come on in."

She picks up an inside-out shirt off the couch, and dirty socks scattered all over the floor.

"Tía!" My nephew and niece run up to me excited. They run up to me and knock me back on the couch with their hugs.

"Go get your shoes. You are going to spend the night with tía." My nephew and niece run off barefoot with my sister right behind them.

I pull myself back into a sitting position on the couch. I yawn and look in the direction of my sister's boyfriend who now sits across from me on a chair watching wrestling on television.

"Did you know that metal has no smell?" He looks over at me, one eye still on the show.

"You know after you've grasped an iron railing, or a door handle, or you've been handling coins made of copper—your hand gives off that metal smell. Well, you're not smelling the metal at all."

I clear my throat and nod.

"That metal smell comes from chemicals in your skin which are changed in an instant by the touch of iron." My nephew and niece each have their shoes on, each carries a grocery bag with their clothes spilling out of the top. I rub the top of my niece's head and smile at her. I look back at her father.

"So when a lady at the store hands you a coin, you're smelling her body odor. See you have to touch metal to smell it." He comes over and gives each of the kids a kiss. He puts out his hand for me to shake it. I give my sister a kiss on the cheek and a hug, I shake hands with her boyfriend, and I smell a mushroom-like odor when I breathe in and taste metal on my tongue.

CB&)CB&)

I am eight, and my sister is seven. Today we will drown in my uncle's backyard swimming pool. We feel our legs, sweaty on the car seats. They stick because we don't have air conditioning in the car. The drive to get here is a long one with too many stop lights. We don't think too much about anything. We only know that it is a hot summer day. We cannot wait to go swimming.

We hardly say hello to our aunt and uncle when we arrive. We head straight for the bathroom with our bathing suits in hand. We tear off our clothes and change into our bathing suits. We walk out the bathroom doors. Our clothes are thrown on the tile floor. Our mom notices. She makes us go back and pick them up. Our aunt, who bought me a comb for my birthday, shakes her head. She is not happy. I use my fingers to brush back my long, straggly hair. I tuck it behind my ears. I walk slowly. Once I pass her, I make a run for the door. I beat my sister. She says it is a tie.

We run outside, free. The sun is so hot. Almost, I think. We are almost there. Soon we will be jumping into the cool water, but our mom makes us wait, again. Now we have to go back and rub on sun lotion. Finally we are ready, but mom is not. Again we have to wait, until uncle volunteers to go with us to the pool. Our aunt yells out something to my uncle about us girls getting too old for tickling. The grass cools the bottom of our feet as we cross the lawn. He opens the gate. He watches as we run past him. We don't care that we are not supposed to run. The cement is hot. We jump in. The water catches us. We feel patches of cold and warm on our skin as we fall free into the deep end. Our feet touch the bottom. We shoot straight up, cutting the water with a quick slice. My uncle watches. He smiles as my sister and I get out and go to opposite ends of the pool. We jump in and swim toward each other again and again and again. Our eyes are open under the water. We see bubbles rising up from our noses. We laugh. We hold hands and kick our long, skinny legs together. We return slowly to the top.

CR SD CR SD

It is the first day of November, día de los muertos. I walk up to abuela's grave. I have violets with me because her favorite color was always violet. Pan de dulce is in my other hand, crumbled sugar falls off the sweet bread marking my path. I have tucked a stuffed parrot under my arm, like José who bit me but always let her put her hand in the cage without worry. Candles line the walkway. I walk alone. I wonder where my family is. They should be here too. Tissue flag banners are dancing in the wind above my head with cut outs of calaveras. No longer is a grave but an altar in front of me, several items have already been left. Marigolds, of course marigolds, the sugar skulls are melting. My hands are empty; I walk forward to see whose picture is standing up in the frame. I feel her—I turn around quickly and almost see someone out of the corner of my eye. That same shadow I see around the house. I walk and I know she is with me, my sister is with me. I feel her enter me, enter and feel complete, very close, the closeness I always yearned for when she was alive. A cross, the one abuela gave us with the resurrected Christ, stands before me. Abuela always said she did her purgatory on earth and felt she lived the crucified

Christ and didn't need one up on a cross.

⚜⚜

I hear road sounds in the background, a horn honking, muffled voices, the voice of my sister's boyfriend telling her to get on the bus. I rub my thumb along the chewed up part of the cordless phone. The kids left the phone out in the backyard and I found Abby chewing on it when I discovered it missing.

"It's been two weeks that mom and dad are taking care of your kids. You said you were taking his mother to Mexico for an operation on a bad knee. Dad ran into your boyfriend's mother at the gas station walking just fine." I feel my voice crack.

"We stayed for a wedding. Look, I'm on my way home. We'll talk then. I've gotta go." My sister cleared the irritation from her throat.

"No, no. You never want to talk. We need to talk now." The kids look up from their homework. I walk outside on to the back porch.

"What's there to talk about? The trip lasted longer than we thought. Mom and dad are fine taking care of the kids, so it really is none of your business. I've gotta go." Her anger grows the anger in me.

"I know there was no wedding, no operation, stop lying to me. I'm not stupid. We grew up in the same neighborhood, same friends. People talk. Is it drugs you're transporting? Is it guns? Mom and dad are tired, too old for this. *I'm* taking care of the kids. They're with me."

I hear her boyfriend telling her to hang up the phone, saying that people can hear our conversation, that they are starting to look.

"I love you, you know that, right? I'm scared for you. Do you get that? I'm scared for you." I am upset with myself for crying, not being able to make it through the whole conversation.

"You worry too much. I've gotta go. I can't talk right now. We'll talk when I get home."

⚜⚜

And then something, a hand, pulls us under. The grip on my ankle is tight. We try to kick free. Our heads pop up for a second. We both gasp for air. We hold on to each other, our knuckles now white. The pressure is too much. Our hands are torn apart. I look around. I don't see sister. No mom to save us either. A whirlwind of pressure sucks me back under the water. I am pulled close to him. I feel his chest on my back. As we come up together, he begins to tickle me. I'm not ticklish. I pretend to laugh because

I don't want to hurt uncle's feelings. I try to swim away, but a strong force now has hold on me. He lets go of my waist. I take a breath. I am relieved for only a second, but then I feel his hands. They are hidden by the water. They slip down between my thighs. A finger and then fingers make their way underneath my bathing suit. My body freezes. I can't move, only wait. Only seconds go by, but one-two-three-four and then five-six-seven-eight of my years sink like stones to the bottom of the pool. I listen, plop after plop as they go down.

And then it is over, but only beginning. My sister swims over to play the game. She has no idea what is next. He first swims around her several times. I am helpless, not knowing what to do or think. He picks her up, places her on his shoulders and then playfully tosses her off. I try to warn her, but I've lost my voice. He swims at her, dives down and swims through her legs. The wave of the water picks her up. I mouth for my sister to swim away, but no sound comes out. The tickling starts and after a minute, he is done. I can see on my sister's face that she is done too. Uncle swims to the steps. His heavy smell stays behind. He pulls himself out and grabs a nearby towel. He dries his head first, then his arms and body. He doesn't bother to dry his feet. He just slips on his sandals and walks away. I look away.

CR☙CR☙

I feel abuela with me too as the three of us walk up to the altar, we are walking down the aisle, up to the altar a la iglesia de san Juan, my sister in her first communion dress. Fr. Ralph sent her out of the confessional because she forgot the act of contrition prayer, "Señor mío, Jesucristo, I am sorry for my sins with all my heart. I firmly intend, with your help, to do penance, to sin no more, and to avoid whatever leads me to sin. Our Saviour Jesus Christ suffered and died for us. En el nombre del Padre, del Hijo, y del Espíritu Santo. Amén." I say the prayer for her. She looks through me back at our parents and then she looks down at her new white shoes.

CR☙CR☙

I am walking from the kitchen with a soda in hand into the living room of my parents' home when the first car drives up. A second one follows and stops just behind. I walk outside with my father. A man wearing a white collar shirt and grey dress pants greets us in the middle of the driveway with an extended hand. I look over his shoulder to see my sister sitting in the back seat of the car. I see her boyfriend in the backseat of the second car.

"My name is Agent Paul Sears. I'm with the ATF, the Bureau of Alcohol, Tobacco, Firearms and Explosives."

"Yes I know what it is." My father accepts his hand, resignation on his face, like he was expecting him to drive up. "What's this about?"

"An illegal firearm registered in your daughter's name has been involved in a murder in Mexico." The agent turns towards my father. "Your daughter says that she is a gun collector and has stored several guns in your backyard shed. Do you know about this?"

My father does not answer, only shakes his head no. He furrows his brow, the crow lines in his forehead between his eyes permanently creased. His hand covers his mouth. The officer asks if he has permission to look. My father remains silent and nods his okay.

The agent walks over and opens the back door and tells my sister to lead the way. They go around the corner to the backyard. My father and I just stand there for several long minutes; his hands hang at his sides, and my hands are crossed in front of me. They return. No guns are found.

"I'm taking them down to the office for questioning. Is there someone who can pick her up?" My dad tells him that he'll get his keys and follow him down. Dad goes into the house.

"Hey look, we are a good family. Know that, okay." I look at the agent not sure what else to say.

The agent pauses for a minute and then steps in closer to where I stand. "We don't want your sister; she's just a little fish. We want the big fish. You know what I'm saying. You're her sister, right? You guys close?"

"You know more about my sister than I do. Tell me what you know."

"Look, we investigate and arrest individuals who illegally supply firearms to bad people, people involved in violent street gangs, firearms trafficking, you know drug-trafficking activities."

I shift the weight from my right foot to my left, distancing the space between us.

"In a nutshell, I believe that your sister and her boyfriend are doing some gun running for the Mexican mafia. Names, that's all we want. Talk your sister into giving us names."

CR&CR&

Our hair is dry, clumped together now. It is time to go home. Part of me stays behind on the steps of the pool and watches the two sisters get out of the water, dry off, and head for the bathroom to get dressed. After a time, I see mother first, as she leaves the house through the back door. Dressed now, the sisters follow behind. I hear her tell the sisters to say thank you and goodbye. First aunt and then uncle leans down for a hug and kiss. The wooden gate creaks as it opens. It makes a big, clang sound as it snaps closed. The car engine starts. Car doors open and close, and then I realize that I am still sitting in the pool. I try to scream, to get someone's attention. I say, "here

I am" and "please don't leave me." Without a voice, nobody hears me. The
sun is setting now. Nobody is returning for me. Nobody notices that I am
gone. The night wraps me. I become invisible. Nobody sees me, except my
sister. Part of her has stayed behind too. She looks at me, but when I start to
swim towards her, she swims away.

C3EOC3EO

*I keep walking with her and to her, to the picture at the altar, I feel something in
my hands and look down, our muñeca Gabriela is brand new in my hands, yes a perfect
offering for . . . , she is changing underneath my fingers. Her shoulders breaking, her
cheek crushing in, her closed mouth stays intact as the rest of her porcelain self crumbles
underneath her clothes. Rags hang lifeless in my hands. I try to hold Gabriela up, to give
her some form, to save her, but dust to dust we return. I place it on the altar on top of
the melted skull candies, broken; I turn what's left of her head away from me, the brown
marble eyes away from me. I have nothing else to offer. I don't know what her favorite
drink was. She never ate a meal in my home, always dropped off the kids and had some
place else to go. I drop to my knees and place my hands on top of what is left of Gabriela.*

*First, I feel my sister leave me, the air sucked out of me, and then abuela follows
behind her. Maybe abuela can help her. Maybe she will talk to abuela. Maybe abuela can
forgive her for not remembering the prayer at confession, maybe she will believe grandma's
words that she is forgiven. Maybe I will believe the words, "You are forgiven." Pan de dulce
fills my hands. Yes she and grandma liked to eat the sweet bread with just a little melted
butter on top. I place the pan de dulce in front of the white communion shoes.*

C3EOC3EO

The kids are in the front cul-de-sac riding bikes when she pulls up. She
honks the horn and they wave and drive up to the side of the truck as my
sister pulls into the drive way. My nephew and niece drop their bikes and run
to her. She scoops them up in her arms and sprinkles kisses all over their
faces.

"Stay for tea?" I stand up and walk towards the truck. My sister walks in
the direction of the chairs in my front yard.

"Yeah sure, I'll have a glass." She sits down. I go into the house and
return with two tall glasses of iced tea. I sit down in the chair beside her.
Our children ride their bikes around the sidewalk. They go to the top of the
driveway and take turns jetting down into the street.

"Emilio, come back. You are riding out too far." I squeeze the lemon and
let it fall back into my glass.

"Gabriel, stay on the sidewalk." My sister takes a long, slow drink of the
tea; a droplet falls out the side of her mouth and runs down her chin. She

wipes it off with the side of her hand. "He is always wanting to ramp up things. His knees are scraped up; he's all boy, that's for sure."

My sister and I sit for a long minute in silence, watching our children ride their bikes too fast. My sister stands up and calls her kids by their names, "It's time to go."

CR&OCR&O

And then one day it happens. Something falls into the pool on my sister's side. I swim closer to see what it is. It is a flower, shaped like a tube. Yellow spikes spill out the middle of its shiny white petals. I reach out for it. I slip my hand underneath the water just below where it is floating. Slowly, gently I pick it up. With my other hand I feel the silk between my fingers. It reminds me of how I felt in my white Easter dress, the one with the yellow sash that ties in the back. I bring the flower up to my nose. A sweet fragrance takes the place of the chemical smells around me. I bring it up to my mouth. I taste it. Sugary nectar brings me back to the alleyway with the honeysuckle planted right up against its chain links. My sister and I would grab handfuls and suck on each of the flowers until every last bit of nectar was out.

I swim over to my sister. I use my arms to scoop up as many flowers as I can and bring them to her. I bring one up to my own mouth and beg her to taste the nectar, or even just smell one, to remember the honeysuckle in the alleyway. She pushes them away. I grab my sister's arm. I pull her towards the shallow end, towards the steps. She doesn't want to come. My legs are tired and barely move. I plead with my sister to kick, just a little even. I swallow water. The fragrance is so strong now and every part of me knows that I have to let go. So I try. I let go of one of my sister's hands first and pray that she remembers how to swim, how to trust the water again. I let go of the other, but then she begins to sink deep into the part of the water that covers up all feelings. I reach out and grab hold of her once again. She tries to let go of me, but I take hold of her wrist. The flowers float between us and I let go. My sister swims away.

I stop swimming and stand up. I am surprised that I can stand. I walk to the steps of the pool. I look up. Warm rays touch my face. I see someone coming towards me. Light illuminates her. As she comes closer I recognize her. She has returned. She is me. She sees me, says she has never forgotten me. She holds out her hand and helps me as I climb out of the pool.

I look back and see my sister, hands clenched to the side of the pool. I clear my throat, and try my voice. It is hoarse, but my sister looks to me as if hearing me for the first time. I force the sound through the choking sensation I feel in my throat. I tell my sister that she is a great swimmer, better and faster than me. She lets go of the edge. I watch her sink. I tell her that I will be waiting for her. I will keep her bike close by so that we can ride together again through alleyways. We will ride fast, not stopping until we are breathless, until we gulp water again from the front yard hose because we are too busy having fun to go inside.

What Nathan Knows

D. Lee

Nathan sits at home alone all day, drawing unemployment, drinking, and talking to his old Army buddies on his cell phone. He watches the TV and the clock move. He knows when Rosa, his wife, comes home from work today, there will be an argument.

He knows it with the same certainty that he knows a "Rock of Love" re-run will come on at 3:30 on VH1. He knows the show is trash that he can live without, but he switches channels to VH1.

Nathan also knows today is *Día de los Muertos*, and muses about the irony as he presses the cold steel barrel of his shotgun underneath his jaw. He rolls the butt stock of the weapon around on the floor and gently moves the barrel of the twelve gauge to position its blast for maximum efficiency. Nathan knows he wants no mistakes when the time comes. He laughs to himself and puts down the shotgun beside the chair to finish his drink.

Nathan knows a lot—except how to escape this tired routine.

At the first commercial break, he gets out of his blue lazy boy and goes to the cabinets to pour himself another Jim Beam and sprite.

Nathan knows Rosa would not be amused with his joking about *Día de los Muertos*. She takes her holidays very serious. Nathan is allowed to joke about her tiny ears and the smell of her feet, but never *Día de los Muertos* and Easter. Those cannot be demeaned.

Rosa is expecting him to accompany her to the church to pray for the dead. But then again, Rosa wants a lot of things from him.

Rosa wants Nathan to sign up for classes at the community college. She wants Nathan to use the GI Bill he received from the Army for his years of service, and the years of *their* sacrifice—numerous Christmases and Thanksgivings spent alone—to better provide for their future family. Most of all, she wants Nathan to be happy; to be productive.

Nathan understands this. Rosa believes her prayers are turning him around to bring the joy back into his life at any moment. Nathan knows how unfair life really is.

During his last deployment, his contract expired and so did three of his friends. He stayed in Iraq while his friends went home to be buried. He came home when the Army said so, and he got out when the Army said so, and now he did what he wanted, God be damned.

Besides, Nathan no longer wants to be productive. He wants to sit in his lazy boy and work through the tangled forest of his mind.

He wants to drink, because sometimes, when he's alone, he thinks it's the only way he can truly be merry. But other times he doesn't want to drink, but the alcohol still lures him with the sweet serenading promises of a heightened enlightenment of the world around him. He knows so much that the shotgun begs him to squeeze the trigger and leave his knowledge behind to this erratic world.

Nathan knows this is what all the fights are about; his drinking.

Rosa asks questions like, "Are you depressed?" And, "Why won't you open up to me?"

Nathan knows Rosa wants to know what happened over there, but really, she doesn't. She wants him to be a good husband and go to church with her. Nathan knows she would be upset if she saw him with the shotgun so he carefully puts it back in the closet.

Nathan used to believe in God. Now he sits, unemployed. He knows his world must be recalibrated now that the gunshots and bombs have gone.

Nathan looks at the clock and feels the coming wrath burrow through his belly like a school of piranhas. Rosa will be home from work in any moment. She will want him to accompany her to the church and pray, and then to the cemetery and visit, and finally back home to talk.

At 5:22 she arrives. Nathan knows because he is watching the clock. Rosa enters with a smile and asks, "Are you ready?"

Nathan twists in his chair to face her. Her smile drops. He knows Rosa can see his glazed eyes, a byproduct of his drinking.

"No." Nathan answers.

"Have you done anything, today? Sign up for classes, laundry, take a shower?"

Nathan answers her by getting up to pour himself another drink. He doesn't look at her. The hurt and disappointment in her voice is painful enough.

"I don't know how much longer I can live like this," she says as she throws her purse on the table. Nathan can hear the tremble in her voice. He hears the desperation in her words, the extension of faith, the ladder of her concession, but can't find the way to climb up and change the monotony of days. "Why do you drink like this every day? Why Nathan?"

Nathan was well aware of his habit. He drank until the fuzziness fluffed the world around him, and he drank some more. He drank until everything was funny, and he drank some more. He drank until the world was dark and he no longer remembered his actions, and he drank some more. Nathan often woke up in his lazy boy; sometimes in the middle of the night, sometimes in the morning.

Nathan wants to grab Rosa by the shoulders, caress her face, and whisper in her ear everything she wants to hear. He wants her beautiful face to be unencumbered with the snarls of anger. Nathan wants her smile to return. The smile he knows so well, the one that lights up her face.

He's tired of the angry words and the arguments. He wants Rosa to relax and love. Nathan knows if he can tell her why he drinks every day, the real answer, she'll forgive him and hold him close. She'll tuck him away in the safety of her arms and keep the world from flooding inside. She'll coo like a beautiful song bird and then he will make a joke until they are laughing so hard they cry. And then everything will be all better, and he can finally be happy enough to become more productive. Tomorrow would be the start of something new.

But the problem is he doesn't know why he drinks. Nathan doesn't know why he needs the alcohol to cloud up everything or the shotgun under his jaw to make him feel alive. Rosa wants answers, and he has none for this.

"Can't you answer me, Nathan?" He notices the tears in her eyes. Nathan looks down and takes another swallow from his cup, searching for the answer within the cold thrust of liquid riding down his throat.

Rosa doesn't give him time to gather his thoughts before her next question.

"Can you tell me anything, Nathan, or are you too drunk?" Her eyes narrow and Nathan pretends he sees fangs starting to grow out of her mouth. "Here's what I can tell you, Nathan. I'm sick of this shit. I refuse to live like this. Get some help. You know how important this day is to me and you just sat around and drank?"

Nathan opens his mouth to intervene on his intervention.

Rosa bulldozes into his attempt, "Don't do it, Nathan. Don't give me any excuses. What you have is a drinking problem. Or depression. Either way, you need to snap out of it."

Nathan looks past her to the TV. It's the commercial with the twins and that shampoo. "I'll sign up for school tomorrow," he tells her.

"I don't want to hear your shit. That's what you said yesterday, and the day before that, and the day before that. Get your ass out of the imprint in that chair and make something happen. Fuck, clean the house. I'm tired of working all day and coming home to this shithole. Grow up and quit being a boy. We want a family; it's time to be a man."

Rosa gets up abruptly and walks to the kitchen. Nathan sighs because he thinks the exchange is over. He thinks Rosa will go to church and pray for the dead and stew and leave him and his late afternoon court shows in peace. He's wrong.

Rosa storms back into the living room from the kitchen, refueled from a fresh idea. She stands in front of Nathan's chair and he's forced to look around her to see the TV.

She points a finger at him. "Get happy, Nathan. Get your shit together. Go get help. Whatever you need to do, we'll do. But don't just sit your ass on that chair and let everything pass you by. I want—I *need* you happy."

"I am," Nathan mutters and continues to try and look around Rosa's hips. This time she rolls her eyes and walks off.

During the next commercial break he hears the door slam. He knows Rosa has left; gone to church to pray, or her parents, or somewhere else. Nathan feels the pressure ease off his shoulders. He knows he can finally be himself. He gets up to pour himself another drink. He walks to the closet and pulls out the shotgun.

Día de los Muertos is a joke to him, but he knows he can't tell Rosa that. He sees the dead every day, floating in front of him as memories and provocateurs. He sees their faces and their spirits and their finished hopes and dreams. His friends are always with him, holding onto his back and whispering in his ear.

He doesn't need to go to church and light a candle for them. He wants them gone. Nathan doesn't want to converse with the dead anymore. Nathan knows he wants to be able to converse with Rosa, to talk to her without wearing this mask of boredom that keeps distance between the two of them.

Their relationship was never like this before the deployment. He wants to go back to the life they had then. Nathan knows he needs to unsee the dead that keeps him awake nights with their ragged gashes and holes from the bombs and bullets; the same undead that haunts his dreams with their constant appearance and begging for mercy.

Nathan knows there is no celebrating the dead. There is only loss and heartbreak, but the dead do not go on and neither should the memories. The dead certainly should not have their own holiday so the people they left behind could second guess all their actions. Nathan doesn't want to remember that day in Iraq anymore than he wants to think of his friends, so why in the hell would he be going to the church to light candles with Rosa? Didn't she know the dead had put them in this situation to begin with?

Would their souls be closer to earth? Would the souls of those he had killed come back for him? Nathan knows they want to drag their murderer down into the underbelly of the netherworld. Nathan has already killed his enemies once in life, he does not want to do it in death as well.

Why couldn't he just tell Rosa about the day his friends died or how he feels about this stupid holiday and this inconsequential life? Maybe he would write it down in a letter, and spell out everything that needed fixing in the world. As soon as he gets out of his easy chair for another drink.

But instead, Nathan finishes watching the reality show on VH1 and numbs his mind while he plays with the shotgun and contemplates making this the day of the dead.

Skin Deep

Kathleen Alcalá

It's not the skin that counts, I kept telling her, it's what lies beneath. And that was the basis of my promise.

It started with a little spot. At first it was rough and red, and I assumed it had come from a strap rubbing on my shoulder. I worked as a photographer, and in spite of the vest full of pockets, still carried cameras, extra batteries, and a reflector in various cases and containers, most of which ended up hanging from me like umbrellas on a coat rack. In fact, I resembled a coat rack then, a long drink of water, a tall tree, a mast on a ship on a calm sea.

But Dolores loved me. She loved me with a love fierce enough to break down walls, mostly those I had built around myself as a solitary person. She loved me beyond convention, beyond reason, beyond taboo. She loved me with the intensity of a strong woman gripping a bone hard enough to crumble it to dust.

And so we come to the crux of the matter. I made her a promise I was not sure I could fulfill.

When I noticed the spot on my shoulder, I rubbed some ointment into it. When that did not help, I began to take vitamins, thinking that my skin needed a little boost. It felt like an act of vanity, a man my age caring whether or not he had good skin. The spot would go away for a while, but it always returned.

One night, after Dolores had carried me to deep waters and back, she lay snuggled into the bony crook of my arm. She turned to kiss me, and her glance fell on the spot.

"You need to have that looked at," she said, drawing a circle around it with the nail of her index finger.

"All right," I answered, and promptly forgot about it.

Some weeks later, I hoisted a camera bag and felt a slight burning sensation. Removing it, I looked under my shirt for an insect or a burr. There was that damn spot. So I went to the doctor.

"Now, who are you again?" asked the receptionist. I did not go to the doctor very often.

"I'm sure it's nothing," he said. "But we'll biopsy it just to make sure."

Applying some local anesthetic, he deftly sliced a bit of skin off the spot and covered it with gauze. "Here, press this," he said.

So I pressed. And I pressed. But still the spot did not go away.

The phone call was bad. I went in for more tests, more little slices, like Ronald Reagan during his Presidency, removed one little slice at a time. The spot had already eaten its way down to the bone. From there, it had spread its devious tendrils throughout my system, the marrow, the nerves, the blood cells themselves acting as tiny carriers of bad news. "Oy to the world," they screamed, "your time is up!"

So I made Dolores a promise.

After the winter had passed, wet and desultory, she took most of my things to the Goodwill. Now other gangly men, some poor, some surprisingly rich, wear my lean shirts, my extra-long jeans, my large shoes. My belts, at least one extra notch on each one, have gone as well, some with the jeans to the same home. Clothes might make a man, but clothes without a man are just, well, clothes.

As the tepid spring turned to summer, Dolores took to sitting in the garden with my books, looking at the photos, remembering the places she had visited with me, or heard about from me. I had been fortunate enough to travel widely, to see places that no longer exist, and record them for others to see and dream over. Gradually, the books I had authored were returned to the bookcases, while my reference books began to migrate to the homes of my friends, and even to booksellers. While Dolores had no interest in taking photos herself, she sometimes took out my cameras and looked them over, caressed the hard carapaces of my Leicas as though they were crystal balls and she could see the future in them. She did not give away my equipment, nor inquire about its value.

As autumn drew near and the full-blown flowers hung heavy on their stalks, the nights lengthened and the wind blew more often from the north. These were interrupted by warm, wet weather from the southeast, the tails of hurricanes, of sailor stories and mothers' nightmares. Dolores began to gather things from the garden.

She assembled a cairn in the front room, on the hearth in front of the fireplace. She spent a long time arranging the rocks, until they looked utterly natural, as though they were part of a glacial rill that had been deposited there eons ago. Dolores was an architect, and her understanding of form resided not in her head, but in her hands. Into this arrangement, she began to tuck dried flowers. She filled a porcelain bowl with shells and pebbles, remembering my affinity for the sea. She placed my fountain pen before the rill, and yes, she placed some of her, and my, favorite photos here and there. Memories of the past, postcards from the Titanic.

On the final day, she made a green curry, and Thai fish cakes wrapped in banana leaves steamed in coconut milk. She filled a mug with piping hot Mexican chocolate, and poured a shot glass full of tequila, the good stuff.

Next, she placed a new shirt and a new pair of jeans in my size neatly on a chair near the door. This puzzled me. What would I do with them? Finally, she placed marigolds, carefully tended in the garden during the waning days of summer, in a vase near the clothes. Then she lit two candles and relaxed into a chair by the hearth. Within minutes, she was asleep.

This being my first time, I did not know what to expect. But as midnight fell upon us, I found that I was standing outside the front door, and turned the knob. The door opened.

The food smelled delicious. I walked straight to the kitchen, where I found that she had neatly cleaned up the pots and pans and put everything away. One place was set at the table. *For herself or me?* I wondered.

When I got up my nerve, I returned to the front room and walked over to face Dolores, who slept peacefully, her hands in her lap. By the unsteady light of the candles, I examined her face curiously, the skin I had adored, so much like my own. I spoke freely of my background in front of others, and she not at all. No one had known us in this town before we moved here, only that we came from a place near the border. Did she look older? I was not sure. Perhaps a bit careworn, perhaps a bit lonely. She had small creases around her mouth. Were those there before? Her breathing was deep and even.

I stood over the offering and inhaled deeply. I tried to remember the smell of each item separately, the complexity of the curry, the rich fish and coconut smell, the mountain and chile smell of the chocolate, the alcoholic jolt of the tequila. I examined the photos. In the few where I appear, I look innocent of my fate, unaware of the spot burning into my shoulder, eventually freeing my soul.

Finally, I could not resist. I tried to raise the tequila in a toast to her, my beloved Dolores, who had not yet forgotten me. But when I reached for the glass, all I managed to do was knock it over. There was the slight noise of bone against glass, of glass hitting stone, followed by the spreading wetness around and beneath the altar. She stirred and I froze. Would she see me if she awoke? Would I frighten her? There was only the smell of alcohol on wet stone.

Finally, she shifted and seemed to sleep again. I relaxed, both relieved and disappointed. I would not be able to hold her in my arms. All that was left to me were the essences of things—of food, of photos, of love. Everything else would run between the bones of my fingers like water.

I walked over to the clothes and put them on. Of course, they fit me perfectly—the narrow jeans and embroidered shirt that she had driven all the way across town to buy. I stood there looking at the empty fabric on the chair. Who knew that clothes had an essence?—then back at the empty food from which I had taken all spirit, and hoped that she would understand that I had been there.

My glance fell on the upset glass of tequila. With only a moment's hesitation, I dipped my finger in the spilled tequila and gently touched her shoulder, drawing a circle as she had once drawn a circle on mine. She stirred again in her sleep, reaching with her opposite hand for the spot, feeling the beginning of the end.

More confident now, I moved out through the front door without opening it. Then I remembered that I had not even tried to kiss Dolores. But when I turned and placed my hand upon the door and tried to pass back through, it would not yield to me. I was unable to re-enter the house. Not this year. I would return to the long sleep, the blissful nothingness that would be my lot until the day I would be united forever with my beloved Dolores. For almost one year I had lingered near her, but now I walked away from the house without regret, my longing sated by her offerings, my cousin's adoration of bony me. Oh Dolores, I kept my promise to you.

The Conscience of the King

Trent Roman

Carlos Galicia drummed his fingers irritably on the round table by his chair as his lieutenants aired their complaints in what had become a daily ritual over these last few months. Outside, beyond the balcony, the day's festivities were in full swing, with music and happy shouts wafting through the hot, still air of his hacienda-style house in central Tijuana. He could only wish that what he was hearing from his men would be as pleasant. Always, *always* they bitched and moaned, and always he was the one who was expected to sort all their problems out. God forbid any of them ever think to actually show some intelligence or initiative and take care of their problems themselves.

"We've had to effectively abandon the eastern district," Carlito Galicia, his nephew by his sister and one of his top lieutenants, was saying. "The boys heard that Los Negros are operating on the other side of the shore and they refuse to go out there."

"Do I have nothing but cowards working for me?" Galicia exclaimed, striking the armrest. "Have these dogs no gratitude for everything this family has done for them over all the years? They take, take, take when times are good, but oh, how easily our generosity is forgotten when we ask them to do a little bit of hard work for once in their miserable lives! You go and tell them: no work, no money, no drugs! It's that simple. If these weasels won't do their jobs, we turn off the spigots."

The side door opened and Galicia saw his butler, Manuel, come in with a bottle of fine *Valle de Guadalupe* wine and a glass on a tray. Finally! Galicia thought it was near half-an-hour since he'd asked for it. Couldn't get good service for any job, it seemed; everything was falling apart. Snapping his fingers to catch the lazy butler's attention, Galicia pointed to the table as Carlito went on:

"With respect, uncle, I don't think that'll be enough. I think an example needs to be made. Right now, the problem is that they are more frightened of Los Negros and the rest of the Juarez Cartel than they are of us, their own bosses. Next time, uncle, the next time they say that they won't go patrol our turf, let me beat on one of them. Better yet, let me put a bullet in his brain. That'll show the men who's in charge. They'll be tripping over themselves to go patrol rather than being the next to incur our displeasure."

Galicia tightened his grip around the stem of the wine glass; it was a good thing the crystal was solid, otherwise it could have shattered in his hand. This was the problem with the younger generation: they had spent all their youth watching action films and gangsters on television, and now their solution to every problem was rooted in brutality and blind violence. This had never been a clean business; there was a lot of blood on Galicia's hands that he knew only God could forgive. But at least in his days they had honour and respect, towards each other in the cartel if to no one else.

"Kill our own men! That's your solution?" Galicia cried out disgustedly, rising from his chair. "And if their fear of Los Negros proves greater still than that of their petulant bosses, will you kill another and another? Perhaps threaten to kill their families like some street gang? What use are soldiers frightened into loyalty when there's only a dozen left?"

He cut himself off, beginning to feel hot and flustered, and sat back down heavily. He wasn't as young—or, to be honest, as thin—as he had once been, and his doctor had told him that he needed to watch his heart. These children would prove the death of him yet!

"Go. Get out. You remind those cowards who has looked after them all these long years, and if that still doesn't awaken their underdeveloped consciences, tell them we'll start hiring those MS-13 dogs to do the dirty work they won't. Let's see how long they hold out at the prospect of starving in the unemployment lines and sending their mothers and sisters to the *maquiladoras.*"

Galicia waved towards the door, clearly dismissing them. They hesitated a moment, glancing at each other, before dipping their heads in a token gesture of respect and turning to leave. Carlito was the last in line as they filed out the door, and, standing in the doorway, turned back around to face him.

"Uncle . . . forgive me, but I am worried about what will happen if we do not begin to start enforcing harsher measures, towards our own men as towards our enemies. I hear whispers on the street . . . They say that Carlos

Galicia is going soft, that he does not have the balls to run a business in the current environment. We need to send a signal that we are just as strong as our rivals."

"Ha! They say that, do they? And I'm sure you've taken them to task for it, yes?" Carlito was silent. "Right. Next time you hear this whispered, you bring the whisperer to me, and I will show him how much strength is still left in these fists." Galicia balled his fists and showed them to his nephew.

Carlito appeared unconvinced. "Beating gossips isn't going to impress our boys, much less the Juarez and the Sinaloa. We're at war; we can't afford to look weak, or we'll be eaten up by the other cartels, or else the government will think we're easy targets and come after us to 'prove' that they're winning. If the boys think we have a weak leader . . . they might start looking for a way to replace you."

"What!" Galicia jumped out of his chair again, aware of the strain across his chest but not particularly caring. "You would dare say such a thing to me?"

"Not me, uncle," Carlito said quickly. "I love you like a father, and it's only because I worry about your position that I—"

"Enough," Galicia said, cutting Carlito off with a sharp gesture. "Get this into your head: I am protected from above, by the boss of bosses and by God Himself. No one will dare touch me without bringing down terrible retribution upon themselves. Only Carlos Galicia can kill Carlos Galicia, and no other. Take that to the whiners and the traitors, if they've forgotten it."

"Yes, uncle—sorry, uncle," Carlito said before ducking out, closing the door behind him. Carlos glared at the door for several moments afterwards, still seething at the suggestion that some people in his own organization might be plotting against him. Him, who had sacrificed so much, given of himself time and time again, for this organization. The violence of these dark days of open war was like an acid, eating away at all the old bonds of family and friendship that had once held them together in the face of a hypocritical world looking for somebody to blame for their ills.

"Bah," Galicia said, trying to wave off his doldrums. He walked over to the small table, poured himself a glass and drank it all in one gulp. Uncouth, maybe, but he needed something to calm his nerves. And it wasn't as though propriety was a concept held in esteem any longer, so why should he bother putting on airs in the privacy of his chambers?

Galicia poured himself another glass, but this time let the wine air out, sloshing it around in the cup as he ambled over to his balcony. The streets below were bright with the festivities, people cheering as oversized *Catrinas* passed through the boulevard, children racing to and fro, pumped up on the sugar skulls and the other candy they had been snacking on all day. For the adults, it was rather tequila and other alcoholic spirits that gave colour to their faces before the stylized spirits of the dead with their ivory-toned visages. From their appearance and clothing, it was obvious that a large number of those watching the parade were American tourists who had, legally or otherwise, crossed the border for the occasion. Some of those, Galicia well imagined, would be hitting the red light district after the more wholesome Day of the Dead celebrations had—pardon the pun—died away. He wished them a pleasantly expensive night; the Tijuana Cartel happily claimed a portion of the money made by the brothels and the dealers.

For his part, Galicia knew better than to partake in the pleasures he peddled, particularly on this of all days. Most people looked forward to having the dear departed visit them today, but Galicia had been in this business too long to count more friends than foes among the dead. He'd gone to the cemetery that morning, in the quiet, respectful atmosphere of the early daylight hours, where he'd left his offerings for his parents, his late wife, and other family members. Then he had taken a quick tour of several other graveyards, where he left, en masse and anonymously, votives for the many soldiers who had fallen under his command, from when he'd been a mere lieutenant in the back alleys to all the boys he had never met who had fallen in these last few years of war against the other cartels.

He had gone home after that and tried to put the dead out of his mind—impossible as that was, given that his house staff insisted on decorating, despite his objections. At least they had respected his wishes that his chambers be left as is. Also, there was the noise from the street outside. In truth, he enjoyed listening to the celebrations—they were at a remove, communal, and so felt safe. It was the idea of having altars or shrines in his home that made him wary. He had no doubt that many of those below would be going home tonight to such shrines—not the tourists, obviously, but the real Mexicans—where lit candles shone on photos of the departed to make it easier for the spirits to find their way back to their old homesteads. But Galicia worried that such a doorway in *his* domicile would prove too tempting for uninvited guests.

More and more, Galicia felt as though the weight of the resentful dead was pressing heavier on his shoulders, a cavalcade of blind sockets and jangling bones. The young ones, like Carlito, couldn't understand how those first fumbling kills in the alleyways were just as much of a gateway drug as any of the wares the cartel smuggled across the border. Your first kills made you feel powerful, invincible, high on the rush of fear and excitement, feeling paradoxically more alive in that moment than at any other point in your life, as though you were absorbing the vitality of those who died at your hands, like Aztec warriors of old eating the hearts of their foes. After a while, though, the rush of the immediate emotion fades away, and you're left to cling to that sense of having control—the ultimate power, that over life and death—in an uncertain world. Murder becomes casual, a routine demonstration of your place in the great food chain of the modern jungles.

But like any other drug, it could eat you up. That's what he kept trying to impress on Carlito, who, nominally, would take over running this particular slice of the Tijuana Cartel whenever the Lord saw fit to call Galicia back to Himself. You couldn't solve every disagreement with death, or else you find yourself with no one by your side, surrounded by vengeful enemies.

Galicia poured himself another drink, closing his eyes as the sweet nuances of the wine played across his palate before soothing his throat with its warmth. Galicia remembered when he had made boss, the pride he felt tempered by the realization that where before he'd had many friends— brothers in arms, really—and a mass of faceless enemies working for rival gangs and cartels, now he had many faceless underlings but personal enemies who knew his name and his face. Some bosses still got off on the killing, although they were executioners more than soldiers now. Galicia, though, looking to trim his list of foes, had tried to wean himself off the drug, and in some ways he still felt like he was in withdrawal to this day, nervous and depressed.

Ordinarily, those worries would just be a buzzing in the back of his mind, but things had gone poorly for the Tijuana Cartel over the last few years of war. Galicia had been one of those who had argued for the alliance with the Gulf Cartel, in the spirit of making friends rather than enemies. Yet Tijuana was not prospering; far from it. With arrests and deaths at the higher echelons, the cartel was slowly breaking apart, centrifugal organization giving way to a modular chaos where pieces of previously safe territory were being usurped by the Juarez, or else taken over by their supposed allies, with Gulf men assuming positions of power in the vacuum resulting from their losses. Galicia acutely felt the precariousness of his position, and Carlito's concerns did nothing more than remind him that he was walking a tightrope above the abyss. This day was supposed to be a festive one, but when he looked out onto the streets, he saw only resentment in the dark hollows of the skulls below, just waiting for him to make a misstep.

In fact, the street below seemed to be falling away, further and further down with each passing second until it resembled a chasm where the dying light of the sun could not penetrate, lit only by the unhealthy neon and ultraviolet glow of the skulls. Feeling light-headed, Galicia turned away from the window, shaking his head. He tried to make his way back to his upholstered chair, but missed a step on his way down from the balcony, triggering an odd sort of half-falling jerk before he was able to catch himself. The red wine sloshed inside the cupola of his glass, overflowing and spilling. Galicia stared at the crimson stain it made on the white marble, finding it difficult to think of what he needed to do about it over the attempt to blanket out the thought that it looked like a bloodstain.

Enlightenment eventually arriving, Galicia ambled uncertainly back to his chair, wondering if he was already drunk. He didn't remember drinking more than a few glasses, but then if he was drunk he wouldn't remember that anyway. He all but fell into his chair, one hand missing the armrest and upsetting his balance once more, though this time there wasn't enough wine left in the glass to spill. He stabbed at the intercom button set into the table at his side and called for his butler.

"Manuel! Get in here; there's wine on the floor."

"Yes, sir," came the muffled reply.

Galicia dipped his head in his hands. He felt as though he was swimming, the room around him refracted and distorted. Looking at the opposite wall, he thought he could see it rippling like a bodybuilder flexing his muscles. It was rather upsetting to look at and was making him queasy besides, so Galicia shut his eyes tightly, then jammed the palm of his hands against them. This wasn't normal, not even drunk-normal. Something was wrong; he needed to see a doctor.

"Manuel!" he cried out, hoping his butler would be on hand. How long was it now since he'd called him up? A few seconds or minutes? Galicia suddenly found that he couldn't estimate the time that had passed, which only deepened his anxiety.

Finally, hearing the door open, Galicia staggered to his feet, fully intending to tell the hired help off for taking . . . however long it had taken him to get here, in what was clearly a crisis situation.

Except it wasn't the short, mustachioed form of Manuel at the door. Instead, framed by the corridor light, was a tall figure in stygian robes and a skull for a face. Shocked, Galicia tried to back up, and instead tripped on his chair and tumbled backwards, somehow managing to do a reverse somersault across the cushion to land on the ground on the other side of the chair. He lay there a moment, disoriented, trying to process what he had just seen and reconcile it with his aching sanity. He *couldn't* have seen what he thought he had seen; surely it was a trick of the wine, or whatever affliction was causing his more general vertigo.

He popped his head back up over the chair, and instantly wished he hadn't. The skull-faced figure had not vanished, or assumed the more familiar form of his servant. Worse yet, the entity had been joined by several more just like it, silently passing through the doorway into his chambers. Galicia watched as they glided into a semi-circle before the doorway, facing him. Galicia thought he heard a loud rapping, before realizing that was the sound of his own heart beating away in his chest. His doctor's orders not to get too excited rose and sank briefly in his mind; though his breath was short and his face warm, Galicia thought he had a somewhat more immediate challenge to his health than his overtaxed heart.

"W-what do you want?" he finally managed to stammer out. He pointed to the window, trying to inject his words with as much of the steely authority he had developed in his years with the cartel. Even to his ears, though, the tremor in his voice was amply evident. "You belong outside; you're not welcome here! Go! Find *your* loved ones and don't bother me!"

They stood there silently several moments more, their dark robes rippling, their forms always growing without ever coming closer to the ceiling. Then one of them spoke, his skull-face blurring as it did so.

"Carlos Glaicia." Its voice was deep and echoing. "We are the dead. And we have come for you. Tonight, you will be leaving this world . . . with us."

"No," Galicia whimpered. "No, please, I cannot; it must be a mistake. I—I am too young. I have too much work to do still . . . ." He drifted off, the blank, bony expressions staring back at him clearly unmoved.

"We are those whom you have killed," the lead skeleton said. "The time has come to answer for your sins." It stretched out an arm; Galicia saw no hand at the end of the black robes. "You have no choice. You will be stripped of your name, stripped of your face, and you will take your place in the darkness . . . with us, for all eternity."

Galicia swallowed hard, passing the back of his palm across his sweaty forehead. The voice of the lead skeleton sounded almost familiar . . . and why shouldn't it? It had said they were the spirits of those he had killed. When he had last heard this voice, had it been begging him for mercy or cursing him to the bitter end? Galicia supposed it didn't matter now; one way or the other, the spirit was surely not well intentioned towards him. These were no friendly angels, come to lead him to the eternal reward with a fanfare of trumpets; Galicia didn't imagine he would much like the place they wanted to bring him to. Particularly not if these vengeful spirits would be his fellow tenants.

Galicia looked around, trying to find some mean of escape. However, even with the room twisting as though seen through an aquarium, Galicia couldn't see any way out. The shades were blocking the doorway and Galicia didn't think much of his chances were he to try and run past. There was the balcony, but that was too high up; there was no way he would survive a fall from there, even if he aimed for the celebrants in the street to try and cushion the blow.

But still. Galicia looked out towards the balcony where the final rays of sun had passed beyond the horizon, not that it seemed to be dampening the enthusiasm of the revelers any. There was something perverse about that, Galicia thought—that the moment of his death should be accompanied by such lively ambiance. The fall would kill him, yes, but was that really such a bad thing? True, the priests said that suicide was a deadly sin, but maybe if he died this way, he would fall back into the natural order of the afterlife and the forgiveness that was his due, rather than this twisted nightmare of being plucked still living by a collection of grim reapers. Galicia estimated the distance from the chair to the balcony, wondering if the shades could move faster than the gentle glide they had affected on entering the chambers. He pictured himself running, jumping off the balustrade, tumbling down into the shadows below . . .

Yet, something inside of him—a last guttering spark of the old aggression—rebelled at the thought of going down without a fight. So, when Galicia darted forward, it was not towards the window he went, but to the low table next to the chair. He put his hand into the hollowed-out bottom of the table, groping for the gun he knew was taped there. He found it, grasped the handle, and ripped it out with the sound of tearing tape. He pointed the pistol at the shades, squinting with one eye to maintain his aim despite the room's irritating tendency to sway from side to side.

Some of the skeletons seemed to retreat or dwindle at the sight of the gun, dark robes blurring as if they were getting ready to run. Galicia frowned; only now that he had apparently frightened some of them did he realize how nonsensical it was to threaten the dead with a gun. Nominally, they couldn't very well be killed a second time; at worst, a bullet might shatter some bones. Was that why some of them were stepping back now? Did the dead fear pain, or . . . ?

Galicia's attempts to reason out his situation through the haze that had settled over his thoughts were pushed out from his mind as the lead skeleton, the one who had spoken earlier, advanced on him, both arms raised as though in anticipation of some corrupt embrace.

"You cannot kill us a second time, Carlos Galicia," the shade said. "You only make your fate worse by threatening us. Put the gun down and prepare to come with us."

Galicia kept the gun trained on the lead reaper for a few more moments then let the weapon drop to his side, since the shade was clearly not intimidated. He glanced over at the balcony again, trying to judge his distances in defiance of the fluid proportions of the room, but with the lead shade so much closer now, Galicia didn't think he would make it before it could snag him.

However, he realized there was still one last exit available to him.

"Only Carlos Galicia can kill Carlos Galicia," he told the skeletal figure before him, then brought the barrel of the gun up and pressed it against the side of his temple, resolved to one last murder. He hesitated a moment, mentally saying goodbye to Carlito, his sister, and all those people and things from this life that he would miss. Then he pulled the trigger, and there wasn't even enough time for the deafening explosion next to his ears to register in his mind before it was blown out the other side of his skull. He crumpled to the ground, dead before his knees even buckled.

"Good riddance, you old coward," the lead figure said, reaching up to remove the hot, rubber skull-faced mask he was wearing.

"You didn't say anything about a gun, Carlito," one of the others said, ripping off his own mask, his tone reproachful.

Carlito spat out the electronic voice changer that had made his voice sound deep and echoing. "I didn't know about the gun," he said, absent-mindedly cleaning the device on his costume. "I was sure he would have jumped out the window—if he didn't have a heart attack on the spot."

"Nearly got killed," his accomplice muttered.

"Oh, shut up. The plan worked, didn't it?" Carlito told him, fingering the wine bottle on the small table. It had been a simple matter to bribe Manuel to lace the bottle with a hallucinogenic which, combined with what Carlito knew of the old man's superstition and guilty conscience, would drive the elder Galicia to the edge. The old man had refused to adapt to the changing times, but still his own bosses protected him. Galicia had told the truth when he promised deadly retribution to any who would dare try to unseat him; even though it was falling apart, the leaders of the Tijuana Cartel still didn't like having their captains knocked off by their own men. But suicide was a different animal altogether; the only one that could be punished there was long past reprisal.

"Come on," he told his friends. "Let's get out of here. We need to be long gone before the staff finds him."

With the elder Carlos Galicia out of the way, Carlito knew he would be next in line to assume control of the family's territory and business. And then he would show them all how this organization ought to be run.

Before the Altar on the Feast for All Souls

Marg Gilks

Doña Pascuala Ek sat in the doorway of her house and waited for a butterfly.

She knew Teodoro would return to her in the form of a butterfly rather than the quicker hummingbird, because that was how Teodoro had been in life: tranquil, a dreamer, his every movement easy and fluid. He'd performed even the most rigorous chore as though his mind was elsewhere, in an easier place.

Pascuala missed Teodoro. He had passed a year ago, May, crossed over to that easier place and left her alone in the small thatched hut they had shared for almost fifty years. The five sons he had given her lived with their families in the other huts of pole stakes and white lime marl that made up their compound so she was never truly alone, until now.

Today was *Hanal Pixan*—her people's name for the Feast for All Souls. Her five strong boys and their wives and the tumbling flock of their children were off at the village churchyard, honoring and remembering those who had crossed to the other side, but Pascuala had insisted on staying at the compound, near the altar lovingly constructed and provisioned for those souls who would find their way home to their loved ones. To Pascuala.

Teodoro had not come last year at Hanal Pixan. She had waited in the doorway until her son, Isidoro, woke her in the first thin rays of dawn the next day. But Teodoro had been new to the other side; perhaps he couldn't find his way back to her then.

Teodoro would come this year. She had seen to it. She had strewn yellow *cempazuchitl* petals in a confetti line from the jungle that crouched behind her son Juan's house, across the hard-packed earth of the compound, to her door. Pascuala could smell the *copalli* candles that the family had lit upon the altar within. She could smell the strong resin odor of copal incense and, like an undercurrent, the sharp bite of spice mingled with the cooler, sweeter odor of fruit from the food offerings in the gourd hung beside the door. The smaller portions in the gourd were for the lost souls, those who roamed in search of families they would never find, but the aroma would guide her Teodoro in to the bounty on the altar. And to her.

The last long, honeyed glow from the sun gave way to the silver-tinged gloom of dusk. The white lower walls of the huts circling the compound glowed, as if releasing the last wan vestiges of light collected during the day into the dark embrace of the jungle. This had been her and Teodoro's favorite time of day, between the end of chores and the oblivion of sleep. In the twilight, Teodoro would talk in his soft, dreaming voice, and Pascuala would rest her head on his chest and feel his words thrum beneath her cheek.

But he was not here yet. Pascuala must do one last thing to ensure that Teodoro found his way back to her.

Spaced at regular intervals beside the path of bright marigold petals were thirteen small paper bags, weighted with sand and scissor-cut with lacy patterns to let the light of the candles within shine through. Pascuala rose and collected an ember from the hearth in the floor of her dwelling, then moved stiffly down the line of paper bags, stooping to light the candles.

It was nearly dark by the time she finished. She turned back at the jungle behind Juan's hut and returned to the stool beside her door to wait for Teodoro.

Pascuala saw the couple standing by the fringe of jungle at the end of the path of marigold petals when she turned to lower herself onto the stool. They were a young white couple, *turistas* in bright crisp clothes that screamed "intrusion" against the worn lines and dusty, faded tones of the compound. The woman's hair was pale, bleached-blonde, as bright and brassy as the glint of gold at neck and earlobes and wrist; the man wore an apologetic smile and a camera around his neck.

Pascuala reeled as though their sudden appearance were a physical blow. The narrow road that ran through the village and past the Ek compound had been widened and paved by the Mexican government two years ago, and now taxis stuffed full of *turistas* from Playa del Carmen and tour buses from Cancún plied the route between the coast and Cobá. The whites had taken the great city of Pascuala's ancestors and made it their own, and now the peace and privacy of her own family's compound was being taken from her by the *ix-tz'ul* and their invasive cameras and handfuls of heavy *mil-pesos* pieces that made beggars of her grandchildren.

She had stayed behind at the compound while her family went to the church in the village so she would not miss her Teodoro when he came. Now these *estúpidos gringos* had blundered in, disturbing the special moment she'd worked so hard to conjure on this one night that her lost husband's spirit might return. Destroying the one chance she had to see him, be with him, just once more.

I cannot wait again to see him. Not another year.

Anger lent Pascuala a moment of agility as she rose from her stool and stalked several paces down the yellow-petal pathway. "Go away, stupid *turistas!*" she called to them. She lifted both arms and waved them at the couple, trying to brush them back into the jungle like the dust she pushed out the door of her hut every morning with a stiff corn broom. "You should not be here; go back to the road and your fancy resorts, where you belong!"

Instead of obeying, the garish woman took a step forward. She would crush the delicate marigold petals strewn for Teodoro and the Ek ancestors. Pascuala watched her approach in dismay.

"Please, can't you help us?" the woman asked. "Our car left the road—"

"I cannot help you!" Pascuala exclaimed. "I am an old woman, alone. Go back to the road and walk to the village. There are men there who can help you push your car back onto the road."

The man stepped forward and put his hand on the woman's shoulder. His smile was sheepish. "I'm afraid it's somewhat worse than that," he said to Pascuala. "The car rolled a couple of times and it's resting on its roof, about a mile up the road to Cobá. We'll need more than a push."

He spoke Mayan. The woman had, too, Pascuala realized. White people did not speak Mayan. She frowned, then sucked in a surprised breath. Could they be . . .? "I don't know how I can help you," she said slowly. "Come forward. Let me see you. Tell me what you need."

The man took the woman's hand and the couple came forward, following the trail of strewn marigold petals to Pascuala. The scattered petals fluttered gently, shifted in small swirls as though something winged flew low above them.

Pascuala watched them approach. They did not look like the survivors of a car crash. Their clothes were clean and unrumpled, as though they had just stepped from their hotel and not stumbled along the rough verge of a road over unknown terrain. There were no cuts or bruises or wounds of any kind showing dark on their pale skin in the failing light. The hair of both man and woman was neat and shiny-clean, not dull with the dust that would have been kicked up during a car accident.

Yes. Pascuala sighed.

"I'm Russell Musgrove," the man said when they stood before her. "This is my wife, Janice." The pair looked at one another as though they shared the most delightful secret, and Russell put his arm around his wife's shoulders.

Pascuala's gnarled hand flew up to touch her lips. "You are newlyweds."

Janice smiled shyly. "We're on our honeymoon."

Pascuala saw the young woman's nostrils flare and her eyes slid past Pascuala, searching out the scent. "Oh, how lovely!" she exclaimed over the family altar within. "And the aroma is so enticing. I had no idea how hungry I was until now."

She took a step toward the *pan de muertos* and mangos and limes, the few confections shaped from *alfeñique* for the children who had not survived, and Pascuala's special *mole* sauce, a favorite of Teodoro's, all lovingly arranged amidst glowing tapers and flowers.

Pascuala opened her mouth to speak, but Russell pulled Janice back to him and said, "That's not for us." Two lines puckered into existence between his brows and he looked to Pascuala. "It's not, is it?"

Poor souls, so far from home, they do not know yet, Pascuala thought, and lifted the gourd that hung beside the door. "This is for you," she said.

"I'm not sure what we should do now," Russell said when they were done. He licked sweet papaya juice from his fingers. "Which way we should go— back to Cobá or on to your village. Is there someone with a car there?"

"There is no car. And Cobá is not the place for you to go. Those who walk in that place would not welcome you." She wanted to weep. *I cannot send them away. They are so young, so lost; they don't even know yet that they no longer belong here. But Teodoro—* "Come inside. Someone will come soon to guide you."

She motioned them into the hut and indicated another stool placed near the altar and set the stool she had brought from the doorway down beside it. But when she started to kneel beside the firepit, Russell exclaimed, "No!" and returned her stool to her. He sat down cross-legged beside his wife's place. They regarded one another for a moment, in the glow from the embers and the tapers on the altar. The penetrating fragrance of the copal incense was stronger inside.

"Who are we waiting for?" Janice asked. "Is your family in the village? Will they be coming home soon?"

"My sons and their families are in the village, at the churchyard, yes. But they cannot help you. We're waiting for someone else." Pascuala looked away from the woman's bewildered blue gaze. Her eyes were drawn to the altar and she lifted a hand to adjust a flower. The hand looked like the paper bags protecting the candles in the compound, the skin brown and crinkled. *I should be in their place*, she thought.

"Who are we waiting for?" Janice asked again.

"My husband," Pascuala whispered. She turned on her stool to face the doorway, and the stream of golden petals that fell away from it into the night. From the corner of her eye, she saw the couple exchange a glance before Janice spoke again.

"Your husband is not at the churchyard?"

"No. He . . . left a year and a half ago." She kept her attention on the doorway. Had there been a flicker of movement out there in the darkness by the jungle fringe? She caught her breath and held it. *What am I doing?* a part of her whispered, *I cannot bear to wait again, not another year! Send them away, let them find their own way; let someone else guide them, let Teodoro come to me, send them away!*

"How can your husband help us, if you don't even know where he is?" Doubt thickened the man's voice.

The breath shuddered across her lips when she released it, and she had to blink rapidly. "I know where he is."

Pascuala heard the hard soles of his shoes scuff across the packed-earth floor as Russell rose. "Thank you for your help, but I think we should head for the village."

Pascuala sat very still on her stool. "*Yes, go,*" she wanted to say; "*hurry, before it's too dark to see your way.*" Before Teodoro comes. He would come this night. She felt it in her heart. *He must. I need him.*

They need him.

She held up her hand. "Wait," she croaked

"I really think—"

She would give him to them this night. Next year, perhaps, she would sit before the altar, waiting not just for a moment with her dear Teodoro, but for his guidance to the other side. Pascuala closed her eyes. "Wait."

"Russ, look at her," she heard Janice whisper. "Maybe we should stay a while, make sure she's okay—"

The jungle sighed.

Pascuala gasped. "Shh, listen! They come!"

The pair stood still, listening. Pascuala heard it again, that breath in the jungle, wafting over the myriad leaves. "Teodoro . . ." she whispered, and opened her eyes.

The strewn marigold petals seemed to lift and take flight, bobbing and fluttering, weaving through the night toward the door of Pascuala's house.

"My God, look at them!" the young woman beside Pascuala exclaimed. "There are hundreds of them!"

"Monarchs," Russell supplied.

Pascuala beamed up at him. "I knew he would return as a butterfly," she said.

The butterflies streamed from the jungle and gathered in a great golden cloud in the compound. A few broke from the flight and capered to hover tentatively before the dark doorways of the other huts before fluttering back to the group.

"What are they doing here?" Janice asked.

Pascuala shuffled to the doorway and stood with her hand on the worn wooden frame, the post smoothed and polished by generations of Ek hands. She lifted the other hand to the butterflies. She could feel the puckered parchment skin over her mouth stretched tight with a wide grin, but she didn't care what the lost ones thought of that.

"They've come for you," she said to them, and beckoned the man and woman forward. "Go to them. They will take you where you need to go."

"Butterflies?" Russell's voice came heavy with disbelief.

"Not butterflies. The Ek are a very old family, and plentiful. Now go; they are waiting."

Russell Musgrove took his young wife's hand in his and led her out into the compound. Monarch butterflies danced around them like flakes of gold in a current. The couple stood with their faces uplifted, glorying in the flight and the flash of bright wings.

"Teodoro," Pascuala murmured, "there is something more important for you to do this night. The *turistas* are lost and far from home and family of their own. Guide them safe to the other side. You are in my heart always, and I will wait for you next year, on Hanal Pixan." She smiled still, but she could feel moisture tracking down the gullies in her cheeks.

The erratic flight of the butterflies coalesced into a tall spiral. The dance of the insects quickened and tightened into a bright yellow tornado with the young couple at its center. The air sighed with the passage of hundreds of wings.

Pascuala could no longer make out the figures of the young couple. They were engulfed in the flight of the butterflies and she wasn't sure if the glint of gold was the woman, Janice's, jewelry and hair or merely the glow of candlelight on butterfly wings.

The sight blurred, and the old woman gripped the door frame to keep away vertigo. Faster and tighter the confetti kaleidoscope moved. Were those individual insects fluttering on the fringes, or was the whole flight fading away?

She could see the white marl of her son Juan's house through the flight now, and the dark backdrop of the jungle. The young newlywed couple was gone. Soon the butterflies would be gone. Teodoro would be gone, and she would be alone again.

Pascuala couldn't help herself; she let a sob escape. "Teodoro, I miss you so," she called softly.

A chip of bright yellow fell away from the fading vortex. A lone butterfly trembled in the air of the compound, then fluttered toward her. Pascuala smiled and held out her hand. "Teodoro," she whispered.

The insect lit on the palm of her hand and rested there, its wings moving slowly up and down. Pascuala wept.

The flight of the butterflies was no more than a pale smudge of color now. The butterfly in Pascuala's palm suddenly lifted and danced two circles around her head before flitting off to rejoin its fellows.

And in that moment Pascuala heard her name, breathed in the flutter of a butterfly's wings.

Ghost Dance

Chip Livingston

I think I'm going crazy when I see my reflection in the camera's lens. I'm surrounded by the dead. Jimi, Marilyn, Joan—face covered in cold cream, hand holding wire hanger high above her head. The Halloween Parade has paused for television crews in front of The Revolver on Duvall Street in New Orleans. I duck inside for a drink, take the elevator to the thirteenth floor.

I walk inside the club without ID. Tonight I don't need it. Tonight I'm invisible. I pass witches, goblins, boys dressed like ghouls. Once we were two of them. Once we both joined the annual masquerade. But tonight is different. Tonight I don a plain white sheet with ink. Circles traced around holes cut out to see through. Another hole through which I drink, from which I breathe.

I wasn't coming out tonight. Didn't plan or purchase a costume. Wouldn't wear one hanging in your closet. What led me to the linens then, to quickly cut a cotton sheet into a kid's uniform? What drove me to this?

Beneath this sheet, your medicine bag hangs around my neck, the tanned leather pouch you made me promise never to open. This is the first time I've worn it. But no one can see it. No one can see me.

I finish my drink, scotch neat, with a gulp, sing the invisible song you taught me, set the glass on the black wood rail, and, still singing, step onto the dance floor.

Beneath this sheet, I imitate you dancing. My feet, awkward at first, soon find your rhythm, and my legs bounce powwow style in the steps we both learned as kids. The steps that never left you. I dip and turn between, around the fancy dancers in their sequin shawls and feather boas. I shake my head like you did when your hair was long, the way you flipped it, black and shining, to the heavy beat of house music. The music hasn't changed much in case you're wondering. I dance in your footsteps; sing the invisible song; close my eyes.

When I open my eyes, I swear I see Carlo. Impossible right, but he's stuffed inside that Nancy Reagan red dress and he's waving at me, sipping his cocktail and smiling. He's talking to Randy, who's sticking out his tongue that way he always did whenever he caught someone staring at him. I start to walk over but I bump in to Joan.

She's glaring at me. Or it may just be the eyebrows, slanted back with pencil to make it look like she's glaring at me. She reaches past me and grabs Marilyn by her skinny wrist and pulls her away, but Carlo and Randy are gone. Where they stood are faces I don't recognize. Faces dancing. Masks I realize. Faces behind masks.

The DJ bobs furiously with pursed lips, headphones disguised as fiendish, furry paws, in the booth above the floor. He introduces a new melody into the same harping beat, and I remember to dance. I remember you dancing. My fingers sliding across your sweaty chest, I find the necklace. The sheet clings to my body in places. The new song sounds just like the last song but I'm being crowded together with strangers. I can no longer lift my legs as high as I want to, so I sway in place, shuffle with the mortals on the floor.

Behind me someone grabs me, accidentally perhaps, but I turn violently, jealously. There are too many people in this equation. Two become one again and again, and ones become twos. All around me real numbers add up to future possibilities. Imaginary numbers. It's why we're here dancing.

A cowboy nods his hat in my direction. But he can't be nodding at us. We're invisible. I think maybe he is a real ghost; he's peering intently into the holes cut out for my eyes. He looks like Randolph Scott, blond and dusty, so I look around for Cary grant as Jimi lifts the guitar from his lips and wails. Randolph Scott is coming this way and I turn my back and dance.

I want you back, Elan. I want you back dancing beside me. I start chanting this over and over to myself. *I want you back. I want you back.*

You taught me the power of words. I believed you. I can even smell you now. Sandalwood oil and sweat. I turn and expect to see you.

Not you behind me.

Not you beside me.

Not you in front of me.

Not you anywhere around me.

I make my way to the bar, but the bar is too crowded. The barman's face grimaces over hands holding folded dollars as he tries to keep the glasses filled. The air is thick with bitter smoke. It's hard to breathe. I make my way for the door, notice the cowboy trailing me. In the elevator, I go down alone.

Into the rain on Duvall Street, we walk out together. One set of footprints splashes our muddy way toward home, then, turning, I realize we are not going home, but passing more pagan tricksters decked out as holiday spirits.

The bells in the clock tower tell me it is midnight. Squeaking from its hinges, the door to morning slowly opens and it's All Saints Day, the Day of the Dead, and I am walking toward Boot Hill, to where you are buried.

We're alone in the cemetery. And the wind lifts the rain in a mist rising up from the wet earth which is claiming me. I remove my sheet in front of the cement memorial that holds your body up above the boggy ground. I remove my shoes. I strip off everything except your leather pouch around my neck, and I dance for you. My legs are free and I whirl and sing.

I'm dancing for you now, because you loved to dance.
I want you back dancing. I want you dancing now.

I'm dancing for you now, because you loved to dance.
I want you back dancing. I want you dancing now.

I'm dancing for you now, because you loved to dance.
I want you back dancing. I want you dancing now.

I'm dancing for you now, because you loved to dance.
I want you back dancing. I want you dancing now.

The Fat Lady Watches Monster Movies Late at Night

Kate Angus

In my dream, I am in a field somewhere desolate like Scotland or Iceland, not that I'm sure. God knows I haven't left the good old US of A but twice, a Caribbean cruise on my honeymoon and a quick trip down to Mexico with Ida a few months ago. I'd stopped going to my job bagging groceries at the Piggly Wiggly. They'd called me twice but I guess they got the message when I didn't call back. Probably they'd heard about what was going on already. Anyway, Leon, my manager, sent me a card and a check for my back pay. The card had a picture of a kitten stuck in a tree, staring up at a robin above it. There was a thought-bubble saying, "Everything's looking up from here." Inside, in his big loopy handwriting, the card read, "There's always a home for you here at the Pig House" and he'd signed it "the Piggly-Wiggly Crew." He gave all the "g"s little ears and snouts and made the stems into curling tails. It was real sweet of him but his wife left him for the man who runs the used Ford lot a couple of years ago so I guess he knew how bad it can be.

I cashed the check but I never wrote him back. What would I say? There was nothing in my life worth telling anyone. I only got up long enough to go to the bathroom or the kitchen. I had all my food delivered. I rolled around that bed in a sea of crumpled tissues and potato chip fragments like tiny broken shells. I lolled there for hours like a greasy weeping beached whale.

I didn't set foot outdoors till Ida got sick of her calls not being returned. She came over, found me there, and booked us tickets for the next flight out—a little dust-hopper from Clarksdale to Ciudad Juarez. She wanted us to go somewhere south of the border, but not too south. Juarez is right across the river from El Paso so there's something familiar on the horizon if you just strain your eyes.

The first night we mostly just drank vats of bright blue margaritas at the hotel bar. On the second day, she dragged me down a series of dirty little streets to an open air market. It was *Día de los Muertos*, which basically means everyone was celebrating dead people. There were candy skulls you could crunch between your teeth and bright marigolds. There were children running around laughing and hitting each other with flowers. Everyone seemed remarkably happy. I knew their lives were probably terrible—full of poverty, cheating husbands, and infected cuts they didn't have the medicine to fix—but the way they were grinning sort of kicked me in the gut. How could they be so happy when I wished that I was mostly dead? Here I was some big fat American tourist come down for a few days from the Land of Opportunity where I had a house, cable television, and nice curtains. They had nothing but dry heat and dirt but, from the way they looked, they had a whole world more than me even though I'm sure they thought that I was the one who had everything. Heck, in some ways I even did—things such as a good dentist and a sage green '93 Chevy that runs pretty nice, but inside me was a huge cave of darkness and crying that I kept trying to fill up with food and these new sights and smells but it wasn't doing any good.

While I kept gnawing on my thoughts like some stubborn dog gumming at his only bone, Ida pulled me aside to show me a stall of clay statues of the saints. There was Peter with his staff and Christopher with Our Lord as a little baby on his back and Our Holy Mother wearing a gown like the ocean—bright blue robes and white. The saints were lush like parrots, painted sleek and green and red.

"I'm thinking about getting a couple of these," she said. "It's a better price if you get four instead of just one or two. They throw in a fifth for free."

How she figured that out is beyond me since she only knows a couple words of Spanish we both learned studying from her book on the plane but Ida's always been one for getting the good deal. She peered at me, looking over the rims of her glasses. It makes her look like an angry owl when she does that, especially with her hair all frizzy from the heat.

"I only want a couple," she said, "so you pick out one for yourself."

It was generous of her to do that since, like I said, she's as tight with money as a frightened virgin's thighs clamped close together on the ride home after prom night. You might be thinking different, hearing how she took me down there in the first place but her husband is an airline pilot so I'm sure she got those tickets cheap.

"I'll take this one for Mother," she said, looking at the Holy Virgin, the one I'd found so pretty with her robes falling around her feet like frothy waves.

Her mother's been widowed six years now after more than fifty years of what she called wedded bliss, though how anyone could have been happy with that woman is one of the unsolved mysteries of the world to me. She spent years picking at me like I was a scab on her family she couldn't wait to peel off and see the skin underneath where I'd been, shining pink and new. There are a lot of things I knew I'd miss about marriage but my mother-in-law wasn't one of them. At family meals, she'd dish out huge portions to everyone else but only give me a smidgeon, saying how important it was for women to keep themselves looking good for their men. She'd say I was "big-boned" or "robust" and then look over at me and smile sweet as saccharine. I could never bring myself to say nothing back since I was raised up to respect the old. I'd just stare out her window to that calm green expanse of golf course she lived next to. I'd look at the men knocking their little white balls down the fairway, saw away at the food on my plate—she always did overcook the meat—and pretend my slice of steak was her tongue.

So Ida put that statue aside, and chose another; this one of Saint Christopher, the patron saint of travel, for her house. Then she took Saint Anne for her hairdresser, Annie, who used to give me blonde highlights, back when I could be bothered to spend the morning being made up pretty, when there was someone I thought would care about the way I looked. Then I saw she'd taken a Saint Rita statue too.

"Who's that for?" I asked her and I'll admit she had the decency to blush.

"You know who it's for, Delores. I don't even see why you're bothering to ask."

I just stared at her, daggers like they'd say, but she didn't drop my gaze.

"You know they're getting married," she said, "so I might as well give her a saint. Give that girl a good role model, some decency for a change."

She was talking about Eddie, her brother, my ex's, new fiancée. Shanti, the little cocktail waitress he met at his regular late night Tuesday night gig, the one I stopped going to because I had to get up so early the next morning for work. At first he seemed sad I wouldn't be going but then he didn't seem to mind and I thought it was because he understood I needed sleep more than I needed to hear him play his music three times a week instead of the two shows I was going to already. I thought we'd reached a good space where he had his life and I had mine and most of the time they overlapped but sometimes they didn't and that was okay. I sure was what my grandmother, God rest her soul, would have called a stupid chicken. Of course he didn't mind our lives had stopped overlapping as long as he could get some on the side. But then having her on the side wasn't enough, he had to tell me about it too, and then he left me. And Ida came to rescue me from near about eating myself to death, which was why I was down in Mexico looking at these saints anyway.

"You could get one too, for your free one," Ida had said to me. "Saint Rita isn't just for marriage. She helps with hopeless love and lost causes too. Maybe he'll leave her or you'll find someone new."

"You can't be asking the Saint to keep his new marriage strong and for him to turn tail and run back to me both. It's too damn confusing," I snapped and turned away.

"I'm sorry, Delores," I heard her say over my shoulder, "but I just don't know what else to say."

I looked at all the statues of the saints spread out in a heavenly chorus across that red table cloth on a teetery market stall. I didn't know which one I wanted. Should I be praying for love or protection? For compassion, wisdom, money, beekeepers, policemen, or for the quiet safety of trees?

Then I saw something I'd never seen before: it looked like Our Heavenly Lady, long robes and a wreath of red roses around the base but under the halo there was a skull.

"*Que es?*" I asked the lady who ran the stall in my meager Spanish.

"*La Santisima Muerte*," she responded. "Our Most Holy Death."

"Huh?"

"She is, I don't know how you say it, Sacred Death? For the women whose men go away."

Well, that about covered it for me. Her robes were pale pink and plum colored like a bruise that's just starting to fade. She had a gold halo over her hood. In one hand she was holding scales and the other hand was empty like maybe she was waiting to be introduced, to shake your hand or to hold it, or for you to put a gift in the wicker basket of her bony palm. Her face looked kind of friendly, though, you know the way some skulls can do, like children's masks at Halloween or something. Their eye sockets are big and dark but nice and it seems like the jaw is smiling at you.

"All right," I said and turned to Ida. "This is the one I want."

"Are you crazy?" she asked, and crossed herself. "That's not a real saint. What are you going to do with her? It's a sin to pray to something like that."

"Maybe I won't be praying," I said, "fat lot of good prayer's done me so far, and fat I am for that matter and, anyway, I'm getting tired of being good."

The woman behind the stall, maybe worried about losing the sale, turned to me and said, "She is for praying. She keeps the men faithful or, if they are not, she judges them."

"Good," I said, "That's just what I need. Just a little judgment maybe since it's way too late now for faithfulness. Wrap her up, please, with the others."

And poor Ida had to bite her tongue at that because she had promised to let me choose the sixth one for myself and anyway it was her spoiled-rotten younger brother, Eddie Dufrey, that aging two-bit balding tenor saxophone player, who had, after eighteen years of marriage, left me a week before my forty-sixth birthday for a girl not more than twenty-three. He sat me down at the kitchen table on a Saturday when I was wearing a bathrobe still, not my good bathrobe even but the ratty old pink one with a coffee stain on the lower right side that's faded now but never did wash completely out, with my hair up in curlers because I wanted to look good for his show later. He told me he'd found true love and was moving into her place after his band finished their set that night.

"But you have true love already," I said to him. "You said you'd found it with me on our third date at Sal's Italian Bistro almost twenty years ago in between the salad and the pasta course."

He just looked at me and sighed. He drummed his fingers on the table and then made swirly patterns in the spilled sugar there. His hands were one of the things I loved him best for. His fingers were long and tapered, thin like the feelers of an insect. A musician's fingers, I guess. Sometimes when we were just sitting on the couch together, I'd bend down and kiss the moist center of his palm. I liked the feel of his hands on me, like he was making music on my skin. Truthfully, though, when we were in bed together, he didn't touch me that much. It's like he was too worried I'd move funny and his fingers would break. Like he had to save them for what was important and it wasn't me.

I'd tried again. "You said you loved me when we got married. In a church. Before the eyes of God and all our friends and family. And you've said it darn near every day since then. Are you telling me you're a liar? That all happened. We're married. I didn't make it up. So how can you be in love with someone else?"

"But I didn't ever love you," is what he said next. "Not really. I realize it now. I couldn't ever really love someone who wasn't a musician. Shanti sings and plays piano. There are things about me she understands that you never could. Even when I did love you, I always knew I needed someone more like me."

"So when the hell did you figure all this out then? Did you ever think to tell me sooner or were you just waiting around, biding your time 'til some other musician came along and swept you off your feet? Maybe I would have been better off with a football player or an acrobat or some FBI-man. But I chose you. We chose each other. That's what the vows said. For richer or poorer. 'Til death do us part. Did you ever think of that?"

He didn't answer. He just stretched his head from side to side to crack his neck, the way he always did, sighed and said, "There's no point in talking about it. I'm going upstairs to pack. I'll come around in a couple of days for the rest of my things."

And he went upstairs and that was pretty much that. Of course there was the awful part of having to call everyone, my friends and family, such as they are, to tell them I'd failed. And there were all the legal papers to sign, and the house that got emptier and emptier and quieter and quieter until I started to fill it up with my own weight. But not all of that had started yet so in the few minutes it took after he told me but before it had really sunk in, while I could hear his footsteps overhead creaking as he moved around our bedroom and decided what to leave behind and what he'd take, I sat downstairs at that table and I licked my hands to wet them and I started scooping up the sugar he'd made patterns in. I ate it all—every last granule that he left. My skin was damp with sweat and spit and all that spilled sweetness. I was crying, but I licked each one of my fingers clean.

But that was a long time ago, or it seems like it now. And I'm just trying to explain why Ida finally caved in and bought *La Santisima Muerte* for me. Of course, she did it because she felt a little guilty, even though Eddie leaving wasn't her fault. But it wasn't just that, like I'd thought at the time. It was her parting gift for me so I guess she wanted me to get something I wanted for once. We didn't talk about the statue again, though she watched me wrap it up nicely in tissue paper, cushioned so it wouldn't get broken in my luggage on the flight back.

Anyway, when we arrived back in Clarksdale and were walking out to my car, she turned to me and said, "Well, Delores, I guess this is it, you know."

I knew exactly what she meant. It made a whole lot more sense that way. She'd never have spent the money to go down to Mexico with me if it wasn't some sort of last blast, a final hurrah for our friendship.

"Don't look at me like that," she said, though I wasn't sure how I'd been looking. Maybe my lip was trembling a little or my eyes were starting to water but it was definitely from the heat. I damn sure wasn't crying. I'd already vowed no one from the Dufrey family would make me tear up again.

"You know it doesn't make any kind of sense for us to stay on like we have been," she said. "You and Eddie are split now. I've got to make space for him and Shanti in my heart. Especially if they have children, seeing as the two of you never did."

It hurt that she'd mentioned our never having children. She knew, just like God knew, how much Eddie and I had tried. I'd been off the birth control for years and tried all manner of injections and hormones and taking-my-temperature-down-there techniques they taught us at the fertility clinic over on Lennox Street. And she knew how raw and bloody my knees got from praying too, after even the doctors said there wasn't any use, seeing as I was an empty vessel, a barren womb and bound to stay that way. But I knew that she was right, too, from her way of seeing things and, God's truth, I knew it would be easier for me too.

Those three days with her across the border, they were hard. She had a voice a lot like Eddie's. They moved the same and their skin was near the same color, like pale sand. Plus there was no way I could be around her without thinking of all those years we'd been in the same kitchen cooking pies and checking on the turkey for Thanksgivings and Christmases. We'd gossiped and giggled like sisters but all that time I'd felt she was my family, the truth is she was his. And I didn't want to hear about Eddie's new life from her: the wedding plans, the new bride sleeping next to him in my place. It wasn't right. The only way I knew I'd really get through all this was by pretending he was dead and having his sister still be my best friend, well, that'd just keep reminding me of the truth I couldn't handle: that he was still living breathing flesh and blood.

So I saw her point. I guess I almost admired her for having come right out and said it which I'm not sure I would have done. I still offered her a ride home but she said no, that it would be too awkward and she didn't mind taking the Super Shuttle back. She hugged me, said she'd pray for me and then she was gone.

I watched her for a little bit, walking fast across the parking lot. She looked back once and gave me a little wave which is more than her brother, my ex-husband, ever did. Then she disappeared behind a bus and I couldn't see her anymore. I want to say the air shimmered for a second from the heat or like a sign in a fairy tale that, well, this is it, this is your life changing, but nothing like that happened. I got in the driver seat of my car and near about burned my forehead when I tried to rest it for a second on the steering wheel. Then I drove away.

But this is a long and winding road to bring you to that dream I had where we started out. I'm slow to get to the point, that's what Eddie would have told you, even when things between us were pretty good. So, suffice it to say, I drove home and never spoke to Ida again, or Eddie either, not in person, though I've spoken to both of them an awful lot in my dreams and, wide awake, just walking around my house or chopping vegetables in the kitchen or in the shower, when I'm soaping myself clean.

I put *La Santisima Muerte* on my bedside table. I talk to her a lot too. I haven't prayed or asked her for anything, not yet, but I like to tell her how my day went, memories I have of my life with Eddie, or what it was like when I was a kid; raising chickens in the 4H club, or the time I got stung by a bee on the school bus, just little snippets of things like that. I moved the TV into the bedroom so it's at the foot of the bed and she and I stay up late watching movies together now.

We've found a real affection for horror movies. Not serial killer things which I think are awful, but the old time monster films. I'd never watch those things with Eddie. He thought they were uncouth, which was a word he liked. Whenever there was a word he was proud of knowing, he tried to sneak it in every time we played Scrabble or even just driving down the highway if someone cut us off. He'd get this expression on his face like he was the best thing since chocolate cake but if I didn't agree or praise him enough then he'd go quiet and sulk for hours. Oh Lord, there were things he did I couldn't hardly stand. He didn't like any kind of music other than jazz like what he played and a little classical, *Bolero* and that sort of thing. He was an inch shorter than me which he blamed me for and he thought I was too fat, which I was I guess, though I was a damn sight smaller then than I am now. He didn't much care for other races, though I guess he did like Asian girls, judging from the magazine I found in his car once. He didn't like homosexuals either, which made it hard when my cousin Steven moved to Austin and found a nice boyfriend.

But there were things I loved him for too. He didn't swear. He smelled like home to me. No matter what he did, I'd pretty much melt whenever I saw him, although I don't like thinking of that now: that syrupy weakening like all the borders of my heart were made of quicksand because of him. The way he sort of hunched over his saxophone like his back was a seashell. He was a good cook. I loved to listen to him play. His body: he was pale and thin and almost hairless. I loved sex with him too, even though I don't think I ever came. If I did, it wasn't big firework explosions like the magazines make it out to be, but I liked how it felt when he was inside me. And waking up the next morning when he'd slung his arm around me to pin me down and keep me next to him while we slept. The way my body felt all numb from not moving and the tingly pain you get from nerves trying to wake up: that was love to me.

I think, growing up big and believing you're ugly, you feel like no one's ever going to want to touch you. So, when someone finally does, you just get so goddamn grateful that you imprint on them or something, like baby birds do on whatever they see first when they crack out of their shell, doesn't matter if it's a dog or their mama, or a scientist using them for experiments in his lab. That's how I was with Eddie. At first, I thought we were meant to be together, that he was the only man I'd ever love. Then I realized it was more that he was the only man I thought might ever love me, so I emptied myself for him like a pocket pulled loose and dangling inside out, not knowing that he wouldn't stay, that, probably from the beginning even if he didn't rightly know it at the time, he was getting ready to leave. Now, I don't know what I think. I tell *La Santisima Muerte* that I miss him sometimes but I don't ask her to get him back. I tell her I hate him, too, but I don't ask her to punish him. She'll do what she wants or nothing. It's out of my control.

Mostly I just like talking to her. It makes me feel less alone.

We watch the midnight movies together: old, new, we like them all. But she, I think, is especially fond of the ones with Bela Lugosi as Count Dracula. I tell her he'd be a nice friend for her, no disrespect intended because who wouldn't want a nice European count and he has lovely big dark eyes. I like Boris Karloff as Frankenstein, especially in the first one before he gets a bride who doesn't really love him or the Wolf-man comes to town. It makes me cry every time. He didn't ask that crazy scientist to make him. He didn't want to be big and ugly and unloved and afraid.

I know what that feels like. Of course I do. That's what I started this thing trying to point out. Sometimes I have these dreams at night where I'm running across a field and, like in real life, I'm big and lumbering but, in these dreams, my fat's all grown over in a forest of thick dark hair. I'm dangerous and devilish, two things I've never been in waking life. And there are crowds of people just over the hill behind me, on horses, hunting me with dogs. They're carrying torches that light up like stars. Pockets of fire like constellations but lower to the ground.

And I'm a monster so I guess I deserve it, even though all I ever wanted was just something to eat and maybe a little affection, a friend who'd put their arms around me and say they really loved me; a mate, someone to raise our little monstrous children with in the dark warmth of our hidden lair. In these dreams, I keep running, my big monster feet crushing the marshland bracken and the hollow gold tubes of dead reeds. I run and run but as I wake up they're usually catching up close to me. Their angry voices come a little nearer each time and I can almost feel their torches singeing the thick fur on my back.

I tell *La Santisima Muerte* all about it when I wake up. She looks at me and, of course, she doesn't say a thing. After all, she goes around all day a skeleton in robes with a halo around her head. Who am I to complain about not fitting in?

When I'm awake, I'm pretty sure I know who the monsters are. It's not just me, but everyone. Ida and her husband in their house with plastic covers on the chairs to make sure no one will sweat or spill anything on the fabric, even though the plastic's ugly and sounds like farting when you stand. And Eddie too, may he be blessed and cursed. He's a monster for what he did to me, which wasn't love me the way I had the right to be loved. But he's a monster in a different way beyond that because maybe sometimes when he's playing he does feel like he's all by himself in a field somewhere of music and no one else can go there except him. That's a lonely way to live. And his little cocktail waitress too, because what kind of crazy do you have to be to hitch up with a man like him, twice your age and ready to divorce? What must have her life been like before him, that he seemed like a good bet to anyone but me?

So, sleeping, I know it's me they're after. The one who lurks around their campfire, waiting to snatch a hunk of bread, a baby, a young man who's wandered too far away from the rest. But in the harsh light of day I know I'm more laughable than to be feared. Elephant-wide, strolling down the aisle at the grocery store with my cart pushed out in front of me like a sail pregnant with wind, laden with chips, ribs, wine coolers and fresh flowers for *La Santisma Muerte*'s base. From outside my house, you can see the TV flickering in my bedroom like the light of faint and tiny stars. We stay up all night, Our Lady of Most Holy Death and me. The fat lady and the Skeleton Queen. We're two of us monsters but you, on the street, looking in at us, let me ask you, what are you?

Bread of the Dead

Ron Savage

I never looked like William Holden, even on my best day—I should've been so lucky. But giving credit where it's due, the old woman did resemble Gloria Swanson, particularly around the eyes, and those eyes could swallow you.

She's coming to visit me today, I'm making sure of that. The old woman won't have a clue, of course. Whether the motivation is guilt or love or just plain arrogance doesn't matter. She'll ignore the rule, too. The one that says, "Never go to Mexico on *Día de los Muertos*, not if the dead have a bone to pick with you."

Right now I am sitting on my fifth floor balcony, looking at the typewritten page in my Olivetti. The new story's doing fine. You can see the *Playa de los Muertos* from here, probably the most popular beach in Puerto Vallarata. When I'm not concentrating on the writing, though, I find myself staring down at the plaza, particularly the two streets that intersect in front of the hotel. I've decided the old woman will be coming from the left, the street nearest the beach.

It's the beginning of *Día de los Muertos*, the Days of the Dead, November 1st, 1951, a year and a couple of months since my own death. This morning I awoke in the hotel with no idea how I got from the grave to the bed. Nada, zero, *no* memories. But isn't that the way of *Día de los Muertos*? Today is All Saints day, tomorrow will be All Souls day, and for the next forty-eight hours the dead get to come back and play, visit relatives and friends, even settle old scores. In Mexico death is a woman, and they love her. *La Catrina, la Flaca, la Pelona*—Fancy Lady, Skinny, Bony, Baldy: Whatever you call it, the Mexicans have always had a little stiffy for Mama Death.

I *do* remember the old woman shooting me, that face-first fall into her pool, and most of the six months or so leading up to my murder. When I think back, none of it was a surprise.

Betty and I were working on a baseball script for Paramount. To be honest, our working relationship had become something more than trying to get through that hideous screenplay. I'd mixed feelings about us, but not about loving Betty, never about loving her. Believe me, the girl was a champ. No, my ambivalence came out of my nightmare situation with the old woman. I didn't want Betty hurt, and I mean physically hurt. The old woman had a butler-chauffeur that really *did* look like Eric Von Stroheim. He would've done anything she told him to do. *"Anything"* is the key word. By this time, I had an intense foreboding about the whole goddamn business. Look, what can I say? There was also . . . well . . . a certain embarrassment, if you get my meaning. Eventually, of course, the old woman told Betty everything, the works, how I was in debt up to my ass, how I was no good and a *kept* man, yada yada yada. So that night I did my own confession to Betty, maybe not every detail, but, you know, the highlights. I didn't lie to her, and I won't lie to you. I *enjoyed* being debt free, living in a Hollywood mansion, no matter how gothic, wearing fifteen hundred, two-thousand dollar suits. Who wouldn't. Though I haven't told this to anyone, I felt a certain sorrow about the old woman, a sadness. I mean, once I actually attempted to leave and she cut on herself. Then there was the butler-chauffeur-Nazi I had to deal with. Jesus-God, you can't imagine the anxiety. I couldn't *just* run off.

I remember taking an envelope with five thousand dollars of the old woman's money and giving it to Betty, asking her to bury me in Puerto Vallarta should things get crazy, which they did . . . *very* quickly.

A year and a couple of months later, here is Yours Truly, sitting on the fifth floor balcony of the Hotel de la Muerte, or whatever it's called, at least for the next two days, more than enough time to settle old scores and finish my story.

Typing on the Olivetti while the last of the day's sun heats my neck and back is nothing short of a blessing. Too bad the living don't ever get what's important. I damn well didn't, and let me say with the complete and absolute knowledge only the dead possess, you damn well don't, either. How wonderful to feel this story moving under my fingers, to feel its life, its purpose.

She'll be here . . . and soon.

She won't know why. She may not even grasp where she's going. But the old woman will command her butler-chauffeur-Nazi to get into that pretentious long black limo and drive . . .

. . . just drive.

Or that's how I imagine it. With the dead, imagination is everything.

Look, it's appeared, *there* on Beach Road. Can you see the limousine? The car is so polished it seems to lose its very color and become part of the sun at twilight. It's no longer dark but golden, sleek, silently racing across the blacktop. The turquoise water of *Playa de los Muertos* is on its left and a wide median of coconut palms and wild roses to the right.

You're on time, old woman.

Do you see me from that red velvet backseat? Has your butler-chauffeur-Nazi mixed your second or third highball?

Here, let me wave.

What her chauffeur doesn't notice is the rusted-out Ford station wagon weaving down Highway 200 at an ungodly speed. I suspect the occupants of the station wagon have also been drinking, the radio is certainly blasting loud enough. In fact, I'm *sure* they've been drinking. Tequila, perhaps, or rum. Isn't rum popular here in Puerto Vallarta? Neither driver can see the other, and the old woman's chauffeur doesn't need to drink for his foot to get heavy. He's a sober speed demon. I'm guessing that the two vehicles should converge at the plaza in less than a minute, the spot where Highway 200 intersects with Beach Road. I could stop the limo, I suppose, signal them to slow down, write it a different way. But maybe the old woman would think I didn't want her to visit, that I'd become stand-offish. It's dreadful enough being dead. Do I really need to be rude?

I hear a tune booming from the rusty station wagon, ". . . *how high the moon*," obviously something new by Les Paul and Mary Ford, the vehicle swerving back and forth over an empty highway. An occasional "*Yahoo!*" and "*Hey, gun this lazy bitch, Billy!*"—shouts inside a dark interior. These boys have got to be going eighty, maybe eighty-five, pretty damn good for that piece of crap. Then Billy guns it a little *too* much, swerves the bitch a little *too* radically, and the wagon hits a metal mailbox and rips the thing off its concrete mooring, pieces of the walkway breaking the window of a small shop. The vehicle does a complete three-sixty as the limo darts onto the intersection, the sun flashing its surface. That's when the rusted-out Ford station wagon smacks the curb at a weird angle and does a ten foot flip. Its nose cuts the limousine's rear like a two thousand pound karate chop. The brutal metal on metal crunch sparks an explosion that literally shakes the hotel. I feel it five floors up through my bare feet, smell the gasoline. A fiery red-orange mushroom wrapped in black smoke billows toward me, so close I could reach out and touch it.

The crazy butler-chauffeur-Nazi leaps from the roofless front seat and heads toward the side door, presumably to rescue the old woman. His clothes are on fire, and I can hear both of them screaming. He grasps the door handle a moment before a second explosion. It sends him and the door at least fifteen feet into the air. When he finally lands, he and the door are consumed by fire. Hell, *every*thing's consumed by the fire. I'm sure of it, the butler-chauffeur-Nazi, the limo, the rusty Ford station wagon and the guys inside it, and, of course, the old woman.

I've always had an unmistakable talent for symmetry.

Ahhh.

Thank you, la Muerte, I feel so cleansed.

Pulling the last page from the Olivetti, I place it with the others and tap them all together on the white metal table to make a neat pile. Then I put the stack next to my portable typewriter.

As I stare down at the plaza, I see the black smoke and the fire begin to dissolve. Parts of the rusted-out Ford have already vanished. The front of the limo is gone, too. The old woman's butler-Chauffeur-Nazi has become no more than a faint shadow in the twilight. I squint at the rear of the limousine, hand cupped above my brow, trying for a glimpse of the old woman. Before I can focus, that section of the car also disappears. It just breaks apart and—*poof!* Amazing. Then the gasoline odor dissipates, giving way to the fresh smell of the Pacific, as though no harsh, burning stench ever existed.

Study the plaza below me now. There's simply no evidence of the crash.

Being a dead writer does have its finer points. The *first* marvelous thing about being a dead writer is about to happen. I lean back in my canvas chair, bare feet propped on the white metal table, hands behind my head. I'm waiting for the show, and I don't have to wait long. This is how it's done on *Día de los Muertos*, when for two days the dead can visit family and friends, when old scores can finally be settled. The living dress up in masks and leave bread for us, but that's not what we eat. The bread of the dead is always revenge. You have to write it, though. You have to write it to make it real.

Here we go, she's on time.

Look, it's appeared, *there* on Beach Road. Can you see the limousine? The car's reflecting the last of the sun, golden like a DeMille chariot, so sleek and silent as it races across the blacktop, the water of *Playa de los Muertos* to its left and a median of coconut palms and wild roses to its right.

If you turn, you'll also see the rusted Ford station wagon heading down Highway 200, weaving back and forth on the empty road, the radio booming out a new Les Paul and Mary Ford number.

Bizarre, isn't it? By this time, you'd think the old woman would realize the rule *does* matter: Never visit Mexico on *Día de los Muertos*, not if the dead have a bone to pick with you.

From the Novel: Sleeping Woman

Sarah Layden

Pollinated summer air filled the Mazda through the open windows. The warm steering wheel felt pliant as taffy beneath Carey's hands. The cloth car seats rubbed against her legs, bare in running shorts. The May morning, hot and sun-beat, had struck her as perfect driving weather. Soon she passed the giant pink plaster elephant with the martini glass in its curled trunk. On the county exchange route, her tires kicked up gravel.

Squares of soybean fields on one side, and perfectly aligned rows of young corn on the other. About a mile down the road stood an unassuming white house next to a slightly larger brick church, both abutting a working farm.

The Williamson family plot took up a small square of earth. No sign, save for the headstones. Perhaps thirty, lined end to end. A freshly-painted white picket fence around a country cemetery seemed like something out of a John Mellencamp video. An idea of Indiana, rather than its reality. No. A way she had not seen it.

Today was Ben's birthday.

Earlier that day at Oakview Mall, she had purchased a poster from one of those shops popular with preteens, which sold black lights and itching powder, and edible underwear in the roped-off adult section. On the way out of the mall, she passed Prisanti's. Glanced briefly at the unremarkable young dough-tosser contained behind the glass. A framed candid photo of teenage Ben wearing a white apron still hung on the wall, next to a laminated copy of his obituary.

Mexico had its altars, its Day of the Dead, when relatives of the deceased brought candies and liquor and toys and flowers to the graves in November, not May. Ben's grave bore no decoration aside from the mottled pink and gray headstone.

BENJAMIN CURTIS WILLIAMSON
May 28, 1974 – February 25, 1996
Beloved Son and Brother
Nunca Olvidado

Nunca Olvidado. Never Forgotten. An empty ledge had room for a vase of flowers. How odd that his family had picked a pink headstone for Ben, she thought, but it made sense, after staring awhile. Smooth granite with bits of rock glitter. Dark flecks and pockmarks like one or both dimples, depending on the smile. The sun glinting off the stone like a wink.

Back in high school, a classmate Carey barely knew, Angelique Smith, had died junior year in a car accident. The newspaper ran pictures of the accident site and the grave, where Angelique's friends had left stuffed animals, necklaces and bracelets, and lip gloss tubes. How wasteful, Carey had thought. She hadn't understood before.

The living need to exhume the dead in memory. To bring sons and daughters and friends and lovers back to life with props. From her black shoulder bag, she removed a can of mango juice with its blue and orange Spanish-language label, which she'd purchased from the new market near Casa Colmo. Ben's juice supply on his dorm room dresser in Mexico, always stocked. She unrolled the poster. In the tacky gift shop, she'd looked for one of Jim Morrison. They were sold out but had several copies of The Doors, and she picked a shot of the lead singer standing front and center, bare-chested and wearing a necklace, his hands splayed before him. The other three band members' heads lined up alongside, much smaller than the singer. She'd brought Scotch tape, but now the idea of hanging a poster on a tombstone, a Doors poster in the middle of a quiet country cemetery, seemed absurd. She placed the cardboard tube on the ledge.

Next, the mix tape she made. Her father's computer had a CD burner she did not try to understand. She liked her antiquated technology, her rudimentary stereo cassette deck used to make this mix, her first. She'd tried to replicate the song list Ben had created in his journal that day on the roof, improvising the music she lacked. Her father's jazz discs, tracks from Ben's CDs as well as her older ones—Indigo Girls, 1980's era-Madonna, The Beatles. Mexican pop, including some Cristian Castro. Years ago that little soccer player, the only girl in a uniform jersey during a neighborhood pickup game, had compared Ben to the Mexican heartthrob. Not an artist Ben would've listened to, but someone Carey wished he could hear.

The gravel crunched as another car approached. She liked to believe her sixth sense told her it was Mike, but she could see a black car in the reflection of Ben's highly polished tombstone. She dropped the mix tape into her bag, hiding it.

They had not been children, the three of them, far from home in a college exchange program, treading the boards of an expensive stage for acting out new selves, but they had been children.

The car drove on. Mike had gone back to Wisconsin weeks ago; they'd since exchanged perfunctory e-mails about the nonexistent progress in Ben's case. The passport had turned up, the man using it fled. The man who might've been present when Ben was shot. The man who might've shot Ben. She could only circle the details for so long.

Her fingers unclenched, and she popped the tape she made for Ben into her own Walkman. Stretching out, the damp grass smelled sweet and pricked at her bare legs. The elastic waistband of her old shorts stretched outward, leaving marks in her skin. Her T-shirt was so old it had grown thin as a paper towel. This had become her uniform when she wasn't working.

She lay slightly to the left of Ben's grave. Not exactly on top. Pillowing her hands beneath her head, which rested at an odd angle on the tombstone's ledge. Perched there, the can of mango juice and the poster. "Penny Lane" piped into her ears. The saver and hoarder in her considered the waste of leaving such a good mix exposed to the elements. She could always make another. She could deliver a copy to Ben's parents, who might grow used to her, and appreciate stories they'd never heard. They might be comfortable enough to finally ask, *What took you so long?* And she might muster the courage to answer.

Stone made for a lousy pillow. Her neck kinked, so she lay flat on the grass. Ben's body was buried beneath her and to the left. There was no avoiding it. A coffin, human remains in a box, soil, worms. What happened to his eyeballs? His lips? She'd imagined and re-imagined what bullets and death had done to Ben's body. Now, lying in the cemetery, she focused on the pink stone. The smell of earth and grass, soybean, the faint hint of manure. Blue sky with flat-bottomed white clouds. She saw whatever she wanted to see. The time Ben stole the tequila shot at the disco, jealous of Luis. She could imagine it was night. Ben flat on his back next to her, tracing a VW Beetle as if it were a constellation. Or the other time on the rooftop, late afternoon, when he hovered over her and smiled. He'd said, God, I love . . . this. And she'd told him, I love this, too.

This. The green grass wiggling beneath her legs as if alive. Eyes closed against the sun, a regal, clanging tone in her ears. She could be anyone, anywhere. She just happened to be here, now. The movie in her mind jumped ahead accordingly. Somewhere on the other side of town, Juan and Elena, her co-workers at Casa Colmo, were preparing a care package for delivery to their parents in Dolores Hidalgo: a thick envelope of cash, Oreo cookies, Polaroids of the shiny new bar top Roberto was installing in their restaurant. Carey had made no promises. But the Morales siblings, ever optimistic, said in unison, "Just in case." Yesterday, the travel agent had offered Carey two days to decide; after that, he couldn't guarantee the fare. She thought of the picture Ben had taken surreptitiously while she ran along the streets of Guanajuato, a girl she barely recognized. She thought of the Alarcóns, her host family, and their walled-in house opened wide for her. And she thought, of course, of Ben. Unceasingly and without censor. Carey didn't need two days to decide. She was buying time, making room on her credit cards. Rearranging the debt.

Carey slept. She dreamt of a rickety bus, a driver named Cesár. She couldn't see his face. He drove along flat roads instead of hills and mountains, and the door remained closed. The bus was full of students. Nobody spoke, everyone faced forward in his or her seat. Ben and Mike sat silently in front of her, though they hadn't been on the bus from Mexico City to Guanajuato. She asked Cesár to show her the Sleeping Woman, the purplish black volcano, and he shook his head. He drove them down a road that bisected two farm fields: on the right, beans tied to tall poles, on the left, thousands of metallic pinwheels blowing in the breeze, a whole farm full of them.

When she woke, the cassette had ended. She returned the tape to its plastic case and set it on the tombstone ledge.

Back in the car, driving along the county extension, she felt empty and light. Her body an absence. She had gone to the cemetery to honor Ben. Mango juice, The Doors, and a mix, in lieu of a church service, funeral, and memorial. It had taken her too long to visit Ben's grieving parents, and then to find his grave. But she thought Ben would've appreciated her visit. That he was somewhere in the universe, "Penny Lane" jangling in his head, posing like the shirtless Jim Morrison while he ogled her bare legs—the thought made her laugh, though the contraction of her stomach muscles was more like a spasm. Ben, in the poses of a young man; Ben, who forever would be a young man. By the day, she grew too old for him. The gap would only widen, never close. She hunched over the wheel, tears clouding her vision, and soon she sobbed. The air in the car wrapped around her, close as a coffin. How she imagined a coffin's air to be. He could be sitting in her passenger seat. He could be alive if not for timing, if not for her mistakes and the mistakes he owned.

She pulled over in front of a dry cleaner's along the short main drag. Left the Mazda unlocked and the keys in the ignition. Couldn't you do that here? She believed you could. This time, she would carry nothing. She was unprepared. Her hair pulled back messily in a tortoiseshell clip rather than a rubber band, no sports bra, and sockless in running shoes. The same shoes the vendor had tried to buy from her at Mercado Hidalgo years ago, dusty with age. But her feet cared nothing of the blisters that would form. They wanted to run.

She had not run in years, but she had been running.

The Effect of Place on Love and Death

Gerri Leen

All you know is the slide of flesh over sheets and the joining of bodies as your lover murmurs his feelings to you. You came to Mexico to be together; it might as well be Cleveland. You wonder if you will ever leave the hotel room.

It is your first time together. He has wooed you; you have been caught. He has the money to fly you down for a weekend in Paradise, to this hotel that lies on the plaza, that has views of the hills surrounding the town. His favorite place, he told you as you boarded the plane. Does he expect it to be yours, too?

The smell of the flowers in the plaza drifts up into your room; your lover has left the window open, and it captures the scent of marigolds, of dripping wax candles, of sweets and breads being baked and sold. These scents mix with the smell of damp hair, of his cologne and your perfume, of sex and heat and touching.

You finally fall away from each other, chests heaving, sweat glistening, and in the plaza below, a hubbub of voices rises to your room. It is the Day of the Dead. One of them, anyway. You're still not sure which day is for what, or why they don't call it the Days of the Dead or the Time of the Dead.

"One day is for the young. One day for the adults. All death is specific," your lover told you on the plane when you asked. As if that explained anything.

"Is love specific?" you wanted to know, but he didn't answer, and by his look, you understood he did not see any reason for you to have asked.

You try not to think about how general you might be to him now that you're not trapped under him, not lying with your legs wrapped around him, giving him a pleasure specific to this room. The ceiling fan blows a cool breeze to sweat-streaked skin, and you know the words he would use to assuage your doubts: I love you; I adore you; I want you.

But for how long?

If love is specific, then your love will belong to skeletons and altars and portraits of the dead. If love is specific, then your love belongs to this place and it will be a lesser thing when you leave it.

"What are you thinking about?" His voice is throaty, raw.

"You," you say. "I'm thinking about you."

He appears to like that. Ego, it seems, does not need time or place; it just is. It endures. As long as you worship him, will he love you? Will he at least need you?

The smell of marigolds fills the room, pungent spice being dispersed by the gentle circles of the ceiling fan. You are not sure you will ever get the smell out of your head.

CB⬧♄)CB♄)

You have roused, showered, dried your hair and perfumed your body. You've made up your face. You look beautiful, both because he told you so and because you can see it in the faces of the men you pass. You thought you saw it in the mirror as you finished getting ready, but your own judgment is usually suspect.

Beauty is relative. Who will you be compared with? What lens will your lover wear as you walk? The gentle filter of love that makes all you do and say witty and enchanting? Or the more harsh reality that says you are not so clever, not so pretty. That you are not what he wants.

You live in fear that he will realize you are not what he wants. You will run before he can realize it: it is your way. You fear being left more than watching love die before it's ready.

"The altars are gorgeous," he says.

All you can see is the gaudiness of the things. Remembrance should be somber, should be respectful. A woman pours out two glasses of tequila; a man sets a brightly painted guitar on the altar. In your lexicon, the only bright thing death brings should be flowers—and not the raucous gold and orange of the marigolds. They should be white flowers. Lilies and roses and other things that glow at night, not in the day. That fill your head with their sweetness—a sweetness that does nothing to ease pain.

"This would be a good tradition to take with us," your lover murmurs, and it should fill your heart that there is an us and a future to fill with things like this incomprehensible festival. But you hear his words and filter them into,

"When we end, we should build an altar to our love."

"Which is your favorite?" he asks, and you point to one at random. It is bright and covered with things from the sea.

"Mine's that one," he says, and leads you to an altar that has a family of dolls on it, surrounded by the remnants of a full life—toys and clothes and books. An old man keeps watch over it all.

You feel a pang. You have told your lover you do not want children. And here is the evidence he wasn't listening.

"It's like my family. See. Two adults. Three boys. Just like Jim and Roger and I."

You swallow the panic and pain that wells up in you. It is all right. It is only his family. His family, not your family—a family you have said you do not want.

"What's wrong with you?" You imagine his tone is less forgiving.

Because this is what happens. You are good at luring; you are not so good at keeping. Interacting with intent is easy, but just being with someone, just enjoying the moment, eludes you.

"There's so much to see. Just so overwhelming." It is almost the right thing to say, so you continue. "I love it."

His beautiful, luminous smile breaks through and he pulls you closer.

There. You have appeased him. For now.

CB&⧉CB&⧉

"Fortune?" a woman asks. "Pay me what it's worth when it's over."

Your lover has gone to fetch drinks. This woman holds out her hand, and you place your palm in it. The fortunetellers are all the same—none of them see deeply enough inside you to get it right.

"You lost everyone you cared about when you were young." This is correct. One car trip, you were too young to go. "But you have never lost a lover."

You laugh. You have lost every one of them and will lose this latest, too. You try to pull your hand away; the woman holds on tightly.

"You chase them away before you can lose them."

You stop pulling. This is truth on all fronts. Can this woman be for real? "Is that bad?"

"Don't you know the answer to that?" The woman gestures toward the altars. "Yours would be empty. Colorless and sad."

"It's not sad to have never lost a lover." This is the mantra of your life; it must not fall in the face of this woman's attack.

"It is sad to have never loved anyone enough to feel their loss."

"I love. I do love." But you know the woman is right. Even your current lover, now that he is caught, is bumping up against the spikes and razors surrounding your heart. He will flee eventually. Glad to escape. And your altar will stay empty. You try again to yank your hand away. "I will not build an altar; I will not gather flowers. I have no one to honor, not anymore."

They all piled into the car and left you. They laughed and waved, and you were stuck with your sitter. They never came back. Their altar would be crushed metal and gravel.

"*The Día de los Muertos* is as much for us as for those who have passed over." The woman drops your hand. "If we make our peace with them, we give ourselves permission to go on."

"I go on." That is the one part you have no trouble doing. Going on is freedom. No one can catch you.

No one can hurt you.

"Perhaps you should tarry a while with your dead, your forgotten, your lost. It might make your sojourn with the living easier."

"And then again . . ." You fish out coins, have no idea if you are being generous or stingy, and the woman's expression as you drop them into her hand tells you nothing. "Thank you."

The woman moves on, and your lover appears. "Who was that?"

He perks up when you tell him; you did not know he was interested in such things. "Is she any good?"

You take the soda from him and drink heartily. "No. She isn't."

"Too bad." His look is wistful. "I'd like to know our future."

You can tell him all about that, but you won't.

CS EO CS EO

Shadows fall across the floor. From below, the sound of singing, humming, low talking fills your room.

"This is the night for children," your lover says as he stares out the window.

"I don't want any," you say, blurting out what has already been stated.

"I know. God, I know." He turns to look at you. "I wasn't criticizing. I was just saying that tonight is reserved for them."

"I'm sorry. I thought—"

"Why did you come here with me? Do you even love me?"

This is how it starts. They question your love. Then they question your worth. Then they leave. No man can be trusted with your heart. And you trust no man with your heart. They are, of course, slightly different things, but being aware of the difference is not the same thing as being willing to bridge the distance.

"Do you love me?" He moves closer, tries to pull you into his arms, but you resist. "Is there someone else?"

This question has been asked before. It always breaks your heart. For you are, if nothing else, faithful. You find it hard enough to love one person, much less two. "There isn't anyone else."

You change into your nightgown, crawl into bed, and turn off the light on your side of the room. When you made love, there was no space between you; now there will be a demarcation, the beginning of the schism.

"I'm going out for a bit." He grabs his jacket and hurries to the door.

You take a deep breath, then beat the thick down pillows into submission before closing your eyes and drifting off.

CB℘CB℘

The fortuneteller sits in the plaza when you wander out, unable to stay asleep. Your lover has not come back.

The woman rises, takes your arm as if you are old friends, and says, "Walk with me."

You resist. This woman is a stranger.

"Honey, please?"

The voice. The lilt of the word. For a moment, you are back in the past, on a porch, waving goodbye to a father and sisters and a mother who would never come back.

Over the years, it has been your mother you missed most, your mother you've had the most trouble pushing down into the murkiness of memory, rather than living in some higher level of pain.

You are afraid to look at the fortuneteller. Afraid to see, in this land of mystery, on this night that belongs to dead children, what might be standing next to you.

Or maybe you are just afraid of what might not be standing there. You want her to be your mother. Want magic to exist and love to transcend boundaries. To be able to push past the walls between life and death and come back to the little girl she abandoned.

Abandoned. Your breath catches at the thought. Your mother died, sitting on the passenger side, the one the other car plowed into. She wasn't driving; she had no choice. There was no abandonment.

But your heart says differently, and you feel the fortuneteller squeeze your arm.

"You're not ready," she says, and she kisses you on the forehead. "Go back to sleep."

You wake in your bed. It's morning and your lover is next to you. His hand is on your arm, lying gently, and you feel a pang deep inside. It is almost painful to feel this safe, even for a moment.

"Good morning," he says. "You were dreaming." His eyes are wary, his smile not a full one.

You slide over, into his arms, hugging him close, and hear him breathe out. In relief? Is he off balance now? Does he wonder why he brought you here?

"I dreamt of my mother." It is not precisely true, but he knows enough of you to understand.

And then you start to cry. You don't want to. You try to stop. But the tears come as if you've never cried in your life. You think he will pull away in the face of this bizarre storm of emotion. You think he should pull away.

He only holds on tighter. When you stop crying, he makes love to you, his eyes never leaving yours, stroking your hair, kissing softly and sweetly, and you cry again because it feels good, and because you wish you were worthy of his tenderness.

You will hurt him. It's what you do. One night and one morning will not change that.

CRITSIORSIES

He takes you away, rents a car and drives into the hills. You drive until you reach a new town, but you can't escape the dead. Altars fill the plaza; the cemetery is busy with women cleaning the graves.

He drives farther, his speed increasing, and you finally put your hand on his arm and say, "It's okay."

He sighs, a sound of defeat. He would have spared you this, you know that. "Take us back to town. There was a restaurant on the way, in that last village we passed. Let's eat there."

You eat outside, and the proprietor is gregarious, his two children peek out as if they've never seen gringos. A small dog plays on the edge of the terrace. The food is hot and spicy and the beer is cold, and you smile at the children and they laugh and duck for cover.

You see your lover staring at you. "What? I do like them."

"Then why don't you want them?"

"It's not fair to them. Life is uncertain."

"It is. But not all families die."

There it is. The bald-faced truth. Not all families die.

"Mine do." That's the other side of this harsh truth. Or at least your article of faith. If you have a family, it will be taken from you. Because it happened before.

He looks down. There is no argument to change your mind, and he is smart enough to realize this. "I love you," he says, as if it is a challenge to the gods.

"I know."

You can see by his expression that this is a shabby response. It's the best you can do.

૭જીૉૂ૭જ

It's you who stands at the curtains now. He sits in bed, reading.

"I'm going out," you say, and he looks at you but doesn't move to get up.

You wonder if he knows this is the end. This is the last moment between you where things might be saved. He is getting too far in, too fast, and to protect yourself, you will strike first.

He will be glad to say goodbye at the airport. He will not want to share a cab the way you did on the way in.

You practically flee the room. Against your will, you cry, and brush tears away as other tourists crowd the elevator. As the next bunch pushes in, you begin to feel claustrophobic, have to concentrate on your breathing to keep from screaming and pushing and kicking.

On the day after your family died, your sitter's mother turned you over to child protective services. The elevator ride up to their offices was long, and the woman let go of your hand as more people pushed onto the car. You remember the panic, the loneliness, the anger—how could they do this to you? How could they leave you?

The woman didn't take your hand again. "You'll have to be a big girl from now on," she said on the walk down the gray and yellow hall to the window where an unfriendly man sat reading.

You feel the need to scream now, for yourself, for that child who did what she was told. Who grew up far too fast.

"It's time now," a familiar voice says as you nearly run off the elevator and through the lobby.

The voice is in your head, and then it's at your side. The fortuneteller takes your hand and holds it tightly. "Come on."

You don't want to go, but you're caught up in the crowd. You're heading for the cemetery and you pull back: you never visit your own family, why visit anyone else's? But the fortuneteller's grip is like iron.

Then she squeezes your hand. "I will tell you a story. Once upon a time, there was a little girl with blonde curls. She laughed and smiled, and she was the pet of her family. They doted on her, her father who would come home and scoop her up. Her two older sisters who liked to dress her and arrange her hair as if she was their doll. And especially her mother. Her mother loved her so much."

"I don't want to hear this story."

"Well, this story wants to be told." The grip intensifies, and you're pulled into the cemetery, past the candles that light every nook and cranny. The graves are decorated, the white stone gleaming, the marigolds filling the air, and a new flower, a white one, adds its own particular scent.

You register that this is beautiful, perhaps the most beautiful thing you've ever seen. But there is too much panic and fear and age-old pain rushing up for you to enjoy the spectacle.

You're drawn into a dark corner of the cemetery, where no graves lie, only grass and trees. Then you see a lone candle burning, held up by a pile of rocks.

"This is for the forgotten ones," the fortuneteller says. "This is for those who have no grave to polish, no flowers to set out, no food to offer."

You sink to the ground, and in front of you the candle gives way to the porch light. You're sitting on the kitchen floor, staring out the screen door at the carport. Your family should be home by now. Where are they?

Your sitter is cranky with you. She's not the girl they usually use. She's older and meaner, and you hope your parents never call her again to come watch you.

The phone rings and the sitter goes quiet as she listens to whoever has called, and then she hangs up and calls someone else, and there are words that hang heavy and dark. "Accident. Everyone. Dead."

You get up and walk to the door, trying to unlock it, to run out to the carport and wait there. But your sitter grabs you and closes the door and puts you to bed with threats of bad reports to your parents if you're not good.

That is the cruelest thing of all. That she would invoke your parents when she knew they were dead. You've never forgiven that girl, would spit on her now if she were here.

Only, it's probably not her fault. She was just babysitting, just a kid herself. The deal was that the parents would come home and she'd be released. Not get stuck with the kid. Not have to take her home to her mom the next day so she could walk her down to the government offices.

"We never meant to leave," the fortuneteller says, and you are afraid to look at her.

"*They*. They never meant to leave." They because they is far away, and we is close, we is a choice, we is your family, and families go away.

"*We*." Her voice is firm and loving and full of sorrow.

You turn and look up at the woman standing next to you. As you grew older, your mother's image faded from your memory, so you kept photos of her close so you'd never forget.

But you did forget. For the fortuneteller's face has not changed. You just couldn't see it for what it was.

"In this place, at this time, the dead walk when the living call." Your mother's smile is luminous.

"I didn't call." But you have. You've been screaming for her in your heart since that night.

"I heard you. We all did. We've just never been in a position to meet." She pulls you into a hug, her arms strong and firm. She is dead; she is alive. She is not gone.

She will be gone, though. This is temporary.

You tear yourself away from her embrace. "You left me!" The words come out in a cry that resembles the howl of a jungle cat. You scramble away, scuttling along the ground as if there is escape on this night that you understand now is for the adult dead.

"Yes, I left you. I'm sorry for that."

"I had to go on without you." Without anyone. Still, now: alone. Alone with this specter who can walk among the living.

"He saw me. Your young man." Your mother smiles. "He's a good one. You should hold on to him." She kneels next to you, takes your hand. "I see a long, happy life. If you just let him in." She kisses you, her lips soft and filling you with warmth. Her hands trail along your face, as if memorizing it by touch.

And then she is gone, her body giving way to smoke that drifts across the space like the black mist from a fireworks display. Your lover steps through the smoke, his eyes meet yours as he takes in the candle, and you, sprawled across the grass, eyes starting to fill.

"Everyone I love leaves me," you say, and it is the deepest truth you own.

He sits beside you and doesn't try to tell you that you're wrong. His arms are strong, his breath warm and comforting, and he holds you and whispers things that have nothing to do with the past. The future, he sees a future for you.

"You don't want me. I'll run. It's what I do."

He opens his arms, letting you go. His eyes never leave yours as he says, "Run, then."

Part of you wants to. Your heart is beating fast and you can feel the call of freedom—of protection. Who will defend you now, if you love him? Who will keep you from losing him?

"Please don't run," he whispers, his voice cracks and his eyes are moist, and you are lost. You clutch him and hold him, and fear that if he doesn't run now, you'll never let him go.

But he is stronger than you are, he drags you to your feet and says, "Let's look at the altars."

You walk together because there is no other way to walk, not with him holding you so tightly or you hanging onto him as if he is the bridge that will see you through life. As you pass altars, as you nod to families celebrating their dead, you gradually loosen your grip on him, and he lets go of you.

Finally you are holding lightly, hands clasped, and every so often he pulls you in so your shoulders bump up against each other. Your panic fades, and it's replaced by something you're not sure how to identify.

You finally decide it might be peace.

"I lied." You smile up at him, a strange expression for the declaration you've just made.

"Yes?" He does not seem worried, either at the dichotomy or the fact you lied. "What about?"

"That fortuneteller? She was very good."

You walk on, the scent of marigolds burning itself into your brain. You hope you'll never lose it.

Gifts in the Dark

Vonnie Winslow Crist

It was almost time to walk to the graves. The sun had vanished behind the Nodin Sea, the streetlamps were being lit throughout the city of Halona, and the pair of owls that haunted Old Kuraks's Medicines & Cure-Alls were calling for the dead.

"The dead," sighed Mari. This year, in addition to her parents, grandparents, great-grandparents, and other long-ago ancestors, she needed to remember Old Kurak, her Beloved, and his granddaughter, Little Nina.

Mari heard the clink of jar hitting jar as her sister loaded the food into the two picnic baskets they would carry to the graveyard. She quickly finished the last four scarlet feather stitches on the small tablecloth she was embroidering, tied a knot, and bit the unused tail of embroidery floss off close to the fabric with her teeth.

"Ready, Jacy," she said to the small white cat watching her sew.

The cat chirped in response. He hopped down from his perch on the stone bench beside her and strolled to the doorway. Jacy paused, turned his mismatched eyes in her direction, and chirped again.

"I know, you miss her." Mari reached down, scratched the cat behind his left ear. "So do I." She stood up, folded the tablecloth, and carried it into the kitchen.

She admired the two picnic baskets waiting by the door. They were painted with pink, teal, and violet birds and black and white skulls. In addition, they were festooned with bright ribbons and tiny bells. She smiled, then tucked the completed tablecloth into the side of the nearest basket. Jacy padded behind her, chattering in cat-speak.

"He knows *Noche de los Muertos* is when we'll remember his mistress," commented Mari's sister, Grace, as she slipped a beautifully carved comb embellished with small ovals of polished turquoise into her gray hair.

"And dear Old Kurak." Mari bit her lip, brushed her deeply wrinkled cheek with the back of her hand. She was glad Grace didn't respond right away. It gave her a moment to compose herself as they both slipped on thick woolen sweaters embroidered with geometric patterns, butterflies, and crows.

She glanced back at the kitchen table. The five pale blue candles burning brightly in her grandmother's candelabra illuminated several platters heaped high with steaming vegetables, fresh fruit, and corn bread. Her great-grandmother's hand-thrown pottery bowl, nearly overflowing with red beans and rice, had been placed at the head of the table. A pitcher of tea and nine glasses sat beside it, and a stack of plates and eating utensils had been placed at the opposite end of the table. Should the dead decide to stop here for dinner, they would be well-fed.

"Mari, it's time."

She nodded at her sister and, using a splinter of wood, lit the pair of white tapers nestled in carved wooded candlesticks on either side of the front door.

"For Grace, First-born," she said, and handed one of the carved candlesticks to Grace.

"For Mariposa, Second-born," her sister said as she picked up the remaining candlestick and handed it to Mari.

"We leave our warm home to bring you warmth," chanted Mari as she swung open the door.

"We carry candles into the darkness to bring you light," her older sister added in a sing-song voice.

The street was filled with men, women, and children. Some were traveling to the cemeteries with offerings. Some were walking to the beach to remember those who were missing at sea. Some were hurrying to parties and parades. Some were headed to the vendors to purchase skull masks, skeleton dolls and puppets, paper flowers, bundles of herbs, candles, fruit juice, and sweets. There was more commotion on *Noche de los Muertos* than on the busiest market day.

"Why wouldn't you accept his offer of marriage?" asked Grace as the two women picked up the baskets with their left hands while still holding the candles with their right, and stepped into the crowded street. "He asked you again and again."

"I wanted to wait 'til Little Nina was grown."

Mari did her best to ignore her tears. In order to wipe them away, she'd have to set down the basket. Instead, she made a kiss-kiss sound at Jacy, who mewed in response, and then, walked beside her right ankle. The cat walked close, but not too close. He'd been used to the long strides and dancing steps of a fifteen-year-old, but with Nina gone, he'd adjusted to the smaller strides and slower pace of a woman in her sixties.

"Nina would've been fine," observed Grace as they were jostled by the parade of celebrants heading up Nokomis Way towards the burial hill. "I think she'd have welcomed a grandmother."

Mari didn't answer her sister right away. She needed to pay extra attention to where she stepped, and she knew Gace should be careful, too. The cobblestones beneath their feet were littered with odd bits of food that had spilled from picnic baskets, flower petals, and scraps of colored paper. Dozens of dogs, some with ribbons tied around their necks, scampered here and there gulping down the dropped food. A gang of laughing boys with faces painted like skulls ran by them carrying skeleton puppets.

"With her parents gone, I didn't want Nina to think I was taking away her grandfather's love," explained Mari as the sisters neared the food vendors who'd set up tables and carts near the entrance to Halona First Settlers Graveyard.

"Nina wouldn't have minded. I think she'd have been happy to have you live with them. She was over Paco's house to visit with you often enough with that cat . . ."

"Mmm, look at the coffin bread," said Mari. She knew the delicacies heaped on the makeshift booths, tables, and vendors' carts by the local bakeries and confectioners' shops should distract Grace. Her sister was famous in their family for having a terrible sweet tooth and little willpower.

"Ah, *pan de muerto*. Do you think we should pick up a loaf or two before we visit the graves?" Grace ran the tip of her tongue across her bottom lip. "Or perhaps a few skull cakes or candied bones?"

Mari laughed and shook her head. After living together for decades, she could read her sister like pebbles tossed on a foretelling mat.

"I think we should wait until we finish at the graveyard."

Grace sighed. "I guess you're right. We'll be carrying less when we walk back down the road towards the sea."

Mari nodded in response. She didn't want to think about the final part of tonight's ritual—didn't want to think about standing on the beach sending the soul candles out to meet the Dark Lady.

They paused at the graveyard's gate, lifted high their candlesticks. The throng of celebrants around them did the same as they entered the graveyard. They joined the people of Halona as they sang the traditional Summoning Song.

Dear ones, beloved ones, we are now here
with honey jars, bread loaves, sea salt and beer.
Dear ones, cherished ones, you are not alone—
bright blossoms and sweet herbs welcome you home.
Candles are borne to your dwelling places
as we pray to again see your faces.
Dear ones, treasured ones, come to us tonight—
return to your children, return to light.

Mari and her sister sang the Summoning again and again. As they climbed to the highest reaches of the graveyard where their family's plots awaited tending, the singing of the other celebrants grew softer.

"Finally," exclaimed Grace as she set her basket down on a tidy grave. "It doesn't seem to be an honor to be one of the first families to settle in Halona when you have to drag a heavy basket up to the top of the burial grounds."

Mari tilted her head. A few gray hairs escaped their braids and fell around her face. "There's no use in complaining. Let's begin decorating the graves, and I'll tell the story of the Great Migration."

Her sister grunted her agreement and began to empty her basket.

"In the Olden Times, on Terra, the First Mother, there were many tribes and many nations. But humankind mistreated the First Mother, and she became sick. There was no cure for her illness, and so she grew weaker and weaker, until she no longer had the strength to take care of the men and women who were her children."

Mari paused while she spread the embroidered tablecloth she'd finished today on their parents' grave and traced a sacred symbol in the air with her forefinger.

"Sweets from the little messengers of the gods," repeated Grace as she dribbled honey on each of the graves of their loved ones.

"Even the Mother sheds tears for the dead," chanted Mari again and again. She followed behind her sister sprinkling salt on each grave. Then, she resumed telling the ancestors' tale: "It was decided that a Great Migration would be embarked upon. All the tribes of Our People combined their languages, their power, their wealth—so when the Seed Ships were cast upon the Ocean of Stars, Our People had a place on each ship."

She set the salt jar back in the basket, picked up a loaf of fresh-baked bread, and began to tear it into small pieces. The white cat at her feet stared up at her with his one green eye and one yellow eye. He seemed to be awaiting the rest of the story.

She spoke again. "The Seed Ships sailed for almost forever in the Ocean of Stars and Our People and all the other tribes of humankind slept the sleep of the dead. When they'd just about given up hope, the Seed Ships reached the Shores of Forever. There, each ship found its island. Our Seed Ship found Earth Settlement Five—a new and unspoiled Mother. This new Mother, known to Our People as Anna Tuwa, welcomed her adopted children as if they were her own."

"And soon they were her own," added Grace. She poured beer on each grave and said in a sing-song voice, "Quench your thirst, Old Ones."

"Yes," agreed Mari. She stood, walked from grave to grave tossing breadcrumbs. "A bit of bread, a taste of life. Assuage your hunger, Old Ones," she sang in a melodious alto voice. Jacy followed her purring loudly.

After she'd finished throwing crumbs upon the graves, Mari continued the ancestors' story. "But Our People did not come alone. We brought many animals with us, stored in glass bottles. When Seed Ship Five reached Anna Tuwa, the voyagers planted the animal seeds and grew the cattle, sheep, horses, chickens, dogs, and . . ." She smiled at Jacy, then continued, "and the cats of the First Mother."

The sisters knelt at the foot of their oldest relatives' graves, placed a votive on each plot, and sprinkled marigold petals around the candle. It made sense to Mari that the pungent-smelling petals of the *flowers of the dead* were bright, sun colors. Wasn't daylight something the dead would miss?

As she lit the candles, Mari again spoke. "We also brought seeds for the totem animals of Our People. We brought the Wolf to remind us to persevere, we brought the Squirrel to make us laugh, we brought the wise Whale, the gentle Deer, the powerful Bear. . ." She stopped for a moment, thought of Old Kurak whose totem had been the bear.

"Go on," urged her sister as they moved to the next set of graves.

"And Turtle, who reminds us of creation and eternal life. And so, Our People settled with the other nations of humankind on our new home where we honor our new mother, Anna Tuwa, but we also honor our ancient traditions."

In silence, they decorated each remaining family grave with marigolds and votives. Finally, they placed a bundle of sage, rosemary, and other sacred herbs beside each candle. Then, both women knelt, lifted their arms to the moon, and chanted the Summoning Song again.

"Dear ones, beloved ones . . ."

When they finished the chant, the sisters stood and prepared to depart. Jacy wound around Mari's ankles mewing. She suspected he wanted her to pick him up. But with the basket in her left hand and the candle in her right, she still had her hands too full to carry a cat.

Though there was no breeze to speak of, suddenly, her candle's flame flickered and almost went out. Grace elbowed her, pointed with a shaky hand at two shadows passing back and forth across their parents' graves.

"They've come back to us," her sister whispered. "Perhaps it's our time to go with them when they return to the Land of the Dead at dawn."

"Look." Mari nodded in the direction of the metal fence that surrounded their family's plot on three sides. The pair of owls who perched over Nina's old bedroom every night had swooped down and alighted on the fence. One of the birds clutched a dead snake in its talons. The owls tilted their heads, the one with the snake dropped its scaly body onto a grave. Then, the pair lifted up and, with a silent flap of wings, flew into the night sky.

"What do you think it means?" There was no mistaking the fearful quaver of Grace's voice.

Mari shrugged her shoulders. "The Snake is a symbol of transformation, of change, of rebirth. Perhaps they were sent to us by the Old Ones to comfort us."

"I don't feel very comforted," muttered her sister as they headed down the hill to the cemetery's entrance.

By the time they exited Halona First Settler's Graveyard, Grace seemed to have forgotten the owls. Instead, she was focused on buying skull cakes, candy bones, and coffin breads. But Mari couldn't erase the look in the eyes of the night birds from her mind. The owls had seemed to be trying to tell her something. But what?

"Are you sure you don't want a bite?" asked her sister as she licked sugar granules from her fingers. "I believe theses skull cakes are the sweetest ones I've ever tasted."

"No. We need to head to the beach before it gets any later."

"I suppose you're right." Her sister gave the skull cakes another longing look and then joined Mari and Jacy as they began the journey to the edge of the Nodin Sea.

Young women dressed in vivid blouses and ruffled skirts scurried by them. Groups of young men tooting on horns, strumming guitars, and banging on small drums marched up and down the roadway. Children ran by trying to get black kites edged with golden stars to lift up in the night sky. Clusters of old women gossiped on the street corners. Mari and Grace waved to many of them.

"The Night of the Dead is one of my favorite holidays."

Mari glanced at her sister. Her eyes sparkled, her forehead glistened with beads of perspiration, and there were cake crumbs clinging to her top lip. *Noche de los Muertos* did seem to agree with her.

"I smell the sea," said Grace as she took several deep breaths.

Mari's throat tightened. Her sister was right. They were almost at the end of Nokomis Way where the cobblestones gave way to pebbles and the pebbles merged with the sand. Before them she saw the hissing froth of the waves racing across the beach and the towering flames of the Lighting Fire.

There were dozens of people milling about the water's edge. Some held torches, others candlesticks. Most had already sent their soul candles out to the Dark Lady. A few were still placing paper boats on the sand, setting a small lit candle in the boat, and letting the waves carry the fragile vessels out into the great darkness of the night sea.

The chant said on the shore was less hopeful than the Summoning Song. The souls of those lost in the waters of the Nodin or the waters of some distant ocean that most of the people of Halona had never heard of were given into the care of the Dark Lady. Tonight, Mari and her sister would send two boats out into the Nodin—one for Old Kurak and one for Nina.

Mari sighed, set her basket on the sand. When Grace's son-in-law, Paco, and the other nestgatherers had returned from the ill-fated nestgathering expedition this spring, the news quickly spread that Old Kurak and Little Nina had died in the collapse of an island cave. Their bodies would never be recovered, never carried with honor to the graveyard of their ancestors. And so, this sacred night, Mari and her sister would remember two people who were dear to them and give their souls over to the Dark Lady.

Mari and Grace each unpacked a paper boat from their baskets. They each lit a tiny candle and set it in the vessels.

"There, there," said Mari to the cat who cried at her feet.

Jacy continued to wail. He batted at one of the paper boats and tried to upset its candle.

"Hush, little cat," crooned Mari. She picked up Jacy, cradled him in her arms as the waves drew closer to the paper boats.

Grace touched her arm. "It is time."

Mari closed her eyes for a moment, recalled Old Kurak's loving face and gentle touch. Then, she thought of Nina's ready smile and quick mind. She opened her eyes, began the Chant of the Lost:

> *Dear ones, beloved ones, where are your bones?*
> *Beneath the cold waves? Across the deep sea?*
> *Dear ones, cherished ones, you're far from home*
> *and so we give you to the Dark Lady.*
> *She will gather your souls and dry your tears.*
> *She will sing you to sleep and hold you near.*

*Dear ones, treasured ones, you're gone forever
and your sweet faces we'll see again never.*

"Old Kurak. Little Nina," said Grace.

"Beloved Kurak. Dearest Nina," whispered Mari.

Together, they repeated the Chant of the Lost as the waves carried their little candle-lit boats out into the darkness. Jacy meowed loudly, squirmed in Mari's arms. She set him upon the sand where he paced back and forth yowling.

Grace put her arm around Mari's waist. "It will get easier as time passes. We still have each other, Paco's family, our sewing, and the cat."

"But is it enough?" Mari could barely make out the light from one of the little boats, but the other seemed to be returning to the shore.

As the paper boat drew closer to the beach, a murmur passed through the crowd. Such a thing was unheard of. For the Dark Lady to send back a soul candle meant that the person remembered was not dead. There was a flash of lightning and a strange phosphorescence shimmered on the surface of the sea. A shining woman rose from the midst of the phosphorescence. She appeared to point at the sisters.

Mari squinted. She could make out two large birds perched on the shining woman's shoulders.

Several village women screamed as the birds took off, soared into the air, and skimmed across the waves towards shore. One of the birds, which Mari could now identify as owls, plucked the soul candle from the boat. It screeched, then flew to Mari, Grace, and Jacy.

The stunned crowd backed away from the sisters and the white cat as the two owls landed and placed the still-burning soul candle in front of Mari. The owl who had not transported the candle dropped a necklace of polished obsidian chips in front of Jacy.

"That necklace belonged to Nina," gasped Grace.

"Belongs," corrected Mari as the owls gazed up at her with their magical eyes. "That necklace belongs to Nina."

The crowd began to chant. At first their chanting was barely audible, but it steadily grew till the night seemed to be filled with the shouts of the living calling home Nina from the Land of the Dead. The owls circled three times above the throng of *Noche de los Muertos* celebrants before returning to their shimmering mistress.

And as the moon-pale cat picked up the necklace with his pearly teeth, the Dark Lady, Queen of the Dead and Comforter of the Dying, sunk into the cold, rippling waters of the sea.

The Dance

Iris Macor

Every motion, fluid, purposeful. A step, a slide, arm pumps briefcase to the rhythm of the heart. Not his heart. *The* heart. Quick, short steps. Shining shoes. Bass pounding three streets away, over in the auto district. Imagination soars to where hundreds of tiny flags flicker in the breeze, alternating reds and yellows, and on the sidewalk a man dances with a sign. An arrow. Come in here and buy, spend, buy, spend, bow to the rhythm of life. It comes in patent leather with a crackle finish. Like snakeskin, only fake. Cop strobe lights fly down the street, shrieking to the beat. A man on foot dances faster.

Not his dance. His dance is boring. Dance, receive, repent, and rot. Rinse, repeat. The man in the suit with the briefcase and the dimpled polite morning grin, him. He may not look it, but he's about to make the baked bones sing. He dances to the office, another day another dollar, and the beat rolls on. Mustard stain on his shirt from yesterday's pretzel. Tries to hide it with his tie. Systematic, doing the robo-boogey.

The girl at the desk smiles when he slides through the door. He tips his imaginary hat, shaggy hair in his eyes. He does not know her name even though she has been at the door for four years. The boss waits for him in his office of oak panels and close-booked wisdom useless along the walls.

An invasion.

"Go." The boss-man says in the long and short of it.

Eugene goes. His steps slow. He watches the pavement, does not step on a crack. Lost in a sea of humanity.

When Eugene stops, the dance halts. Hearts still beat, blood pumps, but everything else slows. Light takes forever to flicker 'walk' and he damns *don't*. A horn blares. It wakes them because it is out of tune. A groggy city pushes forward and Eugene's eyes meet those of his partner. Another step. He spins.

She's busy, bushel of books in her arms. Each step destination driven. She glances at her watch, he watches. She bustles in his direction, moves to skirt around him. He takes her shoulders, spins her, smiles. She giggles nervously.

"Beg pardon," she says, though it ought to have been his line. He does not want her pardon; he wants her number, her name, to dance. Mostly, to dance. Papers fly free from the back of a book in her arms. She jerks the watch up to her face, squints, sighs. Already he is fetching them. Diving between cars, swooping down to return with sheets of yellow legal paper.

"I'm going to be late for my flight," she yells over the sound of horns and air brakes. The airport is one block over. He lifts the books from her arms, the duffel bag from over her shoulder. Her hair shines, her eyes too. He takes her hand. They dance. They run to the end of the street and turn the corner, giddy like drunks. The airport looms like the end.

"I just might make it!" She looks at her watch, huffs to catch her breath. Her cheeks red from the effort. Roses.

"Where are you headed?" he asks. Already a plan. All around them good-byes.

"South America, actually, Patagonian Desert."

"Really? So am I! Haven't bought my ticket yet, though."

"Well, we can stand in line together then. I have to check my bag," she lifts the duffel bag from his shoulder. "Could get on board with it, you know, but I've forgotten it twice in the overhead compartment. It's easier this way." They join the flow of the crowd, the dance of the weary traveler. "You mind?" she asks. He shakes his head and she steps in front of him. "So, are you also going for the convention at the end of the week?"

His eyes blank. "Convention?"

"The nomads? I'm going to present a paper there." She beams, then blushes. "Once I finish it, I mean, which won't happen until it's started." She shrugs. The line shuffles forward and he prays he has enough to cover a ticket because he is done with the means of more.

Worth it.

"Are you a grad student?" she asks.

"Yes." No.

"I thought so; you have the look, the brown suit is a dead give-away." The line moves forward. A baby screeches behind them and a mother groans. Everything gray and dull, except her face.

"What's your name?"

"Deidre." She extends a hand.

"Eugene." He holds her hand a moment longer than necessary. A man clears his throat behind them. They shuffle two steps forward. "Think they'd have any seats left on your flight? I mean, since I'm going to the same place and all?" Here the steps are awkward and unsure.

"Goodness, I would imagine so, not a lot of people going out to the desert, although, for the last leg of it I'm booked in a private plane. A dinky field hopper. But, if you want, I can call after we board, you know, see if there's a seat?"

"That'd be great."

They talk—barely notice their wait while the line moves between the ropes. He buys a ticket at the counter. The clerk frowns as though to say, *why would you want to go there?* He has no baggage. He feigns surprise, his suitcase forgotten in the cab, he explains. He does not mention what is in the briefcase in his hand. Just evidence of lies. Nothing useful.

They do the language dance the whole flight. Break to change planes. Resume. They barely notice the passage of time, the roar of engines. She speaks reverently about the people of the desert. She is staying with them a week to write her paper before the presentation. He listens. He doesn't notice the tiny world pass below them. The wings outside the window rustling restlessly against the wind.

Eugene the grad student is staying with the nomads as well, research for his dissertation. A word he has heard somewhere before, but has only a vague sense of its meaning. Eugene the daytime divorce attorney/nighttime hit man is back on the ground. Dead for all it matters. All that is left of *that* Eugene is his briefcase, liquid in white plastic bottles—natural, untraceable—and syringes that aren't sterile because it doesn't matter.

Eventually they fall asleep. By then he is certain he is in love, but has been mostly sure since he saw her. She falls asleep first; she snores soft like down.

There is another seat on the plane, the little crop-duster. It smells like chemicals. He takes shallow breaths and there is no speaking over the sound of the motor, the propellers fill his ears with wind and keep his hair pushed over his goggles so he can hardly see a thing. They land. When the plane sputters out of sight, it is time for the truth. Some of it.

"I'm not a grad student," he says.

"I know," Deidre replies.

"How?"

"Until I publish my paper at the convention, I'm almost the only one who knows they are there and why. I've been here once before. The fellow flying the plane was my guide when I came the first time."

"Then, why?" He quirks his eyebrow. The briefcase of lies feels heavy in his hands.

"Why are they here? To choose a new chief."

"No, why this?" He gestures to the unbroken night.

"It gets lonely, being the only one. Besides, I like the way you move."

He smirks. Feels pride in his broad shoulders, smooth walk. The dance.

"You'll have to follow me." She leads him through the desert night. Only her and emptiness. Heaven.

A glow of a campfire. Dark-skinned shadows lurk around it, whites of their eyes like shimmering pearls pushed into their faces by tarred thumbs. They are thin, half-nude. They smile and he cannot tell their intentions. But he is suddenly ready for a different sort of dance. He smells roasting meat. Deidre takes his arm. A low beat shivers the sand beneath their feet. Silhouettes of stunted heathen trees, arms thrust to sky.

They pause outside the circle of firelight, a moment in the embrace of darkness. Eyes watch. There is no hiding here. And that's okay. He pauses, pulls her back to him, just beyond the crush of sound from around the fire.

"You don't know me," he says, feeling suddenly earnest there in the barren land. "You might have made a very grave mistake in bringing me here." The music from the fire falls silent as though cued. The break between the end of one song and the beginning of another. In the silence she laughs. It is a song in itself.

"You may find things precisely to the contrary," she says. She points to the orange glow and dons a smoothly curved smile. He looks. The music begins again. Only now, he sees the bones. Skulls mounted on a rack of sorts, one next to the other. Tanned skin stretched between a frame of leg and arm bones. Finger bones strung together on rough rope tied to sticks like rattles. All of it arrayed around the flame. His breath catches. The music rises. He wonders if he will ever leave here. Realizes he has no way to get home, and nothing waiting for him if he did. He returns the woman's grin. He drops the briefcase in the dust, glad to be free of its weight. He extends his hand and asks her to dance.

Into the circle light, their feet move like madness. Hands reach out and brush their skin. They dance. Men, women, and sleepy children join them. The drum pumps—a heartbeat, no, *the* heartbeat. Voices rise together, a dream of alignment, of oneness. When the music stops, he is one of them. They fall down exhausted and laughing. The slender people so full of grace share their joy. No words are needed for communication. The strangers offer water and meat. Together they eat.

Deidre and Eugene share a hut. They sleep on a bed of sand, covered with the soft skin of something. No grains sift through in the night. When they rise, they have dried berries for breakfast and listen to a little girl sing. Time moves faster at the heart of things.

Deidre explains. "Their elder died nearly a year ago. They have the death ceremony the same time every year; to honor those they have sacrificed as well as important figures in their tribe. The replacement will be chosen and the next sacrifice made."

"Who gets sacrificed?" Nothing but idle curiosity. In a way, sacrifice had been half his line of work, before he was a grad student.

"Whoever the new elder chooses, I suppose. We'll find out tomorrow."

Until then, they dance. The bones sit untouched around the fire pit. Two boys stand apart from the rest of them. Children with smooth ponytails and big, dark eyes. They would be the ones, Eugene figures. Just when darkness gives over to day, or day to dark, the two boys dance when all the others have fallen still. They dance as though they were the same person, mirror images.

At night, everyone dances. In spite of the unforgiving ground beneath bare feet. Because of it, maybe. The eldest man sings low, the voice of the earth. A woman sings high, the grating of sand against sand. The man has white hair, the woman none at all.

Deidre watches. After the dancing, when they retire to their hut, she questions Eugene about the things he saw that she might have missed. She takes frantic notes, rubs her temples, tosses and turns restlessly when she tries to sleep. He seduces her and together they dance anew, slow and sweet to calm her nerves. The hut smells like pleasure and chilled sweat. In the morning, they step out. The breeze smells like sulphur.

The people sit cross-legged on the ground, watching the two boys disappear into the desert. All day there is no music, the heart of the world has fallen still. They wait in silence until night.

When the full moon rises, the boys reappear. Their arms are full of bones. All clean, parched white. They sing soft. Girlish voices, lithe bodies. They skip, smile, and spin. They add the bones to the display around the fire, while the people sit in silence and watch. No meat this night.

Eugene sleeps, having grown drowsy at some point while the boys sang on and on. Deidre joins him. When they wake, the boys are still singing. The sun creeps over the horizon and the people sit. There they stay, entranced, until the sun is directly overhead. Then they leap up, voices raised strong to the heavens, growing, growing, as though joined by angels or silver-tongued demons. Then they set to work.

What sort of work it is, hard to say. They saw at bones, bind them together, arrange them around the pit. Deidre leans close.

"Instruments to raise the voices of their ancestors, the songs of the dead," she whispers. Windswept dust stings their eyes but the natives carry on without pause. The whole time they sing and never falter. Not until the sun goes down. The twin boys sit together on the beach. The eldest man stokes the fire. Deidre scribbles. Licks of flame whip, tongue lashing into the night. Eugene forgets the briefcase and feels the music in his blood, the call of the dance in his veins. The music stops.

The eldest makes his way around camp. He needs no words. He speaks with his eyes, foggy brown, the ocean churned in a storm. He takes Deidre's hand, small and white against weathered skin. He puts a flute made of bone in it. Petite bone. A child, maybe, or a woman. He guides her back to her seat on the right side of the fire. The flames have picked up the rhythm. He looks to Eugene. Measures him with his eyes and half conceals a smile. He hands Eugene a long leg bone and guides him to a massive rack of ribs arrayed by length. A question in Eugene's eyes, an answer in his. Soon. The desert is quiet as death. Not so much as the sharp intake of breath. It is the people's turn to watch the newcomers. Teeth shine in firelight.

Time passes. Everyone takes their places according to the eldest's desires. Each armed with an instrument of life and death. He feels no difference between the natives and himself. Except his clothes. His suit is dirty. Tomorrow he will get rid of it.

The two matching boys stand. They sing. The sound and its meaning pump through Eugene's ears, into his mind, his heart. So high pitched that it makes him shiver, delight and fear. The boys bow to each other. They never pause in the song. They part. One stands and sings twice as strong as before. The other glides into the fire and burns with the song on his lips. The smoke is thick and black, and with it the dead return.

By instinct, Eugene begins to play. To make the bones sing. The song clatters and grinds at first until the life returns to the wind-bleached bones. Then the song changes, when it is no longer the bones played by men and women, but singing of their own volition. The howl of wind across desert plains, the whisper of swishing sand, the crackle of flame, the words of the burning boy. All is one. All is none.

A black haze settles over the camp. Faces drift in and out of existence. He recognizes some of them. The voices of the dead drown out those of the living. The fire glows blue, red at the tips, the boy all but gone. Forms rise from the smoke and take their places at the instruments. The real dance begins. Eugene finds his partner.

Their hands come together. Foreheads touch, an exchange of wordless thought. Turn, slide, shimmy to the ground and rise proud and strong into the cloud of the dead, while the bones sing, the drums thrum deep like pleasured groans. Spin, bow. All the same dance, all known by instinct. Kick, sidle. Stomp once, twice, three times all told. Raise hands to the sky then fall to the knees. Rise. Sing and dance of life and death. Bring the dead back to send them to rest. Turn, spin, weep, laugh, sing, sing, sing.

Does the night last only a few hours? Or days? Eugene turns away from faces he knows, not for shame or regret, but respect. No smoke lingers near his partner, as though it is drawn to him rather than her. As it should be. Those faces belong to those he's killed. Their souls are his, as his is theirs. He understands.

After the dance has worn them to exhaustion, the music slows. The fire burns down to embers. The smoke thickens. They kneel in a circle around the glowing coals. The remaining boy scoops a handful of ash and ember from the pit and breathes it in without flinching. Then he begins to sing again. Eugene understands him perfectly. Deidre does not. He sings the dead home, into the hearts of their kin and their killers. Spent, the boy collapses. Smoke rushes into Eugene's mouth. Perfume sweet. It forces his head back. He sees most other men in the circle experiencing the same. Some of the women, too, but not all. Not Deidre. On and on. He thinks he might choke. The smoke thins as it finds its mark. Finally, only a few wisps remain around the eldest's head, then those are gone and Eugene alone is still shrouded in it.

The eldest stands. Plucks a spear from the ground with a skull skewered on its tip, decked in feathers and braids from the heads of virgins. The smoke has given Eugene the ability to know. Eugene the hit man, not Eugene the grad student. The grad student is dead and gone. A man is the sum of his deeds, and Eugene knows that now. When the smoke clears, the eldest stabs Eugene's shoulder with the spear, painting its tip. It does not hurt and bleeds little. Then the eldest hands it off to him. Eugene accepts. He is oldest now, all the years of his victims have come to rest upon his shoulders. All their experience, their wisdom. He is the sum of their years. He is dead. He is living. He is The Elder. The singing of the bones rises to fever pitch.

He raises the spear and they dance. Frantic and disorganized. No longer do they share the dance, but each moves to the song in his heart. They continue without break until the morning comes. One by one, they drop off to sleep where they fall. When they wake, Eugene will lead them on. He belongs here and his partner with him. She slips into the hut to write all that she has seen. She drifts to sleep, pen in hand, drooling on her notebook. He picks her up. She weighs nothing. Sets her on the rough bed. Touches her face, her smooth forehead. It would be one hell of a paper if she only knew. Innocent thing. He dreams the dream of a hundred men.

He rises first, while the rest of the people, *his* people, sleep on the ground. The fire is cold. The ceremony one step from over. After they break their fast, they must move on. He sends the boy to scavenge for food. As The

Elder, he knows it is tradition. While the boy is gone they set fire to the makeshift huts and watch them blaze.

The boy leaves with just a hatchet and pail, but when he returns the pail is full of wild herbs and the boy carries a dead fox, skinned—a meal that only needs heat.

They eat. Then they drink. They pass a wooden cup crusted with dirt. Filled with the water of life and death, each taking a sip until it is gone. Those who have yet to make a kill abstain from the meal. Instead, they break camp while the others partake. They dig with their hands in the hard dirt until they have a hole deep enough to swallow all the bones. For when they return next year.

Eugene feels a little sick. Before they move on, he stumbles away from camp, another part of the dance, bitter and distasteful. He looks for a place to take a piss. All traces of their footsteps washed away, all record of their arrival forgotten already, erased by the wind. Still, he finds where they came in without any trouble. Relieves himself in a bit of scrub brush. Sees a shape in the distance, once brown and slick. He runs drunkenly, falls twice. The dance is all gone from him. He kneels before what is left of the briefcase, split by a curious boy's hatchet. Fingers the empty bottles, the shining needles. Papers that document a previous life drift through the air; one catches in a sudden breeze, then flies away.

The boy, having no kills, had not eaten a bite. Next year he will have many. Next year he will lead what remains of his people when they return to make the bones sing again.

Aztec Catrina

Linda L. Donahue

José Guadalupe Posada etched on the zinc plate with acid-resistant ink, drawing every line of his newest catrina with loving detail. The image honored *Mictecacihuatl*, the Aztec goddess of Death. With her etched catrina portrait and verse, Jose invited her to Earth for *Día de los Muertos*. He dipped the finished plate in an acid solution, embedding the illustration.

This catrina was special, the skeletal image wore a feathered headdress and thick collar encrusted with rough-cut stones, and she seemed to leap higher off each printed page, her bony arms reaching as if to embrace José. Sweat dripped down his neck. The back of the printing shop was always hot. Today it seemed unseasonably so.

The growing stack of *hojas volantes*, flying leaves or one-page broadsheets, seemed to sway, as if eager to be sold on street corners. When the shop door opened, their edges ruffled, threatening to scatter across the scuffed, wooden floor. Yet the stack only waved, dancing in the slightly disturbed air. Atop it all, the goddess catrina seemed to perform the *danse macabre*.

"I see they are ready," said Constancio, one of the *corridistas*, musicians who sang the printed lyrics of the *corridos* while selling the leaflets for a few *centavos* apiece.

José dumped the stack into Constancio's arms. "By the time you run out, I'll have printed another run." José flashed a grin. "I expect her"—he nodded at the illustration—"to be my most popular catrina yet."

Constancio stared at the printed verse. "You did not use my song?"

"Forgive me, Constancio, your words were inspired. I will use your lyrics another day. Today, this song spoke to me. It is an old song my mother used to sing, one handed down from the ancient gods." Perhaps Mictecacihuatl herself had whispered the words in his ear while inspiring José to sketch her in his popular style. Who better to herald *Día de los Muertos* than the Lady of the Dead?

Constancio shrugged, never one to complain, although his songs were biting and satirical. He took the broadsheets, printed on harvest-orange paper, and left quietly, nodding as he read the words printed on the top page.

Outside, Constancio patrolled past the storefront singing. His mellow tones drew José to the doorway. For just a moment, José took some time to lean and listen. But soon he needed to return to his work. Besides the leaflets, he had many other printing jobs to finish.

> *Like the spring grass,*
> *We come only to sleep,*
> *Only to dream.*
> *It is not true,*
> *It is not true,*
> *That we have come to live on Earth.*

A gust of wind wove through the street, blowing off hats, tugging at women's tiered skirts, and making children giggle.

The wind struck Constancio as he sang the verse a second time. Orange *hojas volantes* flew upward, scattered by the wind. Though some of the sheets drifted down, more than half blew to places unknown.

CB&)CB&)

Modern Day, Mexico City

Nine-year-old Galeno stared into the sky. Orange flyers rained down from nowhere. There were no tall buildings on this street. Nor did an airplane drop them. And the sky was clear . . . except for the falling sheets of orange paper.

Galeno's gaze tracked a sheet to where it landed. He peered at the old-style printing, the ink cracked in places, worn away by time. The catrina image, her skull framed by feathers, ensnared his attention. His heart leapt for joy.

The skeletal image defined beauty with pure simplicity of form. Galeno liked drawing skeletons, but his teacher forbade it—except during this time of the year. For the Day of the Dead, skeletons and skulls were everywhere.

It had always been Galeno's favorite festival. This year, he hoped his older sister would visit. She had died four years ago in a car accident and he missed her so.

Galeno squatted before the flyer. Aloud, he read the time-damaged poem.

> *Like spring*
> *We sleep*
> *To dream.*
> *It is true,*
> *It is*
> *We come to live on Earth*

Galeno's pulse raced. Had the dead sent these flyers? Did it mean his sister was finally coming home?

If his teacher saw this, she wouldn't think his fascination with skeletons and death morbid. Maybe she would see their beauty too. She might even understand.

In his ears, the poem vibrated on the wind like faint echoes. A whisper answered, *I am coming.*

Galeno reached for the faded orange flyer. But when the catrina leapt off the page, he lurched back, startled. A female skeleton towered over Galeno wearing a simple fabric wrap and an elaborate feathered headdress and feathered cloak.

Galeno gawked at the sight, disbelieving. At the same time he felt drawn to the incredible figure. She was even more beautiful than her drawing.

The catrina's bones gleamed silvery white as if lit by moonlight, though the sun still shone overhead. She cocked her head, her teeth in an eternal smile. From the dark depths of her empty eye sockets, Galeno knew she could see.

Her sightless gaze penetrated his skin as if she looked at his bones while he looked at hers. He raised his chin and stretched back his lips, smiling to show every tooth.

The catrina clattered her teeth, laughing. Her bones rattled softly in the breeze, a slice of chilling cold on an unseasonably hot day.

Galeno loved this creature. Just as he still loved his dead sister, Orquidea. He offered the living catrina his hand. If she was imaginary, he didn't care. To him, she *was* the embodiment of his sister.

"The parade starts at sundown," Galeno said.

The catrina surveyed both sides of the street.

"It's not here. Come," Galeno said. "I will show you." Still, he held out his hand, hoping she would take it, hoping she would never leave him.

The catrina's head cocked to the other side before accepting Galeno's offer.

Her bones felt colder than ice against Galeno's palm. When her grip tightened, it felt as if her bones sliced into his flesh, paring away skin, muscle, and sinew to the glorious bone beneath. Her gesture made him an equal.

Galeno walked proudly. "The festival is this way," he said, his words a whisper, as if they had come from far away.

Her footsteps fell as light as fog. With her walking beside him, Galeno felt weightless, like a spirit floating beside his great skeletal queen. Like his sister Orquidea used to, now the catrina would take care of him. She would be the queen of the parade and he her page escort, just like in the courts of old he was studying in history class.

As they strolled up the middle of the street, blocked off for the evening's parade, more orange flyers drifted down like giant confetti.

Candy skulls covered silver platters in every shop window. Flower garlands scalloped the streets; wreaths hung on doors. Paper and wooden skeletons dangled from poles. Around the poles danced people dressed like skeletons. By sundown, many more revelers would appear, wearing make-up to transform their faces into skulls.

Galeno smiled at his catrina and pointed at the candy. "You see? The world welcomes you." Again he noticed how breathy his voice, how distant his words.

The candy skulls vanished, only sugary crumbs left behind. Flowers framing the storefront window withered. The dancing skeletons in the street grew tired and laid down.

The catrina pointed toward the cemetery.

"That's where the parade ends," Galeno whispered. "But it hasn't started yet."

Again she pointed earnestly.

"It's not time," he said softly, shaking his head.

He glimpsed his reflection in the storefront window and stopped to stare. Beside his tall catrina stood a boy-size skeleton wearing Galeno's clothing.

He looked down at himself. His body was every bit as glorious as his queen's . . . only smaller.

 CREACREA

With tears stinging his eyes, Constancio printed hundreds of green leaflets. Across the top, he'd used three of Don Lupe's favorite catrinas. Don

Lupe . . . the affectionate name everyone called José Guadalupe Posada.

Carrying the *hojas volantes* into the street, he sang his ballad dedicated to his old friend.

> *We bore his old body on our shoulders.*
> *He bore the world on his.*

From every shop, people came out to listen. Everyone knew Don Lupe. Everyone had missed him these past seven years.

> *He died alone, his clothing worn, his pockets bare.*
> *He gave us much to feed our hearts,*
> *to fill our breasts with courage.*
> *He showed us truth behind the lies,*
> *in the dance of death he reveled.*
> *Whether rich or famous, we all wear masks,*
> *which Don Lupe joyfully revealed.*
> *In death we are made equal.*

Hands dropped *centavos* all around Constancio as people snatched the leaflets. Don Lupe's famous caricatures had always told the story, even to the illiterate. This time, however, the people would listen and remember Constancio's *corridos*.

> *He died alone, this man of ink and paper.*
> *His wife gone and son too,*
> *alone he lay, waiting for death's knock.*
> *On our shoulders he was borne,*
> *carried to the Cemetery of Dolores,*
> *to rest among the paupers,*
> *having only a ticket for a sixth-class grave.*
> *Now it's come,*
> *that seven years later,*
> *his rest shall be disturbed.*
> *No sleep for our Don Lupe,*
> *not while his bones are disinterred.*

Constancio set down the few remaining leaflets. He wiped his eyes at the indignity that such a great artist's bones should be exhumed and tossed in a common grave.

Before he could pick up the leaflets, a bitter wind tore through the street, grabbing them up and scattering green pages across the city. Constancio recalled that same wind having gripped him years ago. Its fingers hadn't been as cold then, when they had lifted the orange leaflets from his arms. Remembering the Aztec catrina's face upon those pages, Constancio raised his tear-streaked face to the sky.

"Hear my words, ancient ones!" he cried. "Do not let your artist be forgotten!"

☙❧☙❧

Orange flyers swirled at Galeno's feet. The sheets followed him and the living catrina, chasing them like stray kittens, and landing in front of them like tossed rose petals before a queen. Before the skeletal queen. And now, green flyers fell from the sky, mingling with the orange.

Galeno escorted his queen toward the Cemetery of Dolores. Everywhere people slept, taking a second siesta. A forever siesta that would be interrupted only by the night's festivities. Then the Queen of the Dead would command her subjects to awaken. She would give them tongues so those so long silent could speak.

Galeno couldn't wait for the queen's first words to pass her lipless mouth. What wonders might she impart?

Fresh flowers decorated the graves. Strands of brightly colored, plastic beads hung from tombstones. Toys rested on children's graves. Candied treats were everywhere. This time of year the cemetery became a magical garden, transformed by the loving care of families who still mourned.

Green and orange flyers skipped across graves like pebbles flung across a lake. The pages twirled and flipped as if the catrinas printed on them performed the Dance of Death.

Had Galeno still possessed blood or a heart, it would have raced. The dead would all soon wake.

He and his queen strode through the cemetery gates.

The sanctified ground cracked. That crack fissured and spread like many fingers reaching across the cemetery. Piles of dirt tumbled aside to unearth its boxed treasures. Like portals to other worlds, gaping maws appeared. From each rose a coffin, some plain boxes, others of carved and polished wood.

Dirt-crusted doors opened, that other world reaching into this one. Skeletons climbed out. Bare bones, some dirty, others shimmering like pearls.

Some wore rags. Others wore clothing still intact, though their flesh had rotted.

The queen's voice, guttural and strong, rode the wind. "When we finish here, we shall walk the entire city, the entire world, and I shall reclaim my throne," she said, her disembodied voice bold, as if coming from the earth, sky, and distant mountains all at once.

Galeno's thoughts traveled as a whisper, "And I shall sit by your feet for eternity."

Skeletons, all equals now, fell in line behind Galeno and Queen Catrina. Proudly, Galeno wove through the cemetery alongside his queen, as she freed more and more skeletons trapped below, their bones buried out of sight, their lives forgotten.

But Galeno had never forgotten. Even before his sister died, he had played in the cemetery, talking to its denizens, cleaning headstones and picking weeds off graves.

Galeno paused beside Orquidea's burial site. Had he been able to weep, he would have cried tears of joy as her grave opened, as she, rid of earthly flesh, stepped into the pale light of sunset. The sun's fading, orange rays bathed her bones making it seem as if a thousand tiny candles lit them from within. Orquidea would like that, Galeno thought. She loved candles.

Galeno took his sister's hand. He had so much he wanted to say, but didn't know where to begin. So silence overcame him. No matter. Words were just sounds passing through air. Holding her hand meant more than words could convey.

The parade of skeletons, accompanied by dancing flyers, continued snaking through the cemetery. As they neared that stretch of common graves where paupers were buried, the queen stopped.

Galeno pointed, knowing so many poor skeletons lay piled atop each other without dignity or recognition. Surely they, too, had a desire to walk the world once again. Perhaps even their desire for the chance to speak was even greater. So why didn't the queen wake them?

Queen Catrina shook her head, her posture sad. Yet she wouldn't approach the graves, their mounds flattened by time.

Seeing again the costumed people sleeping under the poles and street lamps, Galeno pulled at his voice which grew ever distant and asked, "When will they wake from their forever siesta?"

"When they have shed that which traps them."

"When they're like us?" Galeno whispered, his disembodied voice small and puny.

Queen Catrina bobbed her head, the gesture pure elegance. "Soon the world will be as we are."

The world seemed to answer her. The ground trembled, groaning, speaking in a tongue known only to the gods. The soil covering the mass graves peeled back, revealing skeletons by the dozens. These poor souls had no coffin, no home. Their bones rattled, as if shivering from the touch of cool air.

Yet the queen drew back, pulling her feathered cloak after her.

Skeletons climbed from the mass graves. They crawled on broken bones, begging to join the parade. With a nod, the queen accepted them.

In Galeno's soul, he smiled.

One skeleton stood apart. Rags clung to his bones and a strip of leather that had once cinched his waist now hung loose, caught on his hips. He shook his head slowly, sadly, declining the queen's offer.

Queen Catrina drew back another step. A cold fear radiated from her bones, the sort of cold found only on the tallest mountain in the dead of winter. Or maybe the sort of cold found on the moon's ever-dark side.

She shook her head, causing her feathered headdress to flutter. Standing erect and bold, her shadow stretched toward the one skeleton who stood apart. Defiance shone from within the queen as if the sunset sprang from her instead of passing through. "Will you join?" she asked, no, demanded.

Galeno stared at this other skeleton with wonder. Who was he to the queen? Had he been her king? Surely this one skeleton was why she had balked, why she had not opened these graves.

Meaning *he* opened the graves. He must be a king.

With great effort, doubling over and drawing up air through his rib cage, this skeleton king wheezed out, "No." The word echoed, long and drawn out. "No," he repeated.

Queen Catrina raised her finely chiseled chin. "Who dares tell Mictecacihuatl no?"

"You are no goddess," the skeleton rasped. "You are only a catrina of the dead, not the Lady herself. I created you."

Galeno whispered in awe, "Don José Guadalupe Posada." Though the man had never been knighted, he should have been.

This skeleton king, the great José Posada, bowed in recognition of his name.

Galeno immediately felt ashamed. Had he known Don Lupe had been tossed in a pauper's grave, he would have found a way to dig up the artist's bones and give them a proper burial.

Queen Catrina strode toward Don Lupe.

Galeno hugged Orquidea, their bones entwining like tangled wind chimes.

He had so missed Orquidea's embrace. Though he could read, he missed her bedtime stories that helped him sleep, to fall into night's "little death."

Now he could sleep forever . . . yet not sleep.

"This is not your world," Don Lupe said. "Your world is gone and your people have changed."

"My people have changed many times over and the world is never gone. . . unless I make it gone."

Don Lupe stooped in a low bow. As his hand swept the ground, he picked up two flyers, one orange, the other green. He held them before his skull face. Solemnly, he read the poem on the orange leaflet, adding in the missing words.

Queen Catrina stiffened as if horrified, or maybe sad.

"It is *not* true," Don Lupe repeated, "that we have come to live on Earth." And once more he read, "It is *not* true."

Queen Catrina's bones rattled.

Feeling his beautiful queen's trembling fear, Galeno hugged Orquidea tighter, sensing the queen's power weakening. His sister had come from so far, been gone for so long . . . and she couldn't stay. Galeno trembled in sadness. Tears, crystallized like quartz, fell from his eye sockets.

Though four years wasn't so long to have lost his sister, four years felt like an eternity to a nine-year-old. Four years was nearly half his lifetime. And it was only the beginning of all his years to be without her. Galeno trembled harder and Orquidea held him tighter.

Don Lupe snatched an orange sheet from the wind, looked at it, his skeleton peering at the skeleton catrina he had drawn. Then he tossed it aside. He plucked three more sheets from the air and discarded them.

The wind swirled around him, carrying more sheets to Don Lupe. He caught one after another and set it free.

Until Don Lupe held one page without an image, the page from which the queen had pulled a body, the same page Galeno had stooped to read. Don Lupe held that page before the queen then wadded it into a ball.

Queen Catrina crumpled into a pile of bones. The feathers of her headdress and cape disintegrated. Her fabric wrap rotted. The bones dried out, fractured and turned to dust. Only her skull remained intact.

Wind howled between tombstones. It picked up the bone dust and carried it aloft in swirling currents. The orange flyers trailed after it, vanishing into the sky.

Don Lupe crumpled a green flyer, saying, "In death we are made equal. There can be no sleep . . . not while our bones are disinterred." He headed for the common graves.

From all sides, skeletons lumbered back to their earthen homes. They fell into holes and coffins lifelessly, considering the vigor with which they'd climbed out. There would be no talking tonight. No festivities.

"Wait," Galeno whispered so earnestly that it was almost more than breath. "You deserve a better grave, Don Lupe."

Don Lupe cocked his head.

"We will dig you one," Galeno said. Yet only he, Orquidea, and Don Lupe remained.

Orquidea nodded.

After Galeno and Orquidea dug out a grave among those with tall tombstones and statues, Don Lupe whispered, "My thanks. But what of my headstone?"

Galeno grabbed Queen Catrina's skull. Ornate carving covered her skull, much like the decorations on Mexico's ancient pyramids. Galeno held it before Don Lupe, saying, "This will be your headstone."

Don Lupe bowed then climbed inside his grave.

Once his bones were covered, Galeno pressed the skull into the earth. The ground trembled. Nearby stones vibrated then bounced and rolled toward the skull. As they gathered, the growing pile pushed the skull upward, forming a conglomerate pyramid.

When the trembling stopped, the skull perched atop a stack of stones as tall as Galeno. Dark pebbles embedded in the paler stones read, "Here lies Don José Guadalupe Posada."

Satisfied, Galeno hugged his sister. "I will take his place in the common grave." He had no grave of his own and felt his will to move slipping away. Without the queen's presence, the cemetery's magic was fading.

Orquidea gripped Galeno's hand and pulled him after her.

She led Galeno to her coffin, to that portal to another world. Together they climbed inside. She cradled him against her, protecting him as she always had. In nestling against her, he found that sanctuary he'd lost when she died.

The coffin lid closed.

Galeno clung to Orquidea, grasping the most beautiful of all creations. Bones. And his sister. Happily, he rested.

This Side of the Veil

Katie Hartlove

There is something about this time of year that makes me so happy that I feel like I am humming inside. It is the change, really. The moments when I can imagine that I can see my breath in the early morning air. When I smell the first remnants of woodstove smoke from a neighbor's chimney. When the grey and brown geese fly in perfect formation above my head. And I can lie on my back, deep in the dewy field grass, and marvel at the millions of stars that are aligned differently in the night sky. This is the time I wait for all year. This is the time when my senses are so ripe and the boundary between my world and theirs is the thinnest. And we are so close, so in touch with each other, that I swear it is almost like I am alive again.

"I'm not going this year," Irvin said.

I lay in the grass, holding my hand up in the air, enjoying the juxtaposition of the warm afternoon sun and the harvest breeze that caressed the field and blew through my body. I looked up at him, shading my eyes. He shrugged his shoulders and lay back effortlessly beside me. I knew he wanted me to hold his hand and ask him why, but I didn't.

"You say that every year, Irvin." I rolled on my side, propping my head up on my chin. "And every year you do. Then, you're happy."

"For a while, yeah." He rolled over and looked at me, then tried to pull a blade of brown grass out of the ground. When he found he couldn't, he sighed one of those deep sighs that forms in the pit of your belly. "Then, I have to go a whole year before I can see my family again, before I can be near enough to them. So by the time the end of winter breaks me, I'm aching with loneliness from missing them, and by summer, I have a hard time remembering what my wife's voice sounds like or how my youngest boy's smile crooks up to the left. And knowing that seems worse than the aching. I'm beginning to wonder if I should stop . . . you know . . . and just wait for them to pass and come join me."

I mulled that over for a minute. "Isn't it worth it, though? To be close to them for just a few minutes?"

"I'm beginning to wonder. We don't even have a whole day with them, Bessie. We have sun up to sun down. And that's if they do it first thing in the morning. If they even remember us at all."

I paused. It was true enough. My entire family had passed. Some of my family that had passed came to the celebrations they were invited to. Most of them no longer knew the living, as their friends and family were with them now. The living no longer mattered to them. I reclined back and closed my eyes, enjoying the last days of the perfect warmth of the sun I felt in the fall when the veil was thin.

"Margaret Jane remembers me," I said, my voice soft, remembering how we both looked as we walked home from town on Saturday afternoons, laughing about boys or strangers peddling their oddities at the market. "I'll go as long as she remembers me."

Irvin snorted. "She's not likely to remember much these days."

"If you'd lived past the ripe old age of 37, you grouch, you would eventually have gotten wrinkles and grey hair and forgotten a thing or two." I would have punched him in the arm if we were able to feel each other; but now, it was pointless.

"Who're you to talk? You where what . . . 16? You look like you could be her great-granddaughter."

Seventeen, I thought. Seventeen when I left the world. Margaret Jane had been there the day I passed. We were walking on the bank of the creek in the spring after the snow has melted and days of rain had drenched our town. The water was high, and the sodden ground just gave away. Margaret Jane had jumped in after me, and for a few moments, we were able to cling together as we were tossed along in the rushing water. Then, we were torn apart from each other, and I remember the way our hands felt as I slipped out of her fingers and the despair in her eyes as we separated. She would eventually turn up on shore, water logged but alive. And I would be swept further downstream until I hit the rocks and was no longer able to stay above the surface.

Margaret Jane was old now . . . close to 98, I imagined. Her withered body always made its way to the altar in the center of town to light candles, pour some blessed water into a pitcher decorated with red ribbons, and leave a sweet vanilla cake for me. I felt nourished and whole again when she did that. And I got to spend the day with her, close enough that if we were both still of the flesh, I could have put my arm around her and kissed her browned, wind-worn cheek.

Soon, though. Tomorrow. I guessed Irvin got tired of waiting for me to respond, to tell him to stop being a fuddy-duddy. He stood up, stretched, then watched me for a minute. When I didn't ask him to stay, he walked a few steps before vanishing into the setting sunlight.

At dawn I shivered, standing a few hundred feet from the altar. We all waited. There weren't that many of us who still bothered, and there were even fewer living that bothered. Just the older folks, the ones whose younger family members had to help them totter towards the altar, who waited with feigned patience and fidgeted during the prayers and checked their watches.

I heard a deep sigh behind me. I didn't need to turn around.

"Don't say a word, Bessie. Not. One. Word."

I wrapped my arms tighter around myself and waited.

As soon as the sun peered over the horizon, the first of the living made their way to the altar. A woman in her mid-fifties arrived, followed closely by three boys, the youngest who appeared to be maybe 25. Each of the boys carried a candle, and the woman carried a basket with a cake wrapped in a checkered cloth. She carried her Bible, clutched it tight at her breast, and clenched a white handkerchief in her fist. A few tears slipped down her face, but it was not quite the sobbing I had seen her suffer through in the past.

Irvin sucked in a deep breath. I looked over my shoulder at him, and when the last candle was lit and the last of their prayers were said, he was invited over to join them. He started out, walking towards them before breaking into a run, taking several light-footed strides at once. He smiled through his own tears, wrapping his arms around his boys, then taking his wife by her shoulders and kissing her forehead. The living exchanged nervous grins. Irvin's love was deep, and the veil was so thin this year that they must have felt something.

Irvin threw a glance over his shoulder as he walked away with them. He beamed. His radiance was like a beacon, and his family must have known it to some extent. They smiled, too.

The day wore on. By mid-morning, just about all of the spirits had been invited home. They stopped at the altar and drank and ate their fill before embracing their families, their friends. I sat on the ground, waiting. By noon, the spirits who were left near me began to give up, so by the time the afternoon sun began its long descent in the sky, I sat alone, watching the path that led up to the altar. Margaret Jane would come. She'd never forgotten me. Not once.

But the sky betrayed me. It drank the sun, draining it dry, despite its begging, and sucked it deep inside. In protest, its blood-red fingers drug across the sky, reaching out to grab at the moon as it made its ascent. They both hung in the sky, equally low on the horizon.

There was spring in Irvin's step as he approached. When he saw me sitting where he had left me, he stopped walking and looked around. Some of the joy left his body, exiting through the wonderful posture of his shoulders, leaving them sagging.

He offered a hand to help me up. I shook my head.

"She didn't come," I whispered, more for me than for him.

He shook his head. "I know it must be tough for you, kid. . ."

"Really?" I shot back, my voice harsher than I intended. "*You* were remembered, Irvin. You don't know what it is like to have no one, *no one*, think of you. You can't understand what that is like."

"No," he said, shoving his hands deep within his pockets. "I don't know. But one day, I will."

"Then we'll talk about it on that day. And not one day before." I stood, brushed off grass that wouldn't have stuck to my ethereal skirt, and walked away from him, towards the altar.

It was a long, draining walk to the altar when a spirit wasn't invited, but I had to go. I watched the last of the burning candles pool onto the glass plate upon which it sat. My stomach was too sour from sadness to bother to drink the remaining water or enjoy the sweetness of honey rolls or half-melted flan. No vanilla cake for me this year. Nothing for me this year.

I trudged back to the place where I had waited, then walked past it, further up the hill, back to where the veil was once again drawing in. On the rock, just at the edge of the loblolly pines, a shadow sat, hunched over, body wretching in grief. And as bad as I felt, my heart broke when I heard the sobs. I'd seen this hundreds of times before, and more importantly, I'd felt it before, the day after I first passed.

"Are you ok?" I asked, kneeling beside the figure. She had the smell of fresh earth, the smell of those recently dead.

"I think I'm lost," she said, her voice cracking through her sobs.

"No. You're right where you're supposed to be."

"I'm so scared."

"I know, I was too." I wanted very much to put my hand on her shoulder, but it would have passed right through her. "But I'll help you. And there will be others, the ones that will be sent to guide you."

She sniffed and wiped at her face with the back of her hand. Then, she turned up to face me. I recognized her at once, the same sweet face I'd watched age each year as she made her way to the altar.

"Bessie?" she asked.

"So this is why you didn't come today?" I smiled, ashamed at how upset I had been when I thought I had been forgotten.

Margaret Jane smiled a bit and sniffed. "Is this a good enough reason to not show up?"

I chuckled, then sat down at her feet. "Of course. But thank you . . . thank you for showing up for so many years. For not forgetting me."

"Thank you? But I let you drown, Bessie. How could you possibly say thank you to me?"

"You did everything you could. It was my time . . . I've made peace with that. Just like now is your time. It is so much better here than we ever imagined, Margaret Jane. And now, we can be together again . . . just like the old days."

I grinned up at her, hoping to help her get through her first night on this side of the veil.

Flor de Muerto

Camille Alexa

It was bad luck, my little flower, my little angel, that I named you for the *flor de muerto* of your father's people—the flower of the dead. I think I was overcome by my memory of him, your beautiful father, lying naked and godlike on a bed of orange petals as though he had been summoned to Earth from beyond the darkness and the festivities and all the stars in the sky for just one night. One night of warmth and humidity and the soft lapping of the ocean against the shore; the night of the dead, the night of the innocents; the night of your conception, my beautiful flower, my angel, my Marigold.

Let me lie down here beside you. The grass is sweet, my love. It's a mild November night above ground, lush and humid the way it stays here most of the time—a night much like the one on which you were conceived, dearest. Masked revelers careen drunken and boisterous just across the narrow alley separating this cemetery from the small row of cottages beyond. They sound happy. They sound joyous and light and full of warmth. It takes a special kind of person to live beside a graveyard, Marigold. Not everyone has as much love for the dead as I do year round, and not just at this special time of the season. But who would not love you, my innocent, my angel, my little flower? How could they not?

It took me a long time to drive here to be with you this year. Longer than most. I grow weary easily these days it seems, and feel older than I have in the past: this morning I found the first grey threads streaking through my hair. As with most years I did not stop between my home and here. It takes days, this journey, though I never begrudge you a moment of them. I would never.

I grow sleepy. Don't worry, baby; I'll stay here, sleep beside you as I do every year at this time, for this one night. I've brought you flowers and sugar candies, and another of the small wooden horses you loved during your brief time with me here on this Earth. What bedtime story would you like to hear this year, little one? I could tell you of me trying to find your beautiful father—of me wandering, the world blurred by my tears, through two continents trying to find my way back to him after our one night together—as I told you last year. Last year was a bad year for your poor mother, a year of sorrow and tears and of bitterness. That story of my search is beautiful because I tried so hard; because it shows I love him almost as much as I love you. But no. Instead of that sad end-which-was-not, let me start at a beginning. Your beginning. It's a more happy tale.

Did I ever tell you I dreamt of you before your conception? I was asleep alone in my apartment—an ugly thing of glass and metal, all sharp angles with no curves, filled with furniture bought on borrowed money. There are many places just like it in Texas, in Dallas and in other cities in the north where it gets so cold. It's not like here, where golden sun licks the painted surfaces of these tiny wooden houses and makes them sing with the mornings and the dew. Not like here, where unfettered jungle creeps up to meet the ocean in friendly embrace, and birds wheel and soar overhead with equal equanimity and joy. This is why I eventually brought you to live among the red hibiscus and green palms and the azure of a sky which stretches away forever. You see why I had to bring you back to where you began, my darling flower, when the doctors in Dallas told me you were dying. What could I do, as your baby limbs thinned and your bones grew brittle and cold—as cold as grey cement and hard industrial glass and angular boxes crammed full of people always hurrying toward places they don't want to be? What could I do?

This part of the story is one you already know. It hardly qualifies as a beginning, I suppose, though it is a time I relive again and again in my waking life regardless of the pain it brings. I'd done my best, you see, though my best was perhaps tainted by my fears and my bitter sorrow over losing your father before I had him. I had taken us back, me with you inside, to the top floor of the concrete and glass building which challenged the gods, it rose so high. The sun where it shone on us was not the benevolent sun of green jungle, but the harsh cruel ruler of concrete deserts. When one must go out under such a sun, one does not lift one's face to the sky, close one's eyes, and feel gratitude. No. One hunches over to protect one's retinas against the abuse of the stabbing shards of brightness. One feels one's skin scorch and crisp, and feels the soul shrivel inside like a thirsting thing abandoned in the sand, or dry-drowned in the hot bubbling asphalt rivers of the city. Do you remember such heat, baby? I doubt you saw it much, nor felt its punishment against your skin. Such a blistering torture chamber is no place for a baby born of incense and flower petals, of water and sugar and of wine.

And the nights of such a city; lonely and cold, even when the air feels hotter than fire. The air burns your lungs on its way into your center, but the stars are distant if they ever appear, and the Dallas moon is no kinder than its sun. It's as though separate heavens reside over the two hemispheres; as though the gods have abandoned the one but still smile on the other. It was to that place I went to bring you into this world, though I realized my mistake and brought you back here, if perhaps too late. I'm so sorry for that, my love, my flower. Sorrier than I can tell you. I make this sojourn each year as my penance.

But long before that, on a night just a few before you began, I dreamt of a tiny golden bird. I held it in my cupped palms and it sang to me. Its eyes were of the rich dark chocolate—*xocolátl*—of the ancient Aztecs. Its wings fluttered, fanned out across my fingers like the tiny yellow petals of the marigold, the *cempasúchil*, the *cempoalxochitl*. I had been restless and sad for many years, little one; empty, filled only with longing for a thing I didn't know how to name. When I held that tiny golden dreambird in my palms and listened to its song, I knew your sweet little spirit was waiting for me; waiting for me to find you, waiting for me to bring you into this world. When I woke, it was three in the morning. My sheets were drenched with sour sweat and my limbs felt heavy and aching, as though filled with clay. I dressed and took my passport and my car and I drove south, toward warmth and greenery and mystery and life; toward your beautiful father, whom I did not know but felt calling to me across the rivers and the deserts and the many miles between us.

The next day was Halloween—All Hallows Even, All Saints' Eve—and the day after that was Hallowmas, *Día de los Inocentes*, *Día de los Angelitos*. As I'd driven farther and farther south—past tourists and drunken frat boys; past the border towns and the cheap holiday decorations mass-produced by soulless machines in smoke-belching factories—I'd kept humming to myself those little bars of remembered melody from the birdsong in my dream. I felt an invisible cord binding me to your father like a thread tied around my heart, tugging me to him and to your spirit. It drew me across sand and water and around mountains. I drove for three days without unnecessary stops; without eating and without sleeping.

By the third day, *Día de los Muertos*, I could go no farther. My car rolled to a stop in the main square of this beautiful little town. I was like a walking deadwoman, like a zombie, like an inanimate thing with blood and bone but no heart. I stumbled from my car, my legs cramped, my head pounding like thunder, my eyes like balls of jelly, almost useless. I stood in the dust of the road and blinked into the setting sun and I began to cry.

Forgive me, darling! Forgive me now, after all these years, for forgetting for even one moment how much love you had offered me in my dreams, my sweet little sparrow, my golden bird. My Marigold princess. I was so tired. Tired not just from my drive across miles, but tired from a life of emptiness.

It was then your father stood from his seat on a small stone bench by the fountain. He was tall, darker-skinned than you were, much darker than I am, and his gaze burned into me like the fire of distant stars. I had to shield my eyes against the brightness of him—or was it against the setting sun spilling over the edge of the world behind him?

He stepped toward me and opened his arms and when I fell into them he said in his beautiful melodic language: *I've been waiting for you.*

I was dirty. I was dirty inside and out. And exhausted, my love, and uncertain. But he scrubbed all that from me, your beautiful father. As the sun sank away and the thousand lit candles of the *Día de los Muertos* winked on one by one to illuminate the village, he led me past the feasters with their light music and their heavy wine, past the revelers in their masks with their dancing and laughing, to the beach. There he removed my clothing piece by piece, then his own, and we swam out among the winged boats they call *mariposas*, butterflies, which bobbed and floated along the shore, lit with candles like dancing angels. The water—slightly chilly, but quickening my blood and sluicing away my numbness—buoyed me up, held me in the gently rocking cradle of its waves.

When your father led me up onto the shore toward the fire, my bare skin did not cool with the night. Rather, it burned. I felt lit from within, irradiated, glowing; and when your father lay on his bed of marigolds and beckoned me to him I could do nothing—wanted to do nothing—but comply.

And that was your beginning, little flower. Your entry into this world, though you didn't stay long. After I woke the next morning to find your father gone; after I searched for him and wandered all the places I could think of and cried salty bitter tears for him; I returned to the grey boxy cities in the north. It's only these two days now for which I return each year: one day for you, *Día de los Inocentes*, the Day of the Innocents; and one day for him, *Día de los Muertos*, the Day of the Dead. I don't know that he is dead, of course; only that he is gone.

I don't think either of you is gone for good. I sometimes catch a part of your song in the early hours of my dreaming; a trill or two from the little songbird of you which lives in my heart. And of him, whom I never found or saw again after he left me full of you, I dream as well. I dream of dark liquid skin and eyes hotter than embers and arms like branches of a warm mahogany tree. I dream that some year, on this day, in this place, he'll return to me. He will kiss away my tears and lay me on a bed of flowers, and he will fill me with you again so you may be reborn.

This time I'll be more careful. This time I'll name you after the *cuitlaxochitl*, the Aztecan star flower; a flower of life instead of the *flor de muerto*. You shall be my darling Poinsettia, my angel, my baby.

My love.

Dark Shapes

Samael Gyre

D ark shapes slithered through his dreams the way dark nights spidered
through his life, leaving him stumbling through webs too soft to stop
him but too unpleasant to ignore. One such night came back in memory at
the start of every November, when his parents had died. He remembered
the barn ablaze, the scream of trapped horses, and being told to stay in
the house. More vivid still were glimpses of his parents in silhouette. They
became shadow people just before entering the dark entirely, ironically by
dashing into the brightness of the flame to save the horses.

He was still at the window watching when the screams stopped. He was
still there, too, when the barn collapsed, sending firefly sparks skyward to
play with the stars.

A neighbor woman who smelled of corn tortilla and fresh bread from
her baking found him clutching the sill, forehead pressed to the cool glass,
gaze fixed on the smoldering inferno where last his parents had been. He
was thinking about the smoke and wondering if some of it was his parents'
ghosts rising to join his uncle Juan and all four grandparents in the sky.

"That's where it is, isn't it? The sky?"

"Of course, dear," the woman said, neither knowing nor caring what he
was asking, thoughts of Heaven being far from her mind as she gathered him
to her apron and led him to his bed. She gave him a candy skull, its glitter
like the stars, its sweetness anodyne to the bitterness of that night. When
he cracked it with his teeth he thought of his mother and father, their skulls
cracking in the heat.

Taught never to waste, he ate it anyway, gagging, shuddering, and crying.

Whether he slept that night in his own bed or dressed himself or was
bundled into blankets and taken to the neighbors, he no longer knew. What

mattered was him living, in those simpler times, with señor and señora Alvarez from then on, and growing old enough, finally, first to investigate the abandoned house and burned barn and later to leave for the city, where school taught him different lights and shadows.

At long last he headed for the border, crossing legally for an interview in Arizona, a post at a small college, teaching Latin American cultures.

And every *Día de los Muertos* he avoided sweets, crowds, and celebrations, preferring whispers to chatty picnics with his own dead. There had been some Olmec in Rita Alvarez, his surrogate mother, and when November rolled around he felt more like one of those huge stone heads than a plaster saint in the church. Praying on such a day seemed a sacrilege, as did kneeling or bowing in any way to life's cruelty.

Dark shapes hemmed him in, even his students glimpsing them as All Saints approached. As he stood in class teaching ancient cultures to fleeting generations of distracted text messengers and video game experts, his woolen suit itchy as if it had gone from cashmere to burlap in some shadowy transmigration of comfort, he saw them flick their eyes and knew they were seeing the same thing he saw. Dark shapes crowding in, dashing past him, hovering behind as he held up a Toltec or Olmec vase.

"Is it true, professor, you were a farm boy?" one pert girl asked, her blonde hair apparently as natural as her violet eyes.

He nodded, smiled. "Anyone can," he said, then stopped. As he looked at her innocence he saw flames again, shadows moving past them, and this took away any point he'd been about to make.

"I'm sorry," he told them. "Dismissed."

They filed out but for the blonde girl and three of her supporters, two boys and another girl. Two couples, he surmised. These kids approached him and the blonde girl, always the one to speak, ducked her head. "We just want you to know we like your class. It's really interesting." And she leaned down and set a sugar skull and a marzipan skeleton on the desk.

The treats looked homemade.

"Thank you."

It was obvious to him this was not all she, or they, wanted to impart. To help them he said, "You see them, too, don't you? The dark shapes."

They watched him. "Yes," the blonde said. "We see them, too. Are they ghosts?"

"Maybe," he said. He secretly thought of them more as echoes of an emotional sort, or refraction, perhaps.

"Professor," the blonde blurted, "I'm from Iowa and I used to see them all the time at home, on the farm. I thought they were evil spirits."

"Each culture has its belief systems," he said, hating such academic cant even as he used it like a shield.

The other three kids nodded, murmured assent; they all had seen dark shapes flitting around him. Or themselves.

Such a personal country, North America, the professor thought. Advice from the dean who had hired him, rattling in his heat-cracked skull, reminding him never to forget it is always all about them.

"I just think it's so cool that we grew up the same and all and, uh, you know, like, the way the class is going and all," the blonde's boyfriend said, placing a proprietary arm around her waist.

The foursome walked out happy and the professor sat down, sad that he could both see so clearly yet remain so obscure with them, across the cultural divides.

To them, death meant an end, finality, and terrifying darkness. To many others, death meant an expansion of life, a continuation of learning and growth, and a chance to do more good in the world, or worlds.

He liked what he had thought, and stood and wrote it on the chalk board.

A colleague poked a head into the room, his eyes turquoise set in the amber of his tanned wrinkles. "Hey, *muchacho*, you still working? Long weekend, man, let's par-tay."

"Be along in a few minutes," he said, forcing a smile the way his mother used to force the handle on the water pump in their kitchen.

"Angela McTeague got caught in the janitor's closet with Kyle Morton, had you heard?"

He shook his head, imagining the pretty student pinned against a wall stained by mops and disinfectants by a sweaty gym teacher eager to deflower yet another before the guys in the History Department got ahead of him. He forced a laugh and made a banal comment, which pleased his hall-mate, who left whistling.

So happily corrupt, he thought.

He did not add that to his words on the board.

When the school lay quiet around him and only the hum of floor polishing machines echoed in the long hallways, he got up and went to his personal closet. From it, he withdrew the jug and the paper bag. They were of nearly equal heft.

Back at his desk, he opened the half-gallon plastic jug and emptied it into his wastepaper basket, which was still full of crumpled paper, letting the liquid splash all over the desk and floor.

When it was empty, he set it on the soaked blotter. He pulled some matches from his pocket, lit one, and whispered to it, "Go ahead," then dropped it onto the desk. Flames spread with a whuff.

He watched the fire grow and watched first the skeleton and then the skull melt and thought how good the warmth felt, even on such a hot day for the first of November. He then opened and slid his hand into the paper bag, which was smoldering. Raising it to his temple, he pulled the hidden trigger and was slammed sideways off his chair by the bullet's impact.

All around him dark shapes slithered, snakes in gloom, and he could hear them now, speaking to him in their hissing tongues even as his skin blistered, bubbled, and boiled off. They told him the day of the dead is a golden day of reunion, when spirits long since released and those still trapped in flesh can cavort and frolic in sunshine and laughter.

He heard windows shatter as heat burst from the room and thought of coolness against his forehead. He remembered Mrs. Alvarez finding him thinking of smoke and souls.

His final smile outlasted even his skull cracking as his brain boiled away in the heat of the flames.

The Man Who Loved Dogs

Laura Loomis

Bethany kept the two parchments rolled up in the drawer with her important papers, though she hadn't looked at them since the day she married Andre. The first scroll had told her she could trust Andre. And she did trust him. With everything except the second scroll.

Bethany had been seven when her family traveled through a town whose Spanish name she no longer remembered. It was the Day of the Dead, a notion that puzzled and amused her parents, and they happened across a carnival. Bethany pushed her baby brother's stroller underneath the giant skull that decorated the makeshift gate. She looked around her in awe at the costumed jugglers and dancers. Skulls gleamed at her from every side: the dancers' masks, the dolls sold in the dusty stalls. Musicians played drums and maracas painted with bones, singing a cheerful Spanish tune. Even the cookies were decorated with colored sugar to look like skulls.

Next to the fortune-teller's tent hung a banner that said "*POZO DE LAS ALMAS*," and below it, "Well of Souls." The well looked like a real one, but it was filled with rolled-up pages of silver parchment, each tied with a ribbon. The old woman guarding it wore a necklace of gold coins, and a dress that seemed to be made of bright scarves. "Shall we find out our fortunes?" Bethany's mother asked brightly.

"Don't take unless you really want to know," the old woman said gruffly. "The well is never wrong."

Father laughed and handed her some coins. Then Mother pulled out a scroll and opened it with a flourish. "Great loss should make Margaret cherish what is left," she read. "Hmm, that's not really a fortune. More like a proverb."

"How did it know your name?" Bethany asked.

Father read his next. "You will never be alone in life, or even in death."

He rolled it back up with a bemused look, and gave it to Mother to put in her purse.

Father held little Daniel over the rolls of paper, until Daniel reached out and touched one. Father pulled the scroll out. Bethany slid her hand into the well, but accidentally pulled out two.

Mother looked at the scroll for Daniel. "What the hell is this?" she shouted. "That's not funny!" But somehow the old woman had slipped away. The tent flaps moved lazily in the breeze.

Mother grabbed the scrolls out of Bethany's hands, scanned them quickly, then handed one back to her. It read: *Trust a man who loves dogs.*

"The other one was a mistake," Mother said. "You're not supposed to get two." She rolled the second scroll back up and thrust it into her purse. Bethany was certain, though, that the second prediction was the one meant for her.

Her family changed after that day. Daniel was still fed, bathed and diapered on schedule. But their mother no longer sat and rocked with the baby in her arms, cooing and caressing his pudgy cheek. Bethany had been accustomed to showing Daniel her toys, and kissing him until he squealed. Now she was told to stay out of the nursery.

This continued for six weeks, until the morning that Bethany woke to the sound of her mother sobbing. Daniel was buried with a rolled-up silver parchment lying next to him in the tiny coffin.

Her parents' behavior had changed toward Bethany after the Well, though more subtly than with Daniel. She was never allowed out of their sight, yet rarely embraced. It seemed to her that love was rationed. Most of the kisses she got were from their happily oblivious golden retriever.

In college, Bethany decided she wanted to work with animals. Unlike humans, they either loved you or they didn't, nothing held back.

A few weeks after she graduated veterinary school, Bethany was called home with news of a car crash. Her parents were laid to rest under a single stone, next to Daniel. They had bought four plots together, the one for Bethany lying ready for when it was needed.

Clearing out the house was slow going. Bethany found a box tucked at the back of her mother's closet, with four rolls of silver parchment. Two were for her parents, the ones about cherishing what was left and not dying alone. One was about the man who loved dogs. Daniel's had been buried with him, so that left the last one for Bethany: *Your murderer will serve ten years in prison.*

Bethany burned the scrolls for her parents, tossing the ashes into the wind. Hot tears ushered in the beginning of forgiveness for the mother and father who were too afraid to love their children fully.

Did the Well report Daniel's fate, or help create it? Maybe he had found the world to be a loveless place, and decided not to stay. She understood her parents' futile attempts at shielding themselves and Bethany from the agony of loss. But she didn't want to be loved like Daniel, at arm's length, with pieces of the heart held back.

She kept the two scrolls for herself, still unsure whether one or both contained her fate. She thought she'd touched the one about murder before the one about the man who loved dogs. Sometimes she would take them out and read them again, as if she would somehow find a missing word or phrase that explained it. Why would a killer only serve ten years? That didn't seem like a lot. A drunk driver? Road rage? Maybe the sentence would be a plea bargain because her body couldn't be found. Horrible thoughts, and she would squash them down until they were the size of a needle's point. And still they stuck at her, drawing blood.

If the scroll said you would die by drowning, she mused, you could stay out of boats. It might still come true eventually, in some flash flood or freak accident, but you could do your best to hold it off. But what was she supposed to do when her death could come at the hands of any person she met? The rude cabbie might run her down in a rage; even the pleasant man across the hall might be a knife-wielding maniac.

Eventually, after dealing with enough rude cabbies and bland neighbors, she was able to think about people in terms other than their potential for homicide. Even then, she avoided serious boyfriends, fleeing the first time a man raised his voice.

Then, on her forty-second birthday, Andre walked into her office with a border collie named Espresso running laps around him.

Andre was a music teacher, ten years younger than Bethany, and he provided puppy foster care for the K-9 Res-Q. Before Bethany knew it, she became the organization's official veterinarian, treating an endless procession of strays for ear infections and parvo.

It took Andre two years to talk her into marrying him. Seeing how tender he was with his dogs, she knew he had no violence in him. And he loved them all, not just the puppies who would go on to other homes, but the old and sick dogs who spent their last days with him. When she had to euthanize one, Andre would stay with her while she put the needle in, reassuring the animal with his gentle voice and touch until it was over. It was, she thought, the kindest death anyone could wish for.

Finally, one evening, watching Andre on the floor with puppies climbing all over him, she caught a little of his optimism and decided that she didn't want to ration her own love. She moved into his untidy house, with a gigantic backyard for Espresso to run races with the foster dogs. Andre taught her the fox trot; she taught him to appreciate cats and iguanas. In the evenings, he would meditate and Espresso would sit beside him, no doubt thinking profound canine thoughts.

Still, when she told him about the Well of Souls, she only told him of the prediction about a man who loved dogs. She didn't tell him there was a second scroll. It would be too easy for him to close himself off, push her away, like her parents had.

 C380C380

Twelve years into their marriage, she woke in a bright place with swirls of sound around her, urgent words crisscrossing with machinery. Andre's voice broke through the rest of the noise.

"Beth, Beth can you hear me? You're in the hospital. You had a stroke. Honey, don't worry, I'm right here, they're taking good care of you."

She tried to answer him. The words lined up in her brain, then got lost somewhere on the way to her mouth. She couldn't turn her head to look at him. She was trapped, motionless and silent, like an insect in amber.

She blurred in and out, sometimes hazy, other times completely clear on what she wanted to say. Words and gestures remained stillborn inside her. The doctor finally pronounced sentence: she wasn't going to recover. And from there it got worse.

"She may live for years like this. Decades, even."

"Is she suffering?" The pain in Andre's voice sawed through her. He had been awake, as far as she could tell, since the ordeal started. "Is she going to be a vegetable?"

"She's not brain-dead. She's conscious. She's alive."

Bethany thought: *This is alive?*

Andre didn't give up quickly. He took her to specialists, signed her up for experimental treatments, even tried a faith healer. At home he would play music for her, or lie down beside her with Espresso curled at their feet.

The latest doctor, Andre told her as he squeezed her hand, was one of the foremost specialists on conditions like hers. It had taken ages to get the appointment. The doctor's office had a mirror cruelly placed in the waiting room, directly opposite her wheelchair. Bethany's head lolled to the side, and she couldn't even close her gaping mouth. A bit of drool dripped down her chin until Andre noticed and wiped it away. In a room full of sick people, no one else would look directly at her.

Andre caught her eye in the reflection, and gave her a brave smile. She could see the lines forming around his eyes and mouth. This was all the life she was going to get, invisible to everyone but him. After years of fearing some killer jumping at her from the shadows, she wished one would come now.

The doctor told him the same thing all the others had said: there was nothing to be done. Andre, the man of endless optimism, stared at the floor.

"What if we just stopped feeding her? Would she suffer?"

"That would be murder," the doctor said.

Andre stroked Bethany's hair. "She's a veterinarian, you know. If she had a dog or cat who wouldn't get better, she'd end their suffering with that drug, what do you call it?"

The doctor was a kind man. He told Andre, hypothetically speaking, what would be quick and painless.

Bethany's voice kicked at the walls of her mind, trying to get out to warn him. A ten-year sentence.

At home, Andre put her to bed, then took her office key and went out. Espresso, now an old dog without the frantic energy he'd been named for, curled up in his usual spot by her feet.

Ten years. Andre was not a man who would do well in prison, away from his music and his dogs. He would wither away.

When he returned, Andre sat and held Bethany's hand for a while. "I'm sorry," he said quietly. "I'm sorry for being selfish because I didn't want to lose you. Maybe in twenty or thirty years they'll find a cure. But I can't ask you to go on like this, that's cruel. If it was one of the dogs, we'd have done the right thing already."

No. She had to warn him. He didn't deserve ten years in prison.

Andre got up and did something to her IV, then brushed her lips lightly with his before sitting down again. "I love you," he said. "I wanted to just keep hanging on to hope forever. It'll be all right now."

Her arm was starting to go numb. Ten years. She had to warn him. It wasn't right.

He bent down close to her ear. "Honey, I found the other paper from the Well of Souls." He kissed her temple. "I've made arrangements for the dogs to be cared for. It's all right, don't worry about me. Ten years isn't forever. I'll get through it."

As the numbness spread its warmth throughout her body, she had just enough time to realize how badly she'd underestimated his love.

Last Chance

Michelle D. Sonnier

When Jorge answered the door, Catrina hung back for a moment. She thrust her fists into her black leather biker jacket and sneered.

"So are you gonna let me in or treat me like a Jehova's Witness?"

"Come in, of course," he said, stepping aside, slightly bowing and sweeping his hand into the room. She stomped in, her stiletto heels making little pits in the hardwood floor. Jorge winced.

Catrina's hair hung in wet strings from the rain, and her makeup made black and blue rivers down her cheeks. Catrina fished into her breast pocket for her Marlboro Lights as Jorge shut the door behind her. She packed her cigarettes on the heel of her hand, craning her neck to try and look deeper into the apartment. She turned to face her ex-boyfriend, who was finishing with the chain on the door, and slipped a cigarette between her lips. She was bringing her lighter up as Jorge turned to face her.

"You know I don't allow smoking in the apartment," he said.

"Why not?" she mumbled around the cigarette with her hands still cupped and thumb on her lighter.

"It's bad for Mario, and you know that." He jammed his hands into his pockets. Catrina put her lighter and pack of cigarettes away but left the unlit cigarette in her mouth. She crossed her arms tight over her chest.

"I want to see him. Now."

Jorge sighed at the petulant whine in her voice.

"Catrina." He tried to make his voice gentle, but it still came out exasperated. "It's 3 a.m. You know Mario's bedtime is 9 o'clock. We can't wake him up now. He has school tomorrow."

Catrina's eyes narrowed like a cat's. She took the cigarette out of her mouth and drew back into her jacket a bit more. "Well excuse the shit out of me," she hissed. "I was already at work by then."

"You couldn't stop by this afternoon? Or this morning? Why do you always have to be drunk to face your son?" Jorge struggled to keep from raising his voice.

"Stop making me feel like a bad mother." She turned and threw herself down on the couch, then propped her feet up on the glass coffee table. She took a drag off her unlit cigarette. She took it out of her mouth and looked at it strangely like she couldn't remember why it was unlit. She chewed on her lip and looked up at Jorge through her dark, thick lashes.

"Can I at least just look in on him?" she asked softly.

"You know he's too light of a sleeper. You'll wake him up." Jorge dropped into the recliner across from her. Catrina shrugged, tried to drag on the cigarette again, then chewed on her thumbnail deep in thought for a moment. She took her thumb out of her mouth and looked at Jorge.

"I have some money for you." She dug into her jacket pockets and pulled out crumpled wads of bills and started dropping them on the table. First the outside jacket pockets, then the inside. She casually unbuttoned her blouse and pulled a few bills from inside her bra, then hiked up her skirt and pulled the last few out of her garter belt. The money was rainsoaked and mostly ones. "I dance again on Tuesday night. I can give you more then."

Jorge shrugged. "You've never given us money before, and we've managed just fine so far."

Catrina flinched. "You don't have to be so mean about it. I'm doing the best I can." She tried to drag on her cigarette again.

Jorge sighed and rubbed his face in his hands. "Did you keep enough money for yourself?" he asked.

Catrina shrugged again as she sat down. "Salvatore pays the rent and stuff. Until he kicks me out again, all that's covered."

"What about food? When was the last time you ate?" Jorge eyed her sunken eyes, prominent collarbone, and bony fingers. Catrina just shrugged and twirled her cigarette through her fingers. Jorge pulled two tens out of the crumpled pile, smoothed them out on his knee, and held them out to her.

"I earned that money for Mario, not for myself," she said, her voice full of scorn.

"Well Mario needs a mother who's not starving to death. Get yourself something to eat. That all night diner is still just down the street."

Catrina snorted and rolled her eyes but still snatched the money from his hand and stuffed it in her pocket. The silence stretched uncomfortably while they both tried to look anywhere but at each other. Jorge cocked his head at an imagined sound.

"Hold on," he murmured and went to the back of the apartment to check on his son.

While he was gone, Catrina studied the cluster of picture frames on the glass end table. There was one shaped like swirling blue waves with sea horses and cock-eyed letters that spelled "Key West." It held a picture of a sweet boy of five standing at the edge of the city pool in his water wings and grinning. Catrina remembered it used to hold a picture of her and Jorge at a local Key West tiki bar making faces at the camera. The bartender had taken the picture for them and, while Jorge had been merely drunk, Catrina had also been stoned out of her mind. Shortly after the picture was taken she stumbled out the door to throw up in the parking lot.

There was a simple blonde wood frame that held a picture of the same smiling little boy, nine this time, hanging from the monkey bars and squinting into the sun. That frame used to hold a picture of Catrina with a forced smile on a swing in the city park. She'd been desperately hung over that day. There were more pictures of Mario and a few of Jorge and Mario.

There were only two pictures with Catrina in them. In one frame made of silver curlicues, there was Catrina in a hospital bed, looking ill, while Jorge perched next to her smiling and cradling a new-born Mario in his arms. Catrina remembered how much she'd been jonesing for a hit that day. It had been pure hell to stay clean while she was pregnant. In another plain silver frame was a photo of Catrina sitting in the rocking chair in the nursery holding Mario when he was eight months old. In that picture she was wearing a real smile. She'd managed to stay clean after the birth, had to since she was nursing. She remembered it as the happiest time in her life, once she got past the withdrawal symptoms. Then all the happiness went away again when Mario was nearly three and she heard the siren song of heroin again.

Catrina sighed and looked over her shoulder after Jorge, and caught sight of the altar laid out in the pass through to the kitchen. Ever the good son, Jorge had placed photos of his mother and grandmothers, festooned with marigolds, with *ofrendas* of candied pumpkin, sugar skulls, and *atole*. Little votive candles in red and orange and yellow flickered in front of the pictures, casting them in flattering light. The corners of Catrina's mouth quirked up as she remembered making sugar skulls with Mario, during one of her attempts to stay clean, shaping them and carving the names of his foremothers into them. And he would beg for a sugar skull of his own, but Jorge would tell him not yet.

Jorge slid back into the recliner. "He's fine. Must have been my imagination."

"So how have you been?" Catrina finally asked after long moments of silence.

"Fine. Very busy," Jorge said.

"Doing what?"

"Taking care of Mario, working, going to law school . . . ."

"So you're finally going." Catrina smiled. "I guess it's easier to pay for classes without me stealing your money all the time."

"Yeah, I guess it is." He paused. "So how have you been?"

"Okay, I guess," she said. "Salvatore's not hitting me right now, the guys at the bar are tipping okay, the other girls are getting used to me. . . . They're not being as bitchy, you know?"

"Actually, I don't, but I'll take your word for it."

Once again, the silence stretched, and they both stared at the floor. Jorge twiddled his thumbs while Catrina tapped her toes in a staccato rhythm. She stopped and Jorge looked up.

"Let's get back together," she said the words in a rush.

"If you had me you wouldn't want me," Jorge said sadly.

"Try me," she said in a desperate whisper.

"I already have." His lips twisted into a wry smile.

Catrina paused, staring at him. "Couldn't we just try?"

Jorge took a breath as if to speak, then clamped his jaw shut. He reached for the remaining bills on the table and started straightening them one by one. Catrina slid from the couch to her knees and crawled to Jorge until her chin rested on his knee.

"We could work, you know. It wasn't all bad," she whispered.

"That's not the point," Jorge said tightly. "It's never all bad. I wasn't enough for you."

Catrina rose up higher on her knees using her shoulders to pry his legs apart. She slid her hands up his thighs as she rose, her breasts sweeping across his groin. Jorge swallowed hard and shut his eyes tight.

"I promise I'll be good this time," she breathed.

"Don't make promises you can't keep." Jorge turned his face away presenting his cheek to her lips. She kissed him on the cheek, her lips barely making contact. Then she kissed the corner of his mouth more firmly but still gently. His breath was coming faster, and he turned his face back to her. She kissed him full on the lips, pinning him back in the chair with her eagerness. He wrapped his arms around her, returning her kiss with the same fever. When their lips parted, Jorge grabbed Catrina's shoulders and pushed her away.

"No."

"Why not?" she said. "I promise, no drugs, no parties. I'll get a real job."

"That's just what you said last time." His eyes were desperate. "And the time before that. Why should now be any different?"

"Because I'm telling the truth," her voice cracked. "I know I've been wrong and I'm ready to change."

"I've heard all of this from you before, Catrina," he said. "But now it's not just me who suffers. You tear Mario apart every time you walk in and out of his life. I can't be your safety net anymore, I just can't." Their harsh breathing echoed in the silent apartment.

"I gotta go," Catrina said through clenched teeth.

"Fine," Jorge said. He strode across the apartment, opened the door and stood holding it for her. Catrina wobbled to her feet, almost losing her balance on her stilettos. She straightened her jacket and patted her hair, then stomped to the door. She stopped and lit her cigarette and blew a big cloud of smoke right into his face.

"I hate you," she growled.

She passed up the elevator in favor of a quick and noisy exit by the stairs. Jorge shut the door and finished with the locks. He sighed and rubbed his eyes. There would be no more studying tonight. He could never concentrate after a visit from Catrina. He drifted into the kitchen and threw out his cold coffee, capped the open highlighter, shut the book after dog-earing the page, blew out the candles, and went to bed.

C3EOC3EO

Outside, Catrina stood in the rain and watched the lights in the apartment turn off one by one. Then, the apartment was dark. The only light in the neighborhood came from the all night diner down the street to her left. A damp, chilly November wind twirled her hair in lazy swirls. She could hear the sounds of traffic on the highway off in the distance to the right. She ground out her cigarette on the street and reached under her jacket, absently scratching at the track marks on her arm. The most recent ones started to bleed. Catrina stepped out of her stilettos and left them lying in the gutter next to an abandoned jack-o-lantern as she turned toward the highway and started to walk. After five miles, her stockings were torn and her feet were starting to bleed. She started stumbling as she crossed the parking lot of a truck stop right on the edge of the highway.

"Hey Catrina!" called a voice from the darkness. Catrina stopped and turned.

"Oh, hey Bunny. What's up?" Catrina asked with no interest.

"What's up with you? You look like hell. Did Salvatore throw you out again?"

"Nah, just going for a walk. Trying to clear my mind, you know?"

"In your bare feet on a crappy night like this? C'mon, let's go inside. I'll buy you a cup of coffee and we'll talk about it." Bunny tried to take Catrina's arm and lead her into the truck stop coffeehouse.

"No really, I'm okay." Catrina pulled her arm away. "Anyway, I wouldn't want to take you away from business."

"Business sucks on a night like this, you know that. C'mon, talk to me. If it isn't Salvatore who is it? Some john from the bar getting you down?"

"I haven't turned tricks in a long time, Bunny. Nobody seems to want to fuck me anymore, except Salvatore and only when he's high."

"I didn't wanna say anything, but you're a bag of bones and drugged out half the time. Can you blame the guys? Most of them can get a girl like you without paying."

"I know. I . . ." Catrina hung her head and turned to walk away.

"Hey! C'mon!" Bunny grabbed her arm and stopped her. "It's not that bad. I'm just trying to help you here. Look, we'll go back to my apartment, and I'll make you some soup. You can stay with me for a while; I've been pulling down some good cash. We'll put a little more meat on your bones and cut back on the drugs, and the guys will want just as bad as before. You'll have your pick just like you used to."

"Thanks, but I can't do that. It's too much on you."

"Did you say it was too much when you dragged me away from that jerk, Buddy? When he was beating me and taking all my money?" Bunny got right into Catrina's face. "No. You got Eddie to beat him up, and you got me out of there. And how long did I stay at your place? Six months? You never said a word. I'd be dead if it weren't for you."

"That was a long time ago, Bunny. Things are different now."

"Not that different. C'mon, talk to me."

"It's Jorge. . ." Catrina began but her voice caught in her throat.

"What? That yuppie loser you had a kid with? He's not worth getting upset over."

"Yeah, you're right." Catrina pulled her arm away again. "I'm okay really. I'm just going to go hitch a ride home and get some sleep. I promise."

"You're really sure? 'Cause you can stay with me anytime, you know that?"

"Yeah, of course I know it. I'm not stupid." Catrina dug into her pockets and pulled out the money Jorge had given her. "Oh, by the way—here."

"What's this for?" Bunny laughed. "You want me to start turning lesbian tricks? Shit, if I'd known the pay was this good, I would've done it a long time ago."

"Nah, just trying to say thanks. So shut up and take it."

"Alright." Bunny looked at her closer. "Are you sure you're okay? You can stay with me tonight, last chance."

"Don't worry about me. I've never seen things clearer." Catrina forced a smile.

"Okay. Well, see you later?"

"Yeah, sure."

Bunny looked at Catrina for a moment longer, then shrugged and walked away. Catrina turned and made for the highway. The gravel on the shoulder bit into her feet and made them bleed more. Catrina stood on the side of the highway and smiled for real as she looked around at the pre-dawn fog that rose almost to her shoulders. She waited for just the right moment and stepped out into the headlights of an oncoming semi truck.

Bunny could hear the brakes squeal from across the truck stop as the driver locked them up. She cursed to herself and did her best to sprint to the highway in high heels. By the time she got there, the driver was out of his cab and staring slack-jawed at the bloody mess on the pavement in front of his grill.

"What did you do? What did you do?" Bunny shrieked, and she pushed past him and dropped to her knees next to what was left of Catrina, sobbing.

"I didn't see her! I swear I didn't see her! She just came out of nowhere." The trucker's voice shook and cracked.

CREXGRED

Across town a ten-year old boy lifted his head off the pillow when he felt a cold draft that smelled like marigolds caress his cheek.

"Mom?"

But he was alone. Everything in the room was as he expected. His backpack on his desk packed for school the next day, dirty jeans and socks scattered across the floor. His Superman costume from Halloween slung carelessly across his chair, and the hand-made *calacas*, made with care by his Uncle Benito, hung carefully on the back of his bedroom door.

There was a strange creak and the boy whipped his head around with a gasp. Nothing but the old rocking chair his mother used to sit in to nurse him as a baby, slowly rocking back and forth in a non-existent breeze.

The Marigold Path

Teagan Maxwell

"*Aquí! Here!*" The woman was a shadow waving at him frantically from beyond the lights of the camp. The priest had never been a man of the people, and particularly not of women, but there was a note in the fear-pitched voice that he couldn't ignore, like the drone of a pipe organ at a Sunday Mass. The voice commanded him to follow it, like the organ commanded followers to worship. Father Ramirez thought nothing of it to leave his tent and walk towards the woman. When she turned and began walking away from him, he thought nothing of following her.

Here, in the desert outside Juarez, no man had followed a woman in a long time, though many had led them—hundreds of them—to shallow graves.

At dawn, the priest had been meant to honour them. Dawn heralded the beginning of the Day of the Dead.

CRSOCRSO

Father Ramirez had long ceased walking, by his definition of the word. His legs, numb stumps, drove one foot into the warm sand in front of him, tipping his weight forward until the other foot swung forward to re-balance him.

It had been full dark when he had left the camp, but now the desert was dyed a deep pink with purple shadows in the rippling ridges of sand. It seemed to the priest, who had also ceased knowing the time, that it had been that colour much longer than it should have.

With his legs working autonomously, the priest chanced a glance over his shoulder. The man in black and his deformed and shuffling horse were an oblong dark spot against the sun, which crept over the horizon, larger than Father Ramirez had ever seen it, and red as a searing coal. Father Ramirez could have sworn that his path during the night had been straight, but now thought he must have turned without realizing it, else the sun was in the wrong place. He could have sworn the woman had been leading him north.

Another rosary bead slipped through Ramirez's fingers.

Glory to the Father, the Son, and to the Holy Spirit ...

His lips formed the shapes of the words, but only the occasional sharp cough or soft *haaa* escaped his throat. His voice was dried out and damaged beyond repair after hours of prayers in the dry desert.

He had reached for the rosary with a shaking hand after the horse and its dark rider had charged him. Until that moment, he hadn't known whether they were innocent travelers walking the same, strange path, or shepherds. He had stopped and turned to face them, mouth opening to implore for help. The horse's angry scream and the irregular thunder of its hooves as it leapt towards him startled him. His attempt to break from the path and run had been swiftly blocked by a cloud of sand that cleared to reveal the horse, a black and ugly monster up close, and the rider, whose face was hidden by shadows thrown from a wide-brimmed black hat like those favoured by parade *vaqueros*. The animal had an agility that its size and twisted legs did not suggest, the rider, an intuition that his silence did.

"Please," Father Ramirez had begun, but the horse had flattened its ears against its head, and a deep growling noise made all the grains of sand on the desert floor shiver.

Shepherds indeed.

Not seeing any other choice, the priest had turned back to the path where, a quarter mile ahead, the woman stood waiting.

The weight of the rosary crucifix in his hand had granted, as it always did, a certain measure of comfort, and with that, a certain—though lesser— measure of defiance.

"I believe in God, the Father almighty, creator of Heaven and earth." His voice had been clear, pitched to deliver a sermon, win converts, pacify troubled Christian souls. Neither the horse, the rider, or the woman gave any indication of having heard.

It was then he had noticed the sun creeping over the horizon, timidly following the parade.

Now, he felt the Lord did truly work in mysterious ways. He was miles from his camp, and the lack of water and the dry air had already taken a toll on his throat. Even if he had wanted to, and he hadn't, he would never have been able to deliver the Mass he had been set to give this morning in the desert, where there were so many dead to honour on the Day of the Dead.

CRBOCRBO

"Hail Mary, full of grace, the Lord is with thee. Blessed art thou among women."

Father Ramirez heard and felt the growl in the ground again and wondered if he was still walking through Juarez's hidden boneyard. He didn't think so, he was too far north. He still had no idea of the time, but guessed that he could reasonably start looking for the American border on the horizon soon.

The woman had long ago stopped calling to him to follow her, but the horse and its dark rider made certain he did not stray. Her walk, which had been so darting and frantic when he had first started after her, now appeared as automatic as his own, though less tainted by exhaustion. Her poise gave her an air of being much older than her voice, her long bright hair, and the curves to which her dress clung, would imply. She was dignified in a way that Father Ramirez, whose life was dedicated to ceremony and ritual, found humbling. Even the marigolds in her hair did not wilt from the heat and the hours of dry walking.

Another bead slipped through his hand. Having lost his sense of time... he could have been walking for hours, perhaps even days, Father Ramirez was no longer sure which Mysteries he should be praying. With each new decade on the rosary, they all demanded his devotions at once, and his lips loosely shaped a few nonsense syllables before beginning the next round of prayers. Though his mind shied away from the blasphemy of it, Father Ramirez found no solace in the Mysteries in his present situation. The true mysteries were the horse and rider behind him, and the graceful woman in front of him. As the priest began another Hail Mary, he found, for once, that he could not form Mary's image in his mind, but saw only marigold-strewn hair, and a strong, straight back.

CRBOCRBO

The clockwork of the priest's limbs seized up without a sip of water to sustain him. He stumbled once, recovered, then collapsed onto the sand, and did not even try to rise.

Behind him, he heard the horse stamp its hoof, and felt the ground shiver again. He didn't move though his fingers twitched on the crucifix of his rosary and, lacking the strength to even call to mind the last rites, he thought only: *I believe in God, the Father Almighty, the Son, and the Holy Spirit.* The horse's scream dissolved his prayer like a mist and he gave up, hoping it would be enough. His body shook against the ground like a doll as the horse's pounding hooves drew near.

Sand sprayed across his back and he felt coolness on his neck from the horse's shadow. There was a metallic rattling and then a thud as the *vaquero* swung out of the saddle and dropped to his knees beside the priest, grabbing his shoulder and hauling him over onto his back. Father Ramirez kept his eyes closed and let his head roll to the side.

Gloved fingers grabbed his chin and forced him to face skyward, and the priest's eyes opened at the sound of a *pop*. The *vaquero*, head still angled to keep his face just out of sight, held out a flask of water, and poured a cool stream over Father Ramirez's lips.

The water lifted the priest's body out of automatic pilot, and with the new energy and strength of will, he threw up one arm and swept the black hat off the *vaquero*'s head.

His scream came out as a dried-up bark.

Above the *vaquero*'s black shirt, there was the cruel head of a dog. Its nose was flat and out of place; its lips twisted to reveal yellow teeth dripping hot saliva that burned through the priest's shirt. The growl that had made the sand dance, now unshielded, made the priest's head and heart rattle, and shook the entire desert.

"*Xolotl*," said a woman's voice, speaking the language Father Ramirez had only seen written by the ancient Aztec scholars.

The psychopomp looked up, then reached for the priest and took his hat back. He stood up and inclined his head before hiding his terrible face again underneath the black brim. "*Mictecacihuatl*," he said in a voice that only sounded like a more cultivated uttering of his growl. He turned to his horse and mounted without another word.

A long hand of bones appeared before the priest's eyes, and he sat up to get a better look at its owner. Bright hair and marigolds framed a skull which, even with its natural grin, looked grim.

"Come, Father Ramirez."

It was not the frantic, vulnerable voice of the shadow in the night, but there was that note in it still, that organ drone of authority, that had drawn him out of his tent.

Father Ramirez took the hard hand, and stood, his other hand clutching the rosary.

His throat, now lubricated, allowed him to actually say the words. "Glory be to the Father, the Son, and the Holy Spirit ..."

"Please stop." The Lady of Death's voice was gentle, even as it left no room for argument. "This is not the day for your Mary, or your Holy Ghost, Father. This is my celebration, and there are so many dead to honour in the desert." Her head turned slowly, casting her empty sockets over the featureless land. "They are waiting for you, Father. They have questions they will not accept answers to from me."

Without relinquishing the priest's hand *Mictecacihautl* began to walk north again. Father Ramirez followed her, his exhaustion ebbing away to be replaced by a grey state of being, ever with enough energy to keep walking, but never to run, just as the desert ever gave him a place to walk, but never to enjoy. The purple shadows in the rippling ridges of sand lengthened as the *vaquero* and his black horse fell back with the sun behind them. This was purgatory without hope of relief or release.

From Father Ramirez's other hand, the rosary untangled itself from his fingers, and not even the priest himself could be certain whether he dropped it by accident or deliberately. As the loops of beads fell away from him, Father Ramirez whispered his last devotion.

"Hail Mary, full of grace, the Lord is with thee. Blessed art thou among women, and blessed is the fruit of thy womb, Jesus."

The crucifix slipped from his hand, and Father Ramirez never prayed again. *Mictecacihuatl*, whose life was dedicated to ceremony and ritual, finished it for him as sincerely as a bishop. "Holy Mary, Mother of God, pray for us sinners, now and at the hour of our death."

The black horse and the psychopomp followed, and as they passed the rosary, the horse's hoof dragged a drift of sun-pink sand over it, burying the Christian blasphemy in the Aztec underworld forever.

"Amen."

Día de los Musicos

Alison J. Littlewood

The shops were full of bones. I pressed my face up against the glass of
Old Pancho's store and saw skeletons among the pickles, skulls piled
up between baseballs and catapults. My brother was next to me. We tore
ourselves away and our noses left twin smears on the glass.

"Come on," Jackson said, and nudged me in the ribs. We jammed together
in the doorway, then went in. Someone pushed past us. I recognized the
black skirt with pink flowers on it, Mrs. Rodriguez's solid brown legs. She
went out, tutting, and the bell rang. Old Pancho's bell announced departure,
not arrival: I didn't know why.

Jackson stared at the shelves. Where tins had been, there were coffins,
figures in black cloaks, white bones. I could smell the sugar. Somewhere a
fly buzzed and there was a blue flash from the thing that looked like a heater
above the counter. The smell of cooked fly joined the other smells: sweets,
the dry aroma of flour, chilies, and the tang of papaya. Not like home, or
what I still thought of as home. Even the smells were different here. It was
the heat, I thought. And the food, and the dogs, and the dust.

"*Día de los Muertos*," Old Pancho said. He was always *Viejo* Pancho, Old
Pancho; even the really old people called him that. He wore a khaki shirt two
tones paler than his skin. His face was wrinkled and reminded me of the
walnuts they put inside piñatas along with toys and candy.

"We honour the dead," Old Pancho said in English. "Saturday. We go to
the cemeteries and honour our ancestors. Our ancestors who are buried in
this land."

I glanced at him sharply, but saw he didn't mean anything by it.

"We light candles and sing songs. Give them good things to eat. They
deserve a feast once a year, no?" He laughed. "And the *musicos* come. The

players. The dead players, who will give music to soothe their souls back to sleep. Sometimes it is well to be sure that visitors have gone, no? No matter how welcome. You'll see. Your father, he must pay them the tribute. He is the great man of the village now. A rich man, no?"

I frowned. What did he mean, tribute? Dad was a technical project manager in the mines; that was all. But then Jackson pushed me in the back, and I put out a hand to save falling into the shelves. When I looked around, he'd put two fat skulls on the counter and was counting out *pesos* and *centavos*. Jackson always carried the money. I still wasn't used to the currency.

We sat on the step outside and Jackson pushed a skull into my hand. It had an 'H' for Harrison on the top, and his had a 'J'. I tried to bite into it, the hardened sugar scraping against my teeth.

"Don't bite, idiot," said Jackson. He licked his over and over until it shone. "Lick it, 'til your tongue goes through. Then we'll see how many brains you have."

I licked it then casually shook the skull, listening for a rattle from inside. Jackson jumped to his feet. He kicked my foot and ran off, laughing.

ය෬ය෬

"Superstition," said father when Saturday dawned. "A silly ritual, that's all it is."

Our faces fell.

"But you can go and see it if you want. It'd do you good to take in some local colour. You need to start school soon. Make some friends."

I sighed. I had friends; my friends were in England. I didn't want new friends.

"He says you have to pay a tribute," I said.

Dad looked at me as though a snake had slithered into the house.

"That's what he said."

But dad wasn't listening anymore. He had turned back to the papers on his desk.

ය෬ය෬

We went to the store first and bought more sweets, stuffing our pockets with sugary bones. Then we went to the cemetery. People gathered among the headstones: Mrs. Rodriguez in her best flowery skirt; old ladies wearing black all over; kids done up in their best clothes. Jackson nudged me but I didn't need telling. We stopped pushing each other and walked like we knew where we were going.

All around us, faces looked out from the headstones. It wasn't like

England, where they carved words on your grave. Here they had faces, pictures of a smiling lady, a young girl, an old man with white hair. They all looked out and people came to see them. They piled sweets on their graves, and flowers, poured glasses of wine or mescal.

"They return tonight. They will drink your health," a voice said in my ear. It was Old Pancho.

"They return every year. They eat and drink, and so are made happy. Happy enough to sleep again for another year, hey?"

I nodded, though I didn't know what he was talking about. Jackson stood behind him, twirling his finger next to his ear. Crazy. But I daren't laugh.

Then bright, sweet notes came to my ears, and everyone turned to listen.

It sounded like a clarinet, a slow march, ready and wavering and travelling easily over the dry ground. It was mournful and steady and sad. Jackson opened his mouth to say something then closed it again.

Something else joined the clarinet, a deep bass thrumming. There was a dry rattle, too, like cicadas.

"They begin," said Pancho.

A banjo darted out a tune between the other sounds. My leg started to twitch. Old Pancho saw it and smiled.

"It weaves its spell, no?" He held out his hand. "Come."

He led us towards the sound, and the skeletons appeared. They were tall, taller than I was or Jackson. Taller than Old Pancho. Everyone stood in a circle and listened, even the children, their dark eyes fixed on the bones that jerked faster and faster over an old double bass. Men stood with their heads bowed and plump mothers tapped out the rhythm against their skirts. The banjo player's white bones danced over the strings.

I saw that the musicians were wearing black suits. The bones were painted over the top, so that they moved as they did. I let out a long breath and Jackson dug me in the ribs.

The music stopped. The banjo player held up his hand.

"The tribute," he said. And suddenly, everyone was looking at us. Jackson looked around before turning to stare at me, and one by one the others followed his gaze.

"Your father sent the tribute?"

It was Old Pancho.

"He should have come himself," said the man who played the banjo.

"It matters not," said Old Pancho. "This boy has brought the tribute. Have you not, young master Harrison?"

I blinked.

"You must pay them," he hissed.

I turned to look at Jackson. He flinched, but kept his eyes on me. His hands had crept towards his pockets. His fingers twitched under the fabric, searching through the sweets and feeling the edges of the coins he kept there. As I watched, he shook his head.

Old Pancho waited. Then he started towards the players. "I have it," he said. He pulled *pesos* from his pockets and pushed them into the banjo player's hands, pushing his fingers closed around the money. It disappeared into some hidden pocket and yet the player shook his head. He was still looking at me, even when he waved his arm and the band struck up another tune.

This one was slower than the first. It had a dark, ominous air. It seemed to spread a bad feeling among the crowd. They kept turning to me and scowling. Jackson didn't look at me at all.

"They're not happy," hissed Old Pancho.

Jackson nudged me. "Come on," he said, and we backed away from them all, Old Pancho and the families and the music. The sound followed us through the cemetery. I tripped over some edging and almost fell.

"Come on," said Jackson again, and I did; but realized he had stayed where he was, perfectly still, staring at one of the graves.

There were bright flowers piled on it, yellow and blue and pink. There were glasses of wine and milk, and a carriage made of sugar in which the figure of a young girl lay. A large grey rat sat on top of it, whiskers trembling. As I watched, it nibbled the young girl's hair.

Behind us there was a shriek. "Maria, Maria!" a woman's voice rose up, and she pushed past, waving her arms. The rat jumped down from the carriage and it fell, spilling the sugar figure onto the ground.

The rat knocked over a glass of wine, splashing the girl with crimson. The woman shrieked again. "You, you!" she said, grabbing my arm. I pulled away and we ran. As we went, we saw that more rats were coming. They nibbled bones, trampled flowers, lapped at sugar skulls. The last thing I saw as we ran through the cemetery gates was a large black rat atop a skull that was clearly marked with the letter 'H'.

"There's no feast left," I said, back at the house. Jackson still hadn't spoken.

"There's nothing left for the dead people to eat. They'll be angry."

Jackson pushed past me, into his room, and closed the door in my face.

C≋∞C≋∞

I thought about it all that day, scores of dead people coming home and finding no welcome, nothing for them to eat. How many would come, I wondered. Some of the families must go back for generations. It was not a large village, but it was an old one.

Jackson hadn't appeared for dinner. Dad said he wasn't hungry. I toyed with my food, thinking of those dead, empty mouths. I wasn't hungry either, and I could feel the uneaten candy in my pockets, sticking into me as though it really were made of bones.

I went to my room. Out of the open window I saw that night was closing in, the sky streaked purple and orange. A cool breeze drifted through the room. I shivered. Then I thought I heard something; a soft sigh that went on and on, like air flowing over the rim of a bottle.

I could just make out the first faint stars. But lower down, where adobe walls loomed out of the gathering dark, more stars walked in the streets.

They grew brighter, each following the next, towards the cemetery. It was candlelight. And dark shapes moved against the walls, wavering and stretching before subsiding once more.

I caught my breath and leaned out. The figures were closer now. One of them had dark holes where his eyes should be. Another had the face of a devil. Ghosts, all of them, going home.

Then I heard a laugh. Saw a swirl of bright skirt. They weren't ghosts, at all. They were villagers, walking in procession towards the cemetery. They wore masks: Devils. Witches. Skeletons. All were there, moving towards the graves.

My heart began to hammer. What would they do there? Would they drive away the rats? I imagined them leaping about, shouting and howling. I wanted to see. I crept out into the hallway.

Jackson's room was next to mine, but I couldn't hear any sound. It wasn't like him to be asleep so early. I paused. I had never been outside without him. He always went first, leading the way, doing the talking.

I scowled, remembering how he had kept silent, his hands all the time feeling the money in his pockets. Alone, then. I tiptoed down the hallway, pulled open the door, and went out.

The night air was pure and clean, the sky deeply black, the stars brilliantly light. I was used to brightness streaming upward from streetlights and windows, but here the houses were nothing but black shapes. It was the sky that was alive, illuminating everything.

Voices murmured in the distance. I saw a last flicker of candlelight and headed after it, my feet scuffling in the dust. I could smell something too, the faint scent of sugar that was somehow dank and made me think of ruin.

As I walked, the first notes began. They were faint but lithe, and I looked down, half expecting to see them twining around my feet. The cemetery gates were a dark outline. As I watched, a shape, nothing but a shadow, slipped inside.

I hurried after it, wondering who it was. Old Pancho, maybe, or one of our neighbours. But when I reached the gates, the view of the cemetery stopped me short.

It was lit by a thousand candles. They wavered, sending countless shadows dancing among the graves. My mouth fell open.

Then I saw my neighbours, and I saw what they were doing. Music swelled, as though someone had suddenly turned up the volume on a radio.

They danced. In swirls of colourful skirts, with outflung arms, turning and bending and taking hands, they snaked through the cemetery. Behind the gravestones the bones of the *musicos* flashed and darted, faster and faster, flinging wild rills into the night air. My breath came faster. The music got inside my feet, my body, my mind. Then someone caught my hand and I was one of them, feet skipping and flying over the graves.

The line of dancers doubled back and I thought I saw Old Pancho, his mask hanging about his neck, mouth open with glee. I almost fell and the hand pulling me along gripped tighter. There. There was Mrs. Rodriguez, and Mrs. Delgado, and Valdez the baker. Their faces were lit as though from inside, as though they had starlight in their cheeks. I turned and twisted, trying to see who was behind me. The hand felt like bones: a glove, maybe.

The music changed tempo, quicker now, and I had to watch my feet. I glanced up to see Mrs. Rodriguez sending a whoop up, up, into the sky.

Then I saw the figure behind her and almost fell once more.

There was a shadow following Mrs. Rodriguez. Its hand was in hers, and yet it was insubstantial, like breath fading on a window.

The dance moved on. Knees, hands, masks, voices raised, hair flying, skirts flying. The notes went faster and faster and faster, and we went with them.

A shape that was nothing but a darker patch of night held onto Old Pancho's shirt-tails.

I blinked. It was gone.

Then the hand gripping mine pulled, hard, and I flew forwards, away from the line. I staggered, putting out a hand and righting myself against a grave. I was face to face with the picture of a young girl, no more than nine or ten. She was smiling. She seemed to stare into my eyes as the music suddenly, shockingly, stopped.

I turned. The dance had ceased. There were figures all around. But they were not the figures of my neighbours. I looked from one to the next and recognized no one.

A man stepped forward. As he emerged into the candlelight I saw that half his face was missing. I could see the white bone of his jaw. I tried to step away and felt the headstone at my back. There was a woman whose hair flowed down over her body, but between the black pools I could see her ribs.

A girl. I tried not to look. But she was there, a girl I recognized, no more than nine or ten. Her body was smashed, as though crushed in a rock-fall or under the wheels of a truck. She met my eye but did not smile.

"*Banquete?*" said the man. He held out his hand. "*Banquete?* Where is our feast?"

"I'm hungry," someone else said. The words were ill-formed by swollen lips.

"*Hambriento,*" another agreed.

I looked from one to the next. There was nothing in their faces. No recognition. No kindness. Their eyes were flat and glassy.

I felt along the headstones at my back, hands slipping along the smooth stone. It was cold. I pulled them away, and as I did, my hands brushed against my pockets.

"Hungry."

"Our feast."

"Our tribute."

I looked up. Another man had spoken, the tall banjo player. But now his bones shone in the candlelight. Stars gleamed against an angle of his skull. He held out his hand.

I did the only thing I could. I felt for the bones in my pocket, the bones of sugar, the sweets shaped like skulls, cookies shaped like ghosts. I pulled them out and threw them as hard as I could towards the musicians. And when they bent towards their pitiful feast, their only welcome on this night of all nights, I put my head down and ran.

I ran until I reached the cemetery gates. There I paused, but only for a moment. Around the graves, a procession wove. People were dancing, although I couldn't hear the sound. I thought I saw Old Pancho waving his arms. There was Mrs. Rodriguez, throwing back her head; but I couldn't hear her cry.

Away among the graves, figures stood. They raised their hands to their mouths, and sucked, and licked, and crunched on the bones. I thought I could see the banjo player, taller than the others. For a moment, I thought he turned towards me and bowed his head.

I saw no more. I ran home, shut the door to my room, pulled the window closed and barred it, too.

CXEOCXEO

The next day, we went to Old Pancho's store. Jackson said he wanted to buy sweets. I didn't want any, didn't think I could bear the heavy, cloying scent of sugar. But I did want to see Old Pancho. Just to look into his face; to see if he would give any sign that what I had seen was real.

Jackson went in ahead of me, looking at the *churros* and sweet *empanadas*. There were no skulls today. No coffins. No funeral processions winding their way between the tins and packets.

Jackson piled the things he wanted on the counter, but it was me Old Pancho was looking at. I stared back at him, seeing the way his eyes were pale and watery, but knowing and sharp just the same.

I pulled the coins from my pocket. Slowly I counted them out and put them on the counter. Jackson pulled a face, but gathered up his sweets without saying anything. He hadn't said anything when I took our money from his pockets either.

Old Pancho didn't look at the money. He kept staring at me, as though sizing me up. Then, almost imperceptibly, he nodded.

I nodded back. Then I followed Jackson out of the store, to see what the new day held. The sun was rising higher and beginning to glare bright gold in a pale blue sky.

The door closed behind us, and as it did, Old Pancho's bell sounded a single musical note.

La Calaca

Olga Sanchez Saltveit

L a Calaca felt a rumbling in the place where her belly had been many years before. Her fingers, clothed in black suede gloves, poked at the starched bodice of her dark linen dress to find the source. The dress she wore covered her frame like skin, from the high antique lace collar to her six-button leather boots, and from one embroidered cuff to the other. She placed her gloved hand where her soft fleshy waist had been a century earlier, but only felt the cold cavity and then, probing more deeply, the bony inside edge of her spinal column. No guts, just vertebrae. She laughed at her own phantom sensation, releasing a dry huff so cool that it chilled her teeth and made her hollow ribs click like bamboo chimes. The marrow had long ago dried away.

She knew well the reason for the rumble in her bones. Borne of the dry emptiness in her dress, it was her annual hunger for flesh, signaling like an alarm clock. Not unlike the living, whose stomachs grumble when their regularly scheduled meal is delayed, La Calaca woke up every year restless for meat and blood and a glass of deep red wine. If the night went well, as it had in years past, the meal would only form one part of her sensual feast. She would smell a rose in her hair, hear the sounds of piano and guitar, and tango in the arms of a lover or two. Tonight she wished for a long mane of chocolate brown hair.

The people call it *el día de muertos* but ancient souls like her preferred to call it *la noche*. It was a splendid time, *la noche*, when shadows fell through the thin veil that draped across her face and softened the sharp edges of her skull. In those shadowy moments, La Calaca looked almost alive again, and attractive. Her depth, her silence, her vast nothingness were always alluring to flesh-and-blood lovers, men or women, who would follow La Calaca like puppies to even darker locations, a back alley, a smoky room, or to the end of a foggy pier.

La Calaca would begin tenderly, gently stroking her lovers, remembering her long gone body. They could never tell that underneath her dress, gloves, boots and stockings remained only her bones. She preferred it that way; the few times she had dared reveal herself had only frightened her lovers. She wanted them to enjoy their moments with her. Caressing their soft flesh, smelling sweat, and feeling their hearts beat faster under her practiced touch, these proofs of her prowess excited her. Before too long, she would give in to her passion, tugging at their flesh, pulling their hair, biting skin and drawing blood. They would fight to escape, but she was determined. The harder her lovers resisted, muscle to bone, life to death, the stronger she became. The fiercer the battle, the more exquisite her conquest. Looking in their eyes as they finally surrendered, she would absorb their broken wills through her dark sockets, like a child drinking the last of the chocolate milk through a straw. Her skull would fill with a surge of life, and for a few brief moments she was alive again, flesh and blood and ecstasy! The stronger her lovers, the longer these fleeting orgasms of life lasted.

She waited all year long for these moments, watching the green spring buds mature into lush summer foliage, then dry to warm yellows, hot oranges, and fervent reds until they finally fell from their trees. She admired their tenacity, how they held on for dear life. Their last rally against the consuming flame of time whetted her appetite.

When the moon rose on the second of November, La Calaca awoke and ventured into the night of the dead, hungry.

ﺣﻬﺣﻬ

At 6pm on November the second, the lovers Carlos y Patricia were sitting at a table for two in La Cantina de la Cruz, making plans for the future. They had met only a few months earlier, in late spring, on a Thursday morning in the market. She carried a basket of fruit and flowers, and he, a loaf of warm bread. They bumped into each other stepping away from the tables of corn and tomatoes, and her elbow brushed his. Their skin as firm as ripe peaches, they smelled like breakfast and heaven to each other, and when their eyes met for the first time they recognized each other profoundly, in the way that only strangers can. All that was missing to make the morning complete were two cups of café con leche. So, after excusing himself for bumping into her, and hoping to make up for the imposition, Carlos introduced himself and boldly asked Patricia permission to invite her for coffee. He recommended La Cantina de la Cruz facing the *zócalo* and the church and she agreed. He took her basket and they said nothing more as they walked, only glancing at one another from moment to moment to make sure they were still side by side, headed in the same direction. He ordered the coffees but they remained silent through the steaming of milk and brewing of fresh coffee, sitting face to face until the coffees arrived and they took their first sips. Warmed, they began, sharing their names, their birthplaces, their neighborhoods, their family arrangements, and more. As the hours passed, they found themselves sharing things they had never dared reveal to others. His passion for word games, her love of the rain, the things others never seemed to appreciate.

By no means children, Carlos y Patricia had met after years of misplaced affection, giving their hearts to people who invariably gave them back damaged. In those lonely times, they often felt La Calaca's cool breath on the back of their necks, a chilling reminder of their mortality, though of course they mistook it for a winter's breeze. They would turn up their collars and continue onward. They deeply believed (and no heartbreak had yet shaken this faith) that someday they would find love and be loved with all the heat and complexity two souls could impart. On that fateful Thursday morning in the market they found in each other the hearts they longed for. They reached out carefully to touch each other to make sure they were not dreaming, but once assured, they drank each other up body and soul like water to their long drought.

Five months later, their affection showed no sign of weakening. Their trust in each other grew daily, and so, they began making plans. Carlos had worked steadily for years to secure a living but now decided he wanted to go back to school, to finish his accountant's course of study. He wanted to get a better job, marry Patricia and raise their family. Patricia wanted to marry Carlos, too, but not just yet. She wasn't being coy; she was well into her child-bearing years and knew that it would only be harder to conceive the longer she waited. However, she had learned that even the most passionate of love affairs needed the test of time to prove their worth. And so their plans were marked by caution as well as love, by mutual admiration, optimism, and a healthy dose of self-respect. They talked about the entrance exam Carlos was preparing to take and the color of the hallway in his little house, which Patricia felt should be painted a brighter, livelier shade of yellow. They held hands across the table and hoped for the best, as the hours passed and the moon rose full and orange over the horizon.

Through the window of La Cantina de la Cruz, La Calaca saw them gazing into each other's eyes, stroking each other's fingers and smiling. Such romance! She could practically smell their warm blood pumping, and hear their hearts beating under their tender skin. She wanted them, either one, it made no difference, they were equally enticing. She chose them for tonight's meal.

The couple lingered in the little restaurant, watching as others put the finishing touches on the *Día de Muertos* decorations in the *zócalo*, adding fresh *cempasuchitl* flowers and *pan de muertos* to the large altars, hanging *papeles picados* across the streetlamps. Musicians and actors rehearsed their parts for the candle-lit procession from the church to the cemetery. On this night, everyone in town celebrated the sweetness of life.

Carlos could resist no longer. He invited her to his house for dinner. Patricia blushed, for she knew that this evening's dinner would lead to breakfast tomorrow. She nodded and they finally left the cantina. They walked to his home with her hand nestled in the warm crook of his arm. La Calaca followed behind, keeping her distance, for when she neared them, they felt her chilly presence and only huddled closer to each other for warmth. She had played this game for many years with others. She would wait until they separated to approach.

Dinner was delicious, stewed beef and several glasses of red wine as the moon rose higher. They ate lightly, tasting without filling themselves, knowing full well their hunger would not be satisfied by food. Patricia was no innocent virgin; after dinner they moved into his room, where he opened the window a little and closed the door. They fell naturally into each other's arms. Removing layer after layer of clothing, they explored the bodies they had only until then imagined. To their delight they found reality surpassed their imagination. They had touched others before but never felt skin so full of soul. They had been touched by others as well, but had never felt so *felt*. In the flecks of color that spotted their eyes they entered a small grove of fruit trees. Sweetness, color and scent, they swallowed this nourishment whole heartedly. They kissed the taste of ripe mangoes, passion fruit and tangerines on each other's lips. They nearly inhabited each other that night, coming close to making each other their home. Looking up to each other's faces they had to catch their breath. In their eyes they found oasis and waterfall, word games and rain. They felt rinsed clean from the tops of their heads to the soles of their feet.

La Calaca watched through the window, hunger growing, belly growling louder than ever. She put her hand to her waist again but could not stop the noise.

The lovers kissed again and again and again. Their hearts flushed their brains with ideas, dreams, and visions of the future. They tried to speak them but the images were a tangled mess of threads, some so delicate that close inspection might break them, and others so thick they were afraid they would become bound by them. But as the night passed, they unraveled these strands and slowly revealed them to each other: grandchildren running down their yellow hallway, the aroma of chicken, onion, chile and lime on the stove when Carlos returned home from his day of bookkeeping, and dying side by side when the time came. They fell asleep in each other's arms.

Suddenly there was a scratch at the window. Patricia awoke and looked where the moon shone into the bedroom. La Calaca was standing there but Patricia only saw what looked like a thorny bush. She was far more intrigued by the big low moon in the dark sky further off. She rose and walked to the window, letting the moon's light illuminate her bare body. As Patricia breathed in the fresh night air, La Calaca inched closer to the window. Patricia felt the chill and was about to close the window when she heard the faint voice of La Calaca whispering to her. "He's lying to you," she said, "He'll never paint the hallway yellow." Patricia froze and listened as La Calaca whispered every doubt Patricia had ever held. "He'll be like all the others you've given your heart to, gone tomorrow." She stared at the moon looking for an answer, but the moon offered none as it sank lower and lower. "You should leave right now, before he wakes up," urged La Calaca, "Before he has time to break your heart."

Patricia turned to look at Carlos, a flesh-and-blood man sleeping in peace. Tonight was wonderful, as had been the last five months with him, but what would tomorrow bring, she wondered? Before falling asleep she had finally decided yes, she would weave the tapestry of her life with his forever. But she saw her clothes on the floor and began to pick them up. She found her blouse and put it on, then her skirt. La Calaca had hoped Patricia might leave the house just as she was, naked and vulnerable, but all that really mattered was that she leave. Patricia gathered up her shoes and looked around to see if she was leaving anything else behind. She glanced at the bed and saw Carlos looking at her. "If you're going to leave, you should leave when the sun comes up. It's dangerous out there at this hour." Patricia walked over to the window and looked out. The thorny bush seemed to gesture to her, to beckon her outside, and she felt an urge to climb out the window into the freedom of the unknown. "Patricia," said Carlos, "please come to bed, sleep with me." Yes, Patricia thought, she was imagining things, the voices and beckoning limbs; she needed sleep. She closed the window, took off her blouse and skirt, and climbed under the covers next to Carlos' warm body. He embraced her and said, "I love you," and she knew she could never leave him.

La Calaca smiled her cold lipless grin and shook her skull. This pair would not come out of the house tonight; they might never come out at all. She had wasted much of the night but the moon was still up. There was still time. She would find a shady corner near the *zócalo*, on the far side from the church. This late at night, hearts were so lonely, and so much easier to trap. As she walked away, the little house that held the lovers grew warmer.

The Catrinas Will Dance with Any Boy They Like

Lori Rader Day

The bells over the front door ring. My daughter, Faye, leads a trail of girls inside. I'm expecting two of them, friends of Faye's who work the registers and bag and carry out for customers after school. The rest of the girls are from Faye's basketball team. From the back, behind the deli and pastry counter, I can see Betsy and Tina settle their bags under the counter in the reflection of the tilted mirror over the register. They tie their aprons, the long strings circling their waists twice, and the other girls fan out to study the candy selection and the pop cooler. Faye laughs at something Betsy says and replies under cover, her hand over her mouth. Finally she leans into the mirror and waves at me. "Hey, Mom. Practice got cancelled."

"All you girls help yourself to a soda, okay?"

The chorus of their gratitude fills the empty store. The girls shuffle at the sliding doors of the cooler in impatience to get to their favorites. Loose shoelaces dance against the tile.

Faye comes down the aisle with her dark ponytail swinging. When she gets to the counter, I resist reaching over to touch her. She says, quietly, "You didn't have to do that."

"What? We can afford a few sodas. What will you do now?"

Faye, her chin down, picks at a sale sticker on the meat case. "Go home. Okay?"

I hate to think of her alone in the house. I prefer to see her safely in a pack like this, jostling with the other girls. "Homework, right?" Faye nods and goes back up front. The girls from the team file out, leaving Faye, Betsy, and Tina, who put their heads together and talk low until the bells chime again. Faye throws a wave over her shoulder and is gone.

The long aisles of the store fill up quickly with more kids and women trying to get home with dinner. I wrap chops and steaks and scoop hamburger into red-checked paper boats, put salamis and breads through their respective slicers. A couple of hours pass in a blur of familiar faces, and then I catch sight of an unfamiliar one. The woman I don't know waves Gina Gusser ahead of her, her head politely dipping so that her long black hair swings over her shoulders. She is pretty and tan, like she just got back from vacation. Gina wants sirloin sliced just so. I hand out the package and go through the bye-now's and we'll-see-you-soon's with her until she backs into Betsy, who is shelving spaghetti sauce in the center aisle. Betsy stands and walks Gina to the counter, asking about her son.

Betsy wants a date to the school's fall formal instead of going with Faye and Tina. Gina's youngest son, though, is already enlisted and away at boot camp. I wish I could tell Betsy to shush: Gina's voice goes brittle talking about her son with a war going on.

The woman at the counter smiles at me.

"What can I get for you?" I wipe my hands down the front of my smock. She stares. I look down to see I've smeared two streaks of blood across myself. I pull at the ties on the smock and let it slide to the ground. "Yes?"

"I'd like a cake. With a skull on it."

Because of the blood, I think I hear her wrong. "Sorry?"

"Could you do a skull? With flowers? You do the cakes? That's what the girl at the front said." She has a light accent. It isn't helping me decide what she's saying.

She takes a step down the counter and stands in front of the glass case of cakes and pies. She wears loose pants that drag the ground and sandals that make her look barefoot. The thin strap of her leather purse crosses over her chest and settles against her hip. Her hair is long. When she tosses her head, her big gypsy hoop earrings swing. The girls in town don't dress like this. She looks over what we have and then taps the glass toward the middle shelf. "Like that one, but with a skull and some yellow and red flowers?"

I'm still not sure what I'm hearing, but I go down to where she's pointing. It's a quarter-sheet cake, white icing, nothing fancy. I pull it out so that we can both take a look at it.

"A *skull?*" I turn the sheet cake around as though the empty canvas turned just so will help me see it. A skull. What would that look like? Jemmie Morgan's daughter decorated Jemmie's house in southwestern theme, all pinks and browns with dry sticks in a vase in the corner. Above the mantel there's a painting of an animal's skull, the creepiest darn thing I've ever seen. Faye and I went over there for dinner, and I could barely eat with that hollow-eyed thing staring at us. This was just after Carey died, and people were so interested in everything I did and how I spent my dinners and my weekends.

"I have a picture of what I mean," the woman says.

I hear a hiss. Betsy is leaning on the pork and beans shelf at the end of the far aisle. When the woman turns back to the cake case, Betsy hooks a thumb at her and gives me an earnest nod of her head. In this way I know that the woman is Janice and Bill Harding's new daughter-in-law. Janice was in yesterday with a cart full of guest food, more milk and meat than she and Bill would eat in a month. Billy, she said, went off to get married in Acapulco. When she left, the girls left the register and sat behind the bakery racks to moan to me about another of our boys lost to a city girl. You wouldn't think they'd care. They always talk about how they are going to college in two years and won't ever come back to Parks, Indiana, no thanks. But for now they are sixteen and stuck side-by-side to the same five hundred or so people they've known since birth and all the senior boys they liked last year went off to the Army or to college or to Acapulco to get married. These things seem like the end of the world to Betsy, especially. I could tell the girls all sorts of things that should make them feel better—that what worries them today won't worry them in a few days, that the dreams they have for themselves will change as they get older, that someday they might be happy with what would seem like a lot less to them now. But I have lived my whole life in Parks. I have no credibility. I don't know a thing.

Betsy and Tina had complained bitterly about Billy Harding and all the other things about Parks that bound them too tightly until Tina drifted back up to the front door to stare out at Main Street. I slipped Betsy a cupcake from the Martin kid's birthday order. I had made a few extra. Betsy sucked the icing off the wrapper and said, "Acapulco. You know why, right? She's Mexican or something."

"How do you know that?"

Betsy didn't know how she knew, but she knew.

Looking at the woman now, I would have just said Italian three generations back, but, sure, okay, Mexican or something. Dark hair, dark eyes, a tan like she's been sitting on a cruise deck. Doesn't mean anything, though. When he was alive, my husband, Carey, was tan year-round and he liked to talk about his Irish blood. If he really had any, I have no idea. Faye takes after him. She can go golden on a single sunny day. I've heard her friends pinch at her brown arms and tell her what a bitch she is for getting so tan.

The new Mrs. Harding pulls a stiff, folded bit of paper from her purse and slides it toward me. "Like this."

It's a postcard. On one side there is a color photograph of three skeleton ladies, their empty eye sockets and open, full-teethed mouths something worse altogether than Jemmie's painting. They are dressed in party gowns and hold bouquets of flowers. They have long bone necks and wear veils down their backs. Their bald bone heads are wreathed in flowers. I flip over the card. Blank, except for a few words of Spanish in light print. I don't know any Spanish.

"A *human* skull?" I'm not really thinking about the skull or what I'm saying. What comes to mind are the dark dreams: ghosts and other things I don't believe in scratching at my sleep. Less than they once did, of course, but I could still meet the sunrise if I let myself think too much about Carey. Specifically, Carey's thick body reduced to bones, which seemed a cruelty of knowing a little something about nature and decay. I had wished more than a few times that I knew less than I do. I fan myself with the postcard and look at the Hardings' daughter-in-law. "But why?"

She raises an eyebrow. "It's for a holiday. Like Halloween, but not quite."

Halloween is around the corner. I have orders for pumpkin cakes and black cat cakes and bat cakes and fifty chocolate cupcakes with orange icing for one of the class parties at the elementary school, but no one has ever ordered a cake with a dead person on it. Unless you count a vampire. I did a vampire last year. But I don't count it. A vampire is just in good fun.

I study the postcard. "I can do the cake." Of course I can. I've done TV characters that the kids request and movie stars the teen girls moon over. I did a muscle man type for a bachelorette party that looked, even made of icing, pretty sexy. But these dead ladies seem to me they were never meant for icing. Who'd want to eat it? The contrast between their elegant clothes and their flowers and the hollows for eyes. Or maybe it's the way they look like brides who will never make it to the altar. Maybe, simply, the fact of their deadness. They'd turn the butter cream sour. Wouldn't such a cake taste like a dish sponge wrung dry?

I lay the card down and lean on the counter to see the new Mrs. Harding better. She has her chin thrust forward, not embarrassed at all by her request. "I can do it, sure," I say. "I can do just about any cake. People like a pretty cake, though. Who are you feeding this to, if you don't mind me asking?"

She smiles as though we are playing a prank together. "Do you know my new in-laws?"

CR&CR&

"A skull? Mom, that is hilarious."

Faye stands on a kitchen chair in a pair of high heels I don't approve of. She doesn't need gold-sequined shoes with three-inch heels. She's already tall for a girl her age and thick in the arms from lifting weights with the team. I like to think that she's going to the dance with a group of girls because she's not boy crazy, but the truth is that she's sixteen. She's boy crazy. They all are. She's probably the girl who intimidates them, who could knock out their teeth in a game of pick-up. And so she goes to the dance with the girls because the boys don't ask. If she wore shorter shoes, she might get asked to dance at least. I don't mind dressing her up like a queen, though. It's one of the things I've been waiting for.

The loose hem of her dress pulls out of my hands. "Hold still, please. This won't be ready until college graduation if you keep dancing around."

The hem wiggles and bounces. I look up to find Faye shaking her rump to the commercial jingle coming from the TV in the next room.

"Your father would never have let you out of the house wearing this." I say it because that's what comes to mind, but I immediately regret it. I don't want to think about Carey right now. I want to take this dress up a single inch because I know this one unnecessary step will show off the muscles in Faye's legs. I know that at least one boy will not be able to keep his eyes off her, that this might be the last dance she will attend with her girlfriends. I hope for it and fear it. But it's true that Carey would be glaring and shaking his head from his recliner, grumbling about how much money the showgirl shoes had cost. "How many hours of servitude do I have to lay out for that?" he would have said. I would have started in on the calculations—as though facing one of those train-leaves-the-station math questions of Faye's—even as Faye cut him off with a grin, wise to him. She would have made monkey sounds at him until he had to give up the ghost and smile back.

Faye shifts on the chair, her shoes reflecting prisms of light across the kitchen cabinets and into the empty chair at the head of the table. Carey never sat there, but that's one of the spots in the house that make me think of him, like the old blue recliner and his half of the bed and the upstairs guest bathroom, where he shaved and left a mess. When I clean the house, I find myself hesitating in certain spots, as though a good dusting will wipe away something crucial: those little black hairs from his beard that collected in the sink basin. They are long gone, but Carey is everywhere in the house and nowhere at the same time. Most days, that is a compromise I can live with, and we leave the spaces that remind us of him empty.

"Maybe Dad would have *insisted* I wear this," Faye says. She puts a hand at her waist and juts her hip into my face. "Maybe he would have recognized I was too *hot* to keep in the house."

I swat at her butt. "Two more pins and then you can go take it off and get *out* of the house."

"Oh, so he'd be okay with me going outside naked."

I dig the postcard out of my back pocket and hand it to her to keep her busy. She flips it over. "*Día de los . . . muertos.*"

"Those three years of Spanish are paying off."

"Ha, ha. I know this holiday," Faye says. "We talked about this in Spanish class last week. There's a name for these—Catrina. The Catrinas. I remember because the guys teased Catrina Lofton for*ever* that day. I guess she is kind of skinny. These ladies are supposed to remind you that everybody dies."

"How lovely." I put the last pin in place and stand back to check the hem.

"Like, even rich people die."

"I'm sure Janice Harding can't wait to be reminded that she's going to die. A fine message for a pastry to deliver."

"The holiday *celebrates* the dead. I can't remember, though. Do they celebrate them to make them come back or to keep them away?"

"I wouldn't know, honey. All done."

After she goes up to change, I fish around in the junk drawer for a pen and sit at the kitchen table with a scribble pad. The skeleton ladies on the postcard are too much for a cake. I have to scale it back to something I can do in icing. I am figuring three pastry bags of icing, black, red, and yellow, on top of the white. I'll use the star tip to draw the skull, star by star. The star tip lets me fudge the shape a little, and if a star ends up in the wrong place, I can swipe it up with a fingertip and do another one. For the flowers, I'll use a different tip. But I'm not worried about the flowers. I've put plenty of flowers on cakes.

I smooth the postcard from Mrs. Billy Harding—that's how she signed the order form, such a silly new-bride thing to do—and sit to look it over more closely. The skeleton women's dresses are low cut over their exposed rib bones. And here is the thing that bothers me. It's more than the fact that they are dead ladies, and more than the way they are dressed for a party even so. The flesh is stripped from their bones, but here's the thing: They aren't neutral about it. They have expressions, really cranky, pissed-off expressions, as though they hate being always the bridesmaid, never the bride, as though they hate being dead. They don't look like the kind of dead you would want to invite back.

I draw some potato-headed skulls, practicing the shape of the eye sockets. My skulls look like Halloween decorations off the shelf of O'Dell's Pharmacy. Happy to be dead, pleased to hold a skull-full of candy for you, kiddo. I cannot begin to get the long, gumless teeth right. The mouths gape wide, smiling.

Faye comes up behind me and leans on my shoulder. "Those look . . . are they supposed to be scary or not?"

"All I have is the postcard."

She sits opposite me and puts her feet up on another chair. She wears the gold shoes with her shorts and t-shirt. I go back to the skulls. Some of them are making fun of me, their dead eyes somehow winking. I'm beginning to wonder how I'm going to get this cake done, after all. A skull is harder to draw in icing than I guessed. I picture Janice Harding standing over the finished product. One hand on her hip, the cake knife from her wedding silver in the other. Her lips tight with distaste as she tries to decide where to cut. I wish I could be a fly on the wall at the Harding house on Sunday, just to see Janice fake her way through a Day of the Dead party.

"Mom!"

"What? Sorry, what?"

"I said I looked it up in my textbook."

"Looked up what?"

"Mom, listen for a change, will you?" She takes a gold shoe off and places it upright on the tabletop, then the next.

I flip the notepad over and put down the pen. "Okay, I'm listening."

"Guess which it is. Is it to come back or go away?"

I don't know what she is talking about. "For who to come back or go— oh, you mean—"

"Yeah, the—you know." She flicks the postcard closer to me. "The dead. Their spirits."

Faye and I only have the one dead in common. She's staring at me across the table with eyes the same gray-green as his. I hadn't given any thought to what Mrs. Billy Harding's holiday was meant to do, and I'm surprised. Not to find that I can't guess the answer, because why should I? No, I'm surprised to find myself wondering which I hoped it was. If I had the choice to wish for Carey's spirit to make a move, would I wish for it to come back or to stay away? His body, fine. If I could have him back whole—his hard-to-buy-for long arms and thick wrists, the spot on the back of his head that had finally gone bald and shiny, the rank smell of him when he came home from a longer haul than normal, the whole of him as he had been—I would. No question. But a ghost version of him? Didn't we have that already?

To bring back the spirits or make them go away. It wasn't much of a choice. "To make them go away?"

It's the wrong answer. Faye swipes her jeweled shoes off the table into her arms and heads upstairs.

CB ED CB ED

It's hot in the bakery, but Betsy and Tina are settled on the back sink counter, comparing notes on the fall formal. The back pocket zippers on Tina's fatigues rattle against the metal countertop so that I keep looking over to make sure it's not someone tapping at the alley door with a delivery. I brush at a thread of sweat running down the side of my face with the crook of my arm. This morning I've already finished a surprise order of sweet rolls for the ladies group that meets across the street in the back of Sheffield's restaurant. Sheffield's oven is on the fritz, they said. The ladies have to have their sweet rolls. I'm practicing drawing with the star tip and a pastry bag of pink icing. Pink, because that's what I have left after finishing the roses on a little dinner cake Mary Anne Michaels wanted for her parents' anniversary party tonight. The pink icing barely shows up on the sheet of parchment I'm working on. The girls sit a few feet away and don't pay any attention to the death masks I make. In pink on white, the skulls are a fresh horror. A baby shower cake gone horribly wrong.

I have the Halloween orders done, too, as well as all the things people have come to expect: the popcorn balls, pumpkin cakes, orange cupcakes. Black cat cookies, the cats' backs arched. Halloween is tomorrow, but all the town's festivities are tonight. I have to go down to the O'Dell's Pharmacy for candy for the bell-ringers. The kids will start coming around early, but I'm out of time on Faye's dress, too. If Faye didn't have practice after school today, she could get the door, but I'll have to do both—bringing the empty white dress to the door like a ghost that got too close to my sewing needle.

"I'm going to wear a gorilla's mask, I swear," Tina says.

I look up. Betsy, picking at her cuticles, says, "Shut up, you will not."

"You don't like your dress for the dance, Tina?" I say.

"I don't like dresses, period. Or dances. What is Faye wearing?"

I mime a scoop-neck, then a skirt from the hips. "White, to the knee, gold shoes. She didn't mention the shoes?"

The front door jingles. Tina elbows Betsy and they throw a hand of rocks, paper, scissors for who has to go up and man the cash register. Tina, paper, slides off the counter and heads for the front.

Betsy looks after her. She says, "Tina is a lesbian."

My throat constricts a little. I think I might choke on my own saliva, but then manage to calm down. Deep breath. So what if she was, right? "You seem to know a lot about everything."

"Okay, not a lesbian. I don't know. A tomboy, I guess."

"Faye is a tomboy."

"Not that kind of tomboy."

I try to imagine which kind of tomboy Faye is and what kind Tina is. She's right—not the same. But I couldn't put it any better than that. I guess it's hard for Tina here if she turns out to be a lesbian. Parks is not the sort of place where difference goes undetected. Take the new Harding bride. They'll probably not stay in town, but if they did, it might be a hard place to live for someone who dresses like a fortune-teller and orders cakes with skulls on them. People talk.

I wonder what people say about me. About Faye. What was there to say about Faye? I was her mother, so of course I didn't know. "Betsy," I say, looking hard at the icing skull I'm working on. "You know stuff. What do you know about Faye?"

Her eyes flick at me, away. "What do you mean?"

I'm not sure. I guess I mean anything. Betsy seems to know things and I seem to know nothing. What does she think about? What does she worry about? At home, Faye is as happy and strong as she's ever been, unchanged. That can't be right. Her dad was there one morning and, then, by four that afternoon, gone, crushed in his delivery truck by a tractor-trailer hauling one half of a pre-built home. A closed coffin, a plot of land bought sight unseen, and he was under the ground in three days. She was twelve at the time, and things moved too fast. Too fast for me: I wandered wherever someone told me to go, stood where they placed me. I was picked clean to the bone. One day, a month or so later, I snapped to attention: Faye was making monkey sounds at me over her morning cereal bowl. To make me smile, an old trick. Just remembering it could make me smile. I don't want to know anything that would take those monkey sounds away from me.

"Never mind. Tina's not really wearing a gorilla mask, is she? It'll ruin the pictures."

"Nah. Some of the kids said they were wearing costumes, but I don't believe them. Faye and me want to look pretty. Not like ghosts or stupid vampire-girls. We're getting our own flowers, even."

I meant to get a corsage for Faye to wear, but she's ahead of me. "I like that you girls are all going together."

Betsy sighs. "Yeah. All the moms do. Next dance, though." Betsy twists her mouth and knocks on the countertop.

"I'm sure a boy will ask you next time." I hand her the parchment paper. "Want some icing?"

She takes the paper eagerly and digs a finger through the icing. Doesn't notice the knobby-headed skulls at all. She pops a dollop of pink into her mouth and hums with happiness. Betsy is not a tomboy; she's a different kind of girl, a girl like I used to be. They used to call them late bloomers, the kind of girl who wears teddy bear sweatshirts a year too long, whose t-shirts pull awkwardly across chests they were hoping for but still not quite expecting. The kind of girl so busy shopping around for a different kind of girl to be that she hardly notices that she's already who she is. Or maybe that's the kind of girl all girls have to be, for a while.

Cঠৡৎৠ

Carey used to dress up to hand out candy. One year he was a mummy, wearing a long strip of bed sheet he'd torn up and stitched together. One year he was a hobo, and when he answered the door, he asked the kids on the porch for treats before they could ask him. Another year he was a vampire, opening the door so slowly and emerging from the dark foyer onto the porch with such a dark presence that the first few groups of kids to come around had nearly fallen backward down the stairs. They wouldn't reach for the candy. We had a lot of leftover candy that year.

It was always my job to take Faye around. I never dressed for it—I liked to spend the time on her costumes. A princess, a witch, one of the characters from the show she liked the year she was eight, a ballerina one year, but it had been so cold she'd had to wear her winter coat. She got tired of it about the same time her dad died, so after that, we'd gone to the door together, no costumes, to hand out candy to the smaller kids.

This year I'm on my own. When I pull up to the curb, kids are already scouting the neighborhood for porch lights turned on. Groups of middle schoolers in lazy costumes and empty pillowcases, families guiding smaller children up each sidewalk and down the tree-lined streets. The Bradleys are passing by, but I stop them. Their daughter has dark hair like Faye. She's dressed like a princess, with a wand, and remembers to say thank you when I drop some mini chocolate bars into her plastic jack-o'lantern. "You're welcome, darling." She flutters her wand at me. The three of them continue onto the next house. I try not to watch too long.

Inside, I pour the candy bowl. The three of us could demolish a bag of the mixed like this. Carey liked the plain. Faye likes the crispies. I like the ones with almonds and peanuts. I sit at the kitchen table and stir the bowl with my hand. I pull out a plain one. I think maybe I'll pull out all the plain bars and hand them out first. I could get pretty sad if, tonight, all that's left are the plain bars. Outside I hear feet shuffling by. I haven't turned the porch light on yet, so they're still passing me by. I think about the way that Terry Bradley held his daughter's pumpkin bucket for her, guiding her gently with a hand on her shoulder. Just the way Carey guided Faye in all things—softly, so that she hadn't really known he'd been doing it.

I feel turned wrong side out, more itchy in my skin than I had been in a long time. I know it's loneliness. When I'm alone, I can collect in my head all the other times I've been lonely. Backward and forward, because I can already feel the empty house around me and feel the day coming when I don't expect Faye home in an hour. And now, of course: I hear scuffing shoes under eye-hole-cut sheets outside, and it's a lonely sound, as though the children's shoes scrape at the thin layer of earth that separates us from what is underneath, and what is underneath is nothing. The world isn't the sturdy place we think it is. It's a pumpkin shell, hollowed-out and fragile. Instantly I can call up the image of Carey's empty grave with the coffin strangely majestic off to the side. I can recall without any difficulty the feeling I had then that the earth was shallow, that the coffin, placed inside the deep grave, could do nothing but fall right through and fall forever. I feel as though I might fall forever. I glance out the windows to find my feet again. The street is going flat and gray, my thoughts turning day to night.

"Is it Dia de the damned dead already?" I say into the bowl of candy. If Carey were here—and then I know what I will do.

In the closet upstairs, I find my wedding dress. I think if I suck my stomach in a little, I can still zip it. I dig through Faye's makeup bag until I find the eye shadow she bought to do smoky eyes. I do smoky eyes on both of mine, sponging the shadow wide into my brow and in the circles already under my eyes even as my hands still shake. She has a face powder that is much too light for either of us. I use that over my cheeks and forehead until I'm as pale as I can hope for. There's the problem of my hair. I slick it back with handfuls of water and use some of Faye's mousse to plaster it wet and flat to my head. I don't have any flowers, but I have the veil to go with the dress. I push the combs through my hair and stand back from the bathroom mirror to have a look. I don't look as scary as the postcard, but still, pale and hollow-eyed as a ghoul. I stare into my own eyes until I find myself strange. What would Carey do if he saw me? Wouldn't he laugh? Wouldn't he call me crazy, proud as he could be? For a moment, I can remember him behind me, the weight of his arms around my shoulders, the scratch of his two-day beard against my cheek.

Downstairs I finally turn on the outside light for the trick-or-treaters and walk around the house barefoot. I don't feel like sitting down. The candy bowl on my hip, I wander out of the kitchen to the front door and then through the house again to the back porch. The tree in the Calavans' backyard is changing colors, the leaves peeling off one at a time. I help myself to an almond chocolate square and stare out the window until the doorbell chimes.

Quickly to the front again. I see through the curtain that it's Gina Gusser and her grandchildren, the children of her oldest son. I suddenly feel ridiculous. I'd brought Carey's spirit back for a moment with this get-up, but nothing has changed. He is still gone, and I'm still who I am. It's too late, though. Gina hears me coming and urges her grandchildren, a tiny pirate and a butterfly with rosy cheeks and sparkly wings, to hold out their pumpkin buckets.

I open the door and the children take a step backward. Gina looks up, concerned, and her face turns to horror. "What—?"

"Carey always used to dress up. Do you remember?"

Ask a woman of fifty-eight in this town of only a few hundred people if she recalls an occurrence of a mere five years ago. These women remember everything. Gina's face shows me that she remembers quite well, that she remembers perhaps more than I do. I am a widow dressed in her wedding gown, a yellowed veil, and the eyes of the dead, standing on her front porch and frightening the children.

"Is that your—? A dead bride? Is that—?" Is it funny, she is about to ask. And it isn't. It's not what I meant at all. I remember the way her voice grew strained talking to Betsy about her youngest son, the one going to war in a few months. Death is not funny to Gina Gusser. She needs a Catrina to remind her of the facts.

I grab a handful of candy and drop it into the pirate's pumpkin. The little girl takes flight, darting down the steps to avoid me.

Gina escorts the boy off the porch, glancing back, uncertain. I set the candy dish on the porch and retreat. The door closed, the porch light off before they're down the sidewalk. By the time Faye arrives home, her cheeks still pink from a hard practice, I am clean-faced and dressed in the soft, forgiving clothes of a woman my age—not a Catrina, not a bride—hemming a dance dress in the dark.

CB⧣⧤CB⧤

"We should have got a limo," Tina says.

"Oh, and who has money for that?" Betsy says, protecting Faye, who is still upstairs. Faye doesn't work because of sports. She gets an allowance, but I never see her spend it. Betsy and Tina make enough money at the store to have gone in with some other girls to get a limo. Those girls drove past twenty minutes ago, turning the festive air of our front yard heavy. We'd been having a good time. The air is sharp in our lungs. The birch in the front yard rains gold leaves onto the ground, creating a carpet fit for royalty. Some of the neighbors find excuses to stand on their porches and look fondly across the street at us. They want to see Faye.

Faye never mentioned getting a limo, so I know she was protecting me from having to say that we couldn't afford it. She thinks we don't have enough of anything since her father died. This is the first true secret thing I know about my daughter, and I didn't need Betsy to tell me. I'd have considered paying for a limo. The store does okay and there's the insurance, untouched, for her college. We have enough of just about everything we need. I'm embarrassed that she's worried for us, and relieved that she thinks the worst thing that could happen is that we might go under financially. She's still young enough to worry about the problem that can be fixed. She can still look around her and not think the ground is cracking.

As it is, the three girls are riding to the dance in the back of Betsy's parents' SUV. Betsy's mother, Ginger, stands in the yard with me and takes test shots of the empty street with her digital camera. As soon as Faye shows herself with the flowers she got for them all, Ginger and I will take our photos and they'll go.

"Girls, it's just a dance," I say. "Wait until your prom and I'll pitch in for the limo."

Betsy clutches at Tina's arm, who smiles. Tina did not bring a gorilla mask. She wears a green dress that might match the camouflage pants she wears to work. She's the sort who doesn't like to admit she enjoys this sort of to-do, but she's going. She has on dainty green shoes to match her dress. Her hair, normally spiky, is prim and girlish. Betsy is in pink. Her dress could be made of icing, it's so light and frothy. Her hair is out of its ponytail, long and blonde and curling. They are darling, so fresh and so young that I want to hug them to me.

Ginger and I exchange smiles, and then she turns back to her camera, studying the lens fiercely.

The screen door bangs and we all turn. Faye is wearing her white dress and gold shoes. Her legs are killers, just as I knew they would be. Tina whistles and Betsy giggles. Faye has a band of fresh yellow roses like a saint's aura on her head and two more rings of roses on her arm, one in pink and one in white. She looks like a bride. A happy one. Behind me, I hear the neighbors cooing in approval. Faye take the steps cautiously, one arm out for balance and her free arm waving across the street. Like a beauty queen, trying on her tiara.

"Where did you get *those?*" Betsy says. She reaches gratefully for the pink one when Faye offers it.

"I made them." She helps Tina adjust her halo of white buds.

"You *made* them?" Betsy sets her crown upon her head. She can't leave it alone. Her hands fuss at it, her eyes rolling in her head as she adjusts it. She turns to Tina. "Oh, T. You look like an angel. And Faye. You look like, I don't know, a Greek goddess or something."

Faye blushes and glances over her shoulder at me. She does. She looks like an angel and a Greek goddess and a bride and a beauty queen and a young woman about to go dance with any boy she likes. But she also looks like a Catrina, and she knows I know.

The girls turn this way and that, straightening each other's roses and smoothing each other's hair. The dance is happening in my front yard.

After Faye leaves for the dance, I'm going back to the store to finish up Mrs. Billy Harding's cake. For the first time since she ordered it, I'm sure I can make one. Three Catrinas, wreathed in roses, the petals falling behind them. I understand the Catrinas now. They're supposed to remind us that everyone dies, but they also remind us that everyone lives. Faye saw it first, and she's the one who's been guiding me all this time, softly, so that I didn't know.

The girls link arms in front of the birch and smile for us. Ginger and I back up into the yard to get the shoes into the picture, and we move down the sidewalk toward them until we are face to face and the girls blush and Faye says, "*Mom.*" We make them stand under the golden boughs of the birch until it seems impossible that they will stay another minute and impossible that they will go. We ask for their smiles and make stupid jokes and refer to boys whose names we've heard thrown around, all to get them to laugh and nudge one another. All to force one more moment from them, just one more, before they are gone.

Contributors

Dru Pagliassotti is the author of the award-winning steampunk novel *Clockwork Heart* and the horror novel *An Agreement with Hell*. Her short stories have been published in a variety of zines and anthologies, and she is currently co-editing *Day Terrors*, a horror anthology from The Harrow Press. A professor of communication at California Lutheran University, Dru also recently co-edited the scholarly volume *Boy's Love Manga: Essays on the Sexual Ambiguity and Cross-Cultural Fandom of the Genre*.

David J. Corwell y Chávez's short fiction has appeared in *Cloaked in Shadow: Dark Tales of Elves*, *Dead in Th13teen Flashes*, and *Tales of the Talisman Magazine*. Other stories ("The Harvest" and "Gremma's Hands") are scheduled for publication in *Daily Flash: 365 Days of Flash Fiction* (Pill Hill Press, December 2010) and *Voices of New Mexico* (LPD Press/Rio Grande Books, early 2011). He is a 2001 graduate of the Odyssey Fantasy Writing Workshop, a 2005 graduate of the Borderlands Press Writer's Boot Camp, and a 2006 graduate of Seton Hill University with a M.A. in Writing Popular Fiction.

Maxine Anderson is usually a playwright and sometimes a journalist, and she does not make very much sense very often. She would rather eat watermelon than cantaloupe. She was born a Southerner with no Southern heritage, and is a writer and student at Emory University. She has never been a farmer or a waitress at an all-night diner, but thinks there should be more stories about farmers and less about waitresses.

Chris Blocker is currently working toward an MFA from the University of Nebraska. He is a graduate of Washburn University and Indian Creek Elementary. He lives with his family in Topeka, Kansas.

Edward DeGeorge is a film producer and consultant who lives in the Chicago suburbs. As an Assistant Organizer for the Filmmakers in Action Meetup Group, he participated in the making of the short film "Before Mirrors." His fiction has appeared most recently in the anthologies *Damned in Dixie*, *Hell in the Heartland*, and *Spooks!* His comic book writing has seen print in *Big Bang Comics*, *Dr. Weird*, and *Y's Guys*.

Sheri Sebastian-Gabriel's work recently appeared in *Twisted Dreams* and *Six Sentences*. She is currently working on her second novel. A Georgia native, she lives in New Jersey.

Maureen Wilkinson is a British Author. Her interests range from travel to antiques. She has been told she has a warped sense of humour because she likes to hang naked by her toes in a tree and frighten the motorists. It's when walking her German Shepherd her mind travels its own strange paths. Some of her many credits include short stories published in *Flashme, Champagne Shivers, The Deepening, Literal Translations, Susurrus, Skive* and *Bound Off*, etc. Northern Ireland Arts council has just published four of her flashes in a newly released anthology.

Mary Fernandez received her Master's in Social Work from Arizona State University and her Bachelor's degree in Psychology from the University of Arizona. She is a 1st place prose winner for her short story "Los Gallos," published in *Sandscript Art and Literary Magazine*, 2008 edition. She lives in Tucson with her husband and two sons.

D Lee resides with his wife and child in Raleigh, North Carolina. His work has been published in *Bartleby Snopes, Mississippi Crow*, and *Candlelight Anthology*. He's currently working on his transgressive fiction novel titled, *American Terrorist Manifesto*. He likes buttons, things with buttons, and ice cream; though not necessarily in that order.

Kathleen Alcalá is the author of five books set in Mexico and the SW United States which have twice received the Governor's Book Award, the Western States Book Award, and others. Her work is forthcoming in *What to Read in the Rain* from 826 Seattle, and the long-awaited *Norton Anthology of Latino Literature*. She teaches Creative Writing at the Northwest Institute of Literary Arts.

Trent Roman is a writer from Montréal with an interest in all types of fiction strange and unusual in addition to academic interests in archaeology, anthropology, history and a number of other fields. He is fascinated by what makes people tick at both the intimately personal level and the sweeping societal level, and enjoys every opportunity to pursue such questions through the means of fiction.

Marg Gilks' writing credits span twenty years and include poetry, articles, and short stories. Her short fiction has been shortlisted for the Carl Brandon Society Kindred Award, earned Honorable Mention and quarter finalist status in L. Ron. Hubbard's Writers of the Future Contest, and has been recognized in assorted readers' choice polls. She's a freelance editor who operates Scripta Word Services, helping other writers polish their prose and hone their writing skills. Contact her at editor227@scriptawords.com or visit http://www.scripta-word-services.com/.

Chip Livingston is the author of the poetry collection *MUSEUM OF FALSE STARTS* (Gival Press) and the chapbook *ALARUM* (Other Rooms Press). His stories and poems have appeared most recently in *Potomac Review*, *The Literary Review*, *The Florida Review*, and *Ploughshares*. He lives in New York City and Montevideo, Uruguay. Visit him at www.chiplivingston.com.

Kate Angus's work has appeared in *Barrow Street*, *Subtropics*, *Gulf Coast*, *North American Review*, *Third Coast*, and *Poet Lore*. She teaches at Gotham Writers' Workshop and LIM College and lives in New York.

Ron Savage has published more than ninety stories worldwide. He is the recipient of the Editor's Circle Award in *Best New Writing* and was nominated for the Pushcart Prize. He also has been a guest fiction editor for *Crazyhorse* and is the author of the novel *Scar Keeper*. Some of his publications have appeared in *Glimmer Train*, the *North American Review*, *Shenandoah*, *The Baltimore Review* and the *Magazine of Fantasy and Science Fiction* to name a few. Learn more about his mystery novel at http://www.ronsavage.net

Sarah Layden's short fiction can be found in *Stone Canoe*, *Artful Dodge*, *The Evansville Review*, *Zone 3*, *PANK*, *Wigleaf* and elsewhere, with poetry in *Margie*, *Reed Magazine*, *Blood Orange Review*, *Juked*, *Tipton Poetry Journal*, and the anthology, *Just Like a Girl*. Excerpts from her novel *Sleeping Woman* also appear in *Freight Stories* and *Cantaraville*. Find her online at www.sarahlayden.com

Gerri Leen is celebrating the release of her first book, *Life Without Crows*, a collection of short stories published by Hadley Rille Books. In addition to *Día de los Muertos*, you can read more of her stories in such places as: *Sword and Sorceress XXIII*, *Return to Luna*, *Sniplits*, *Triangulation: Dark Glass*, *Footprints*, *Sails & Sorcery*, and *GlassFire*. Gerri lives in Northern Virginia and originally hails from Seattle. When she's not writing, she walks dogs at an animal shelter and watches horse racing. Visit http://www.gerrileen.com to see what else she's been up to.

Vonnie Winslow Crist, MS Professional Writing from Towson University, has had speculative fiction in print magazines: *Tales of the Talisman*, *Ethereal*

Tales, and *Cemetery Moon*; online: Echelon Press eShorts, *Aoife's Kiss*, *Ensorcelled Magazine*, and www.spacewesterns.com and in anthologies: *Dragon's Lure*, *While the Morning Stars Sing*, and *Sideshow 2*. Her speculative poems were recently printed in: *Champagne Shivers*, *Illumen*, *Scifaikuest*, *Ancient Paths*, *Sea Stories—Hibernal 2009*, *EMG-Zine*, and *Heroic Fantasy Quarterly*. She is a columnist for *Harford's Heart Magazine*, an illustrator for *The Vegetarian Journal*, editor of *The Gunpowder Review*, a contributor to *Faerie Magazine*, and a long-time fan of science fiction & fantasy literature, films, and television shows.

Iris Macor was once lost in the desert where she found a petrified alien's head. It watches her sleep at night and may be malicious. Her work has appeared in *Everyday Weirdness*, *Niteblade*, *Grey Sparrow Journal*, *Boston Literary Review*, *Keyhole Magazine*, *The Shine Journal*, and others. She blogs (infrequently) at http://idiotwithapen.wordpress.com/

Linda L. Donahue, an Air Force brat, spent much of her childhood traveling. Having earned a pilot's certification and a SCUBA certification, she has been, at one time or another, a threat by land, air or sea. For 18 years she taught computer science, mathematics, and aviation. Now, when not writing, she teaches tai chi, belly dance, and writes non-fiction articles. You can find Linda's twenty-plus stories in various anthologies from Yard Dog Press, Sam's Dot Publishing, Fantasist Enterprises, Elder Signs Press, Permuted Press, Ricasso Press, Morrigan Books and Kerlak Publishing. As well, Linda coauthored a story with Mike Resnick for Martin Greenberg's *Future Americas*, available from DAW Books. Also, find Linda's stories in MZB's *Sword & Sorceress 23*, and in Esther Freisner's anthologies, *Strip Mauled* and *Fangs for the Mammaries*, published by Baen Books. Read Linda's first published novel, *Jaguar Moon*, available from Yard Dog Press as half of Double Dog #5 and the novel *The 4 Redheads: Apocalypse Now!* which she co-authored with 3 other redheads. She and her husband live in Texas where they keep rabbits, sugar gliders and cats for pets. www.LindaLDonahue.com

Katie Hartlove holds a master's degree in professional writing. Her poetry and short fiction have appeared both online and in print. She works as a freelance editor.

When not in a grand shack on ten wooded acres near Austin, Texas, **Camille Alexa** writes in a grand shack on the mossy bank of the Tualatin River near Portland, Oregon. Her work appears in *ChiZine*, *Fantasy Magazine*, *Escape Pod*, and *Pseudopod*. Her first book, *Push of the Sky*, received a starred review in *Publishers Weekly*. More information and an updated bibliography can be found at http://camillealexa.com.

Samael Gyre—An adult, intelligent discussion of life's darker aspects, rather than a literary Hallowe'en fright show, is what I prefer my writing to be. If it also knocks the reader flat, all the better. Recent credits include the magazine *Tales of Moreauvia*, *Terra*, *All Possible Worlds*, *Scared Naked*, and *Talebones*, and the anthologies *Bitten*, *Northern Haunts*, *Ruins Metropolis*, *Barren Worlds*, *Love & Sacrifice*, *Jigsaw Nation*, *Cold Flesh*, & *Poe's Progeny*.

Laura Loomis is a social worker in the San Francisco area. Her fiction has appeared in *On the Premises*, *New Delta Review*, and *Many Mountains Moving*. A story in *Margin* was nominated for a Pushcart Prize.

Michelle D. Sonnier first knew she wanted to be a writer in fourth grade. Since then, she has made up stories—first in other people's worlds and then her own. Her specialty is dark urban fantasy fiction. In her stories a dentist learns the not-so-pretty truth about the Tooth Fairy and Baba Yaga has to break herself out of an old folk's home. Michelle is currently at work on a collection of short stories connected to Baltimore, with strange carnivals under the Jones Falls Expressway and mermaids performing magic in Inner Harbor. She lives in Maryland with a husband and two cats, and has modest dreams of being a critical darling and smashing commercial success.

Teagan Maxwell is based in Toronto, Ontario, Canada, and currently lives with her boyfriend, and their pet rats. She spends her days as a chipper, cheerful office monkey, while dedicating her nights to writing, music, drawing, sewing, or whatever else catches her eye. She enjoys twisting reality for her entertainment, and yours.

Alison J. Littlewood lives in West Yorkshire, England, where she hoards a growing collection of books with the word 'dark' in the title. She loves writing and dreaming, and is currently working on a novel. She has contributed to *Black Static*, *Dark Horizons*, *Not One of Us*, and *Read By Dawn 3*. Visit her at www.alisonlittlewood.co.uk.

Olga Sanchez serves as an Artistic Director for Miracle Theatre Group, Portland Oregon, which is dedicated to Latino arts & culture (www.milagro. org). She is an actor, director, writer, and artist-educator, originally from NYC, where she received her BA in Theatre from Hunter College and served as Co-Artistic Director of the People's Playhouse. In Seattle, she served as a founder and Artistic Director of Seattle Teatro Latino, for which she wrote and directed several works celebrating the beauty of Latino cultural heritage, including RETRATOS LINDOS, a touring show of Latin American children's stories and songs. She is currently working on a new work, VIVA DON JUAN! for Miracle's celebration of *Día de Muertos* (Day of the Dead), as well as writing a 12-episode *radionovela* for Behavior Works. Her play REUNIÓN and other short plays have been published by Rain City Press, Seattle. She is the creator of several Miracle arts education programs: *Milagro at SEIS*, bilingual performing arts workshops for students of the Spanish English International School at Roosevelt High School, *Posada Milagro*, a community-based holiday program, and *Cuentos y Teatro*, a Spanish-language summer acting camp for children. She is also a co-founder of Los Porteños Latino writers group, sponsored by Miracle. Olga holds a Masters in Human Development, with a concentration on Bicultural Development, from Pacific Oaks College NW. Olga has served on panels for the National Endowment for the Arts (NEA), Theatre Communications Group (TCG), Regional Arts & Culture Council (RACC), among others.

Lori Rader Day's stories have been published in *Good Housekeeping, Crab Orchard Review, TimeOut Chicago, After Hours, Big Muddy*, and *Southern Indiana Review*. She won the 2008 Chris O'Malley Prize in Fiction from *The Madison Review* and has an MFA in creative writing from Roosevelt University in Chicago.

CPSIA information can be obtained at www.ICGtesting.com
Printed in the USA
LVOW080437300911

248413LV00002B/4/P